Illusion of Control

The Way Back

Loraine Haynie

ISBN: 978-1-6653-0823-6 - Paperback
eISBN: 978-1-6653-0824-3 - eBook

These ISBNs are the property of BookLogix for the express purpose of sales and distribution of this title. BookLogix is not responsible for the writing, editing, or design/appearance of this book. The content of this book is the property of the copyright holder only. BookLogix does not hold any ownership of the content of this book and is not liable in any way for the materials contained within. The views and opinions expressed in this book are the property of the Author/Copyright holder, and do not necessarily reflect those of BookLogix.

Library of Congress Control Number: 2023923486

Cover Concept: Loraine Haynie
Cover Design: Gina Dyer
Photography: PeopleImages.com_YurlA.
                    Mike Blanchard
                    Gina Dyer

0 4 0 5 2 4

Acknowledgments

First, I must thank my husband, Billy, for enduring the interruption of sleep early in the mornings, as I crawled out of bed in darkness to start my day first with God, and second creating stories.

Even when a story flows easily for me, as it did in this book, there are a multitude of ways to misrepresent its message with unrecognized flaws. To mitigate the plethora of potential errors, my team of supporters was on the job. Every successful author needs a team to make sure any errors are caught and corrected.

My First Readers were there with this book. My dear friends, Anita Scott, and Fran Fields, both with educational backgrounds and friendship kindness, agreed to take on the challenge again amid their busy lives. It's a comfort to have close friends who can be honest and offer advice and correction with love.

Two new first readers offered a variety of in-depth evaluations and critique. Brenda Austin, who has supported my other books, offered encouragement and support of the storyline and characters. Linda Martin, with a journalism background, gave the book a line-by-line critique and evaluation. I am thankful for her attention to detail and value her input.

The support of the Northeast Georgia Writers is a comfort as well as a source of knowledge about the publishing world. A group of fellow writers, published and unpublished, offers understanding about the writing process and the frustration of getting the job done. A stand-out for me, Kim Megahee, was there with advice and help before I knew I needed it. I appreciate his love of writing and publishing and for formatting this book for me.

Cover designer, Gina Dyer, read my thoughts and desire for the cover and produced a cover that represents the story beautifully. Thank you, Gina, for your talent, patience, and keen awareness of what I'm seeing in my head. You are my go-to cover designer.

The latest support for my writing comes from BookLogix, who published the book. This is the first time I have used a professional company to do the hard work on the backend. They off-loaded the technical work from my plate and produced a first-class product.

Of course, the ultimate support comes from readers who purchase my books and support me by telling others about my work. Thank you.

Trust in the Lord with all your heart
And do not lean on your own understanding,
In all your ways acknowledge Him,
And He will direct your paths.

—PROVERBS 3:5-6

Chapter One

You can't right the wrongs of the past!

Ashleigh held her sign high as she walked across the steps of the Fulton County courthouse in Atlanta, Georgia. She believed in the ideologies of the young professional women with her. They wanted to call attention to the inequality of women in the workplace in 1989.

Their low-key protest signs highlighted the need for employer compliance with the ERA's 'equal pay for equal work' legislation approved by Congress in 1972. Ashleigh was proud to be part of this movement.

The spring wind whipped her sun-streaked brunette hair in her face, temporarily blocking her view of the onslaught of raucous women, followed by local TV and newspaper reporters.

1

The composition of the crowd had morphed into a rag-tag group of crude, unemployable women. They were encroaching on the top step of the courthouse. The early morning's wind blew in a drizzle of rain which battered banners in the hands of flippant protestors smiling and yelling.

Ashleigh grimaced as she heard, "We won't be held prisoners anymore. We are free to change the course of women's lives all over the country. We are tired of being bound by men's control. We are taking control."

With those words the entire first line threw down their banners, unbuttoned blouses and pulled them off along with their bras. Ashleigh stepped away from them in tandem with the original group of women, horrified at what the day had become.

"What have we started?" she cried as bras came floating down, covering the bottom steps. This is not what the professional women's club intended, when they decided to make a statement about today's unfair pay practices.

"Let's get out of here."

The original group gravitated to the edge of the crowd, avoiding contact with the mob, which spilled across the steps and descended into the street.

Over her shoulder Ashleigh saw six patrol cars fill the space in front of the courthouse blocking her escape. She ducked her five-foot-two body beneath a large sign held by a topless young woman. The police officers began separating the fully clothed women and allowed them to leave, while they held the bare-breasted women for indecent exposure.

Sitting in a nearby coffee shop, the group bemoaned the outcome of the day's events. Tall, auburn-haired. impeccably dressed Saundra Barrett was a third-year lawyer in the largest law firm in town.

"If my partners see me on TV, I will be laughed out of the practice."

Patricia Longino put her gaunt face in her hands as her slender, five-foot-six frame leaned toward the table, her dark hair falling forward.

"How did this happen? We had good intentions. Now, no one will ever believe that. How many customers will I lose in my tax business?"

Martha Wilshire stretched her five-foot-four, slightly dumpy frame, shaking her kinky blonde hair.

"I will probably lose my teaching job!" She held her head high and slipped out of the coffee shop.

Ashleigh sighed. "We had hoped to start a movement addressing 'equal pay for equal work' for today's women. We never intended, or expected, to put it out there the way those women did. Their display undermines our chance of being taken seriously.

"This backward look at equality for women might have been a huge mistake. However, the social mores of the 1960's kept women in teaching or secretarial jobs, or in the kitchen. We were only trying to draw attention to the fact that, even though the ERA was passed in 1972, Georgia has still not ratified it, which makes it more difficult to ensure protection for equal pay in this state. For heaven sakes, we're almost in the 1990's."

Saundra joined in. "That rowdy group of women was trying to make a mockery of our demonstration. Their interference took the focus away from us and showed women being irresponsible, proving to men that we don't deserve equal pay, because we are not equal. They believe we are nothing but hormones and sexual objects, who can't be taken seriously."

As the group dispersed, Ashleigh realized their faces would be shown on TV. Reporters had swarmed the grounds. The six o'clock news might headline the event. TV stations looked for something sensational to begin their programs each night. Bare-breasted women were sensational. The protest motive would be lost in those pictures, even though breasts would be grayed out.

She would be linked to the group. No one would listen to her explanation.

If her conservative boss saw the story or heard about her being in it, he would not be sympathetic. He built his company's reputation on honesty, Christian principles, and sexual purity.

The day had turned into the likeness of the women protestors, who assembled with the New York Radical Women's Organization, demonstrating against the Miss America Pageant in 1968.

This was going to be a big story.

Ashleigh worried. I can't afford to lose my job. I've earned my position. I'm tired of fighting.

On the way back to her office, Saundra rushed up to Ashleigh.

"I heard that someone in the group notified a friend at the local newspaper yesterday there was going to be a protest in front of the courthouse this morning. The liberal paper jumped at the chance to highlight a potential confrontational event involving women. The early morning paper's article inspired the mob of women who overtook our demonstration and turned it into a circus."

Ashleigh was sorry she had involved herself in this group of women. She did not know them well. They met at a monthly meeting of the Young Businesswomen of Fulton County. As they were leaving the meeting, they started a casual conversation about that night's program topic on 'inequality of pay for women'. They decided to meet later to continue the conversation and those meetings evolved into them taking a stand for women's rights. She never wanted this to be a major event. She only wanted to highlight the inequality of position and pay for women. Now she saw her career collapsing in front of her.

She had worked her whole life to be accepted to Southeastern Tech's Architectural School. She knew it was a long shot since Southeastern was perceived as a male college. Even though the feminist movement had encouraged women to seek higher education in professional fields, the institutions of higher learning didn't make it easy for any of them to be accepted as students. The fields of architecture and engineering were still considered male careers. Ashleigh's acceptance to Southeastern Tech was based on her making better grades, taking harder courses, achieving a higher SAT score, participating in more community events and social activities than most male students.

Fortunately, she was accepted, graduated with honors, and was offered a job with an established city planning firm. Working as an architect, influencing the architectural style of the Atlanta skyline, was her dream job. She quickly advanced to senior level development at Stockton & Associates Architects and City Planning Agency.

When she learned a male graduate from South Carolina University, hired at the same time, started at significantly more money, it was a slap in the face for her. She was a quiet young woman, who believed that talent and ability, along with education, made men and women's pay equal, if work product was equal. She was not happy with her pay, but she loved her job. She was not prepared to lose it.

She immediately thought of calling her brother, Phillip, who always had good advice for her. He believed in her talent and wanted her to have a chance at success just as he had. There was no way she would call him long-distance, wherever he might be this month. His Marine Corps security clearance didn't allow family to have a location or phone number for him. Her only option was to place an emergency call to his headquarters and leave a message. This situation didn't rise to that level of importance.

She couldn't call her mom because her parents were on another cruise, this time up the coast of Europe. They had been gone a month and still had another month before returning home. She was left calling her best friend, JJ, who was a court reporter and didn't have an assignment today. However, she was probably still asleep this morning.

It was too late to dwell on her choices. She was getting exactly what she had wanted, the control to manage her own life without interference from her family. Today's event struck home what that reality meant. She opened the door to her office and focused on her job for the remainder of the day.

On the way home, Ashleigh picked up a salad at the local eatery and hoped to have a relaxing evening. Kicking off her shoes inside the door, she reached for the TV's remote control. She enjoyed watching the news each evening as she ate her dinner. She felt like an adult in her compact one-bedroom apartment in midtown Atlanta. The sound of shouting and horns honking drew her eyes to the chaos displayed on the screen.

There she was in all her adult life, painfully alert as she watched the overzealous women yank off their bras and shout hateful and unflattering words into reporters' microphones. The camera did not record her exiting the turmoil with several other fully dressed women. Her fears were realized. How would she handle the taunts at work tomorrow? Maybe no one saw the coverage. Maybe they would respectfully refrain from teasing her.

She knew that in her office of young architects, draftsmen, engineers, and lawyers there would be no mercy. This night was going to be long and sleepless, and it began with the first ring of the phone.

It was JJ. "Ashleigh, are you okay? I saw today's protest on the TV just now. Oh my, how do you feel?"

"Embarrassment, fearful of losing my job, terrified of my parents seeing the report, regret for participating in the rally. Is that enough feelings?"

"You want me to come over?"

"No. I'm going to take a cold shower and cover up in bed. But thanks. Talk with you tomorrow."

"Coffee, first thing?"

"Sure. Let's stop at the coffee shop down the street from me to avoid any of my coworkers."

"Okay. See you at eight. And Ashleigh, I'm so sorry this happened."

"Me too."

The cold shower didn't stop her mind from circling back to the morning's events. I'm so naïve. I should have known the protest would bring negative responses. The reason for the rally was positive. It was intended to bring hope to women who felt they were trapped under the glass ceiling, never to emerge.

I feel out of control, like I did at Southeastern. The guys had all the support because of the large number of male students. The women were left to find resources and locations to have meetings and social activities. I knew we were entering a new era because I was accepted to the school. They had to wait for things to move slowly for monetary support for women's sports. Basketball and soccer were seen as men's sports. It was only when the women's team won the regional championship that the attention to their game was broadcast.

Struggling for every inch of accomplishment, the women did not give up. They started more clubs, sports teams, and expanded living situations, during her years earning her bachelor's and master's degrees.

She never dreamed she would be in the same fight in her job.

Chapter Two

The alarm brought Ashleigh back to today. She chose her most conservative navy-blue suit and gray blouse to match her eyes and added full-coverage shoes. Maybe her motives wouldn't be too obvious with this outfit. After her shower she donned the rainy weather ensemble, with a last look in the mirror. The drive to work would prolong her misery.

She ran into a coworker at the elevator. "Hi, Ash. How's your morning?"

"We'll see, Jason. I'm not in the office yet."

She looked at him with a wistful shrug. He always seemed to be where she needed him. He made her acceptance easy into the male pact of architects. He always treated her as an equal. Even though he was a structural engineer, rather than an architect, his position was highly regarded by the architects. They could not be successful without his support.

"Hey, don't worry about the news coverage from yesterday. You looked good on camera." His attempt to boost her mood fell flat.

"So, you think everyone saw it?"

"Oh, yeah."

Her face bloomed crimson. "Maybe I should call in sick."

"You'd have to face the troops tomorrow. Can't hide forever. And by the way, I'm proud of you for taking a stand on your beliefs."

He fist-bumped her shoulder and headed to his office, down the hall to the left.

Ashleigh's office was at the end of the hallway to the right, where she would be outside of his protection and support. She made the treacherous journey trying to ignore the battering.

"Way to go Ash." Dan yelled the first of the chants from his office to the right.

"Lookin' good, Ash." Across the hall, Bob stuck his head out the door and offered a high-five.

"Did you get the names and numbers of the bra throwing women?" Joe held out a pad and pen toward her, as she reached the end of the hazing.

There was no sneaking into her sanctuary. Mr. Howard Stockton's secretary stood at her door.

"Hi, Angela, you need me for something?"

Angela lowered her eyes, "I don't need you. Mr. Stockton wants to see you in his office."

Ashleigh turned to open her office door. "Thanks, I'll head that way after I hang my jacket."

"No. He wants to see you now."

"Okay." She feigned a business attitude and walked confidently to her boss's door.

Howard Stockton's commanding voice was loud. "Come in, Ashleigh. I wasn't sure you'd show up today. I must give you credit for that. Do you have something to say to me?"

He walked toward her; his six-foot-two frame dwarfing her tiny frame. His dark brown eyes belied his superior countenance. He was a fit man for his age, with a full head of grey hair. He propped on the corner of his desk without offering her a seat.

"I hope you know that I was not part of the unruly protest yesterday. I should have warned you that I planned to rally on the courthouse steps. I wanted to bring attention to the inequality in pay and position for women, who have the same background and education as men and turn out an equal work product."

He frowned at her. "I didn't know you were unhappy with your pay. It would have been better for both of us if you had met with me about your concerns."

"I wasn't sure you would sanction my attendance at the event."

"I certainly would not, but it would have been best for you to give me a heads-up, so I could prepare for it. I've gotten several calls about the protest. Only a few callers recognized you. I can manage those clients without too much disruption.

"Ashleigh, you are a very talented architect and I have great plans for you in this company. I want you to know that you will be up for a pay review and possible increase in six months. That should solve our problem. Now, you may get to work. We do have a deadline on the Deerfield Project."

She feigned acceptance. "Howard a review in six months will be appreciated. However, I feel my current pay isn't in line with other third-year architects."

"What do you mean? The other young girls, uh women, make far less than you do."

"I am the only female architect. It isn't fair to lump my pay with other women who are clerical, secretarial, and bookkeeping employees. My education and work product are comparable to every other third-year man in this firm."

"We don't compare women's pay to men's pay. Men have families they must support. Women only support themselves. When they have children, their husbands pay the bills, and must make enough to take care of the family."

"That's the problem. I worked as long and hard getting my education as any man. It costs me the same to pay rent for my apartment as a man would pay. My groceries cost the same as a man's groceries. Gasoline costs me the same per gallon. How is it that I am supposed to live on less. I am not dependent on a man. I am self-supporting. What I'm paid should not be determined by how much I spend. It isn't for a single man."

Ashleigh wanted to say, "Camden is not married and has no children. He graduated when I did. Why is his salary much higher than mine."

She didn't say those feminist things.

"We obviously have a difference of opinion. You have a choice. You can work within our rules or go somewhere else. I would not give you a good reference because you're making trouble for my firm."

"Thank you, Howard. I'll let you know my decision in the morning."

Ashleigh didn't stop at her office on her way out of the building. She had a lot of thinking to do. By the time she reached her car, she was trembling all over with anger, frustration, and fear.

She called JJ, asking to meet for dinner.

Chapter Three

They met at their favorite family restaurant at six. Ashleigh needed comfort food and conversation. JJ didn't always have sage advice, but she never let her down. She always listened with concern and love.

Their friendship began in Ashleigh's second year of college. JJ did not attend Southeastern Tech, but they met while each was on a blind date with a Tech student. Their sense of humor was compatible, and they lived near each other growing up, even though they had never met. They had attended the same grammar school and high school, with two years between JJ and Ashleigh. They even had a few mutual friends. Their values were the same and their independence was matched escapade by escapade. That's why they never considered living together. Two independent souls would not be happy in the same apartment.

Ashleigh arrived first and waited for JJ before ordering, even though she was starved. Stress made her hungry. JJ showed up in work clothes, overdressed for Ashleigh's jeans and sweatshirt. Neither one cared how the other was dressed.

"Tell me all about it." JJ slipped her high heels off under the table and leaned toward Ashleigh, her long dark hair resting on her clasped hands on the tabletop. Her sparkling blue eyes focused on Ashleigh's face.

"I have a choice to make tonight. I accept the situation with my job and pay, hoping for a good review and pay increase in six months, which means I will still make less than Camden. Or I leave the company with Mr. Stockton's threat of giving me a 'troublemaker' reference."

"Well, that's an easy choice. You leave!"

The waiter appeared to take their order, causing a lull in the conversation.

"I love you JJ. I wish it were that simple. I don't know the long-term harm that decision will make on my career."

"With your talent, you can work anywhere. Any company would be thrilled to have you for an employee, outside of the fact that you are a top-notch architect."

"You're always my cheerleader. I need to talk with God about this, but I, also, needed my best friend tonight."

Their meals arrived to interrupt their conversation. They enjoyed small talk while eating.

"I hate to rush off, but I need to get ready for work tomorrow. I'm covering a trial in Cartersville Thursday. I probably won't be home Thursday night, but I'll talk with you tomorrow."

"Thank you for making me laugh, and for not shaming me for inhaling all the fried chicken and mashed potatoes on my plate! I haven't had that much to eat in years!"

"Did you see my plate? I couldn't compete with you, but I'm not going home hungry."

"I'll call you in the morning and let you know what I'm going to do."

Her overstuffed stomach encouraged a long walk on the apartment building's treadmill in the rec room. God listened to her problems and worries. At the end of her five miles, she knew what to do.

***

Howard Stockton cast a knowing smile at Ashleigh as she entered his office. "Well, you're here bright and early. I'm glad you took the night to think about your decision. You will be glad you didn't rush into an unwise choice. I assume you will be staying here."

"Yes, I have made my decision, Mr. Stockton."

"Why are you addressing me as Mr. Stockton? I am Howard to my staff."

"I am not your staff any longer, Mr. Stockton. I can work a two-week notice, or I can leave now."

"You can't be serious. You don't want to give up this opportunity with my company. You can have a long, fruitful career here."

"Maybe it would be long. I'm not sure about fruitful. I appreciate the opportunities you've given me these three years. I no longer feel it is a good fit for my future. Would you like me to stay to finish the proposal and plans for the Deerfield Project?"

"Certainly not! I don't want you to take any more ideas than you already have in your head about our clients and projects. You are making a big mistake, Miss Justice."

"Maybe so. I hope to see you at the annual architecture awards banquet next year."

The walk down the hall and out the door confirmed Ashleigh's decision. She was free. She would find a better fit for her talent and her personality. She felt lightheaded and powerful at the same time. She had no fear of what tomorrow would bring. God is in control of tomorrow.

When she reached the outside door, Camden was entering the building. "I saw your little exhibition on TV. It was below you and your position here to be part of that foolishness. I hope Howard got you straight about that."

"I'm straight all right. Good luck in your future as one of many good architect associates at Stockton & Associates. I'll see you around."

Her anger bubbled up on the walk to her car. She was glad to be rid of this male competitor. In every project they worked on together, he would wait until the day before each milestone meeting with the client then show up at her office, pretending to want clarification on her part of the project.

She quickly learned that he had not done his share of the work and would take her progress, morph it to suit his style and present it at the client meeting as his work. She was always the follow-up presenter at these meetings. Clients expected to hear from the male architects. Being the only female architect at the firm, it was expected she was not the lead architect, even when she was.

The walk to her car gave her time to realize she would not be dealing with Camden and his incompetence any longer. She smiled as she slid under the steering wheel and closed the door, accepting responsibility for her first big decision in her career.

Chapter Four

She beat afternoon traffic and arrived home in time to take a long walk in the park across the street from her apartment. When she talked with JJ this morning, they planned to meet at the local restaurant/hangout for young professionals. She had plenty of time to complete her walk before joining JJ.

Spring began taking over the dry ground, shooting red, yellow, and pink sprouts of new birth in nooks and crannies along the trail through the park. What are the names of these dainty flowers? How many times have I walked in this park enjoying their beauty and never thought to learn their names? I vow to learn their names this year. I do know that is a cherry tree and those are azaleas. It is amazing, the blessings God showers on us.

Her spirits soared and she was singing by the time she unlocked the door of her apartment an hour later. She showered and pulled out comfortable slacks and a loose blouse to wear to the restaurant. As she modeled before the mirror, she felt free, wearing something other than business attire while socializing with her peers.

JJ showed up at the same time. "Wow, it's a weeknight and you aren't in a suit and heels! I'm liking this change in you."

"It already feels like I've moved in a positive direction. The next steps will be harder. My brother, Phillip, will be supportive. Telling Mom and Dad won't be easy. Dad will freak out. Mom will be worried about how I can afford to be out of work for a while.

"Eventually, that may be a problem. For now, I'm okay. Beginning with my first paycheck, I've saved more than half my salary each pay period. I can wing it for a little while, but I don't want to spend everything I've saved. I need to start making contacts immediately."

"Hey, take a breath. Enjoy some down-time for a week or so. Re-think what you want in a job. Don't jump on the first offer."

"You're right. It's time to re-imagine me. Let's eat."

As the evening turned into night, regulars stopped by their table.

"Ash, you look great!"

"Didn't know you had anything other than business attire."

"Are you on vacation?"

She didn't think about work one time during the evening and was not the first one to leave.

However, when she got home, she began thinking about what her routine for tomorrow would be. Do I sleep-in? Or do I use the early morning to begin my search? When do I tell mom and dad? What will Phillip think?

I need my regular routine for a while. I still need structure for my day. Little changes can come with decisions I make along the way. I'll think about that in the morning. Tonight, I'm going to sleep with no deadline haunting my dreams.

Chapter Five

Without the jolt of the alarm, Ashleigh woke fully rested to the song of birds outside her bedroom window. She laid still until the tweets from a resident cardinal drifted away. The clock showed she awoke fifteen minutes after her normal alarm time.

Not bad, newly rescued architect! It's coffee and bagel time.

There was no need for a robe this morning. The sun warmed her bedroom and kitchen with rays filtering through uncovered windows. That was the benefit of third floor living in newly renovated apartments in mid-town.

Her mom, Christine, was anxious about her living situation in Atlanta, because of mid-town's history of gangs and run-down businesses. Once she saw the local telephone company start renovations on their building and a local police precinct open on the next block, she told Ashleigh she felt better about the safety of her building, which held eighteen apartments for young professionals.

When she thought of her mother, Ashleigh pictured the graceful movements of the five-foot five-inch woman silently gliding into a room, somehow immediately attracting everyone's attention. Rather than seeing her, you felt her presence, even though her beauty caused many men to stare inappropriately. Women were drawn to her open friendliness and warm countenance. Ashleigh missed her wisdom and advice this morning.

I can't lean on her advice, even if she were here. I've taken charge of my future. I need to decide my next move. I can't have it both ways, being an adult and strong enough to decide to quit my job but looking to parents to solve the predicament I've gotten myself into. It's good that they are far away from me.

Coffee refill before her shower and time to watch the streets fill with pedestrian and vehicular traffic gave her joy and thankfulness for her life.

I have time this morning to read my Bible and thank God, who has made my life full and blessed. I need to ask Him what He has planned for me.

She decided she would not rush into a job search today. She put on jeans and a lightweight sweater. It was early March and still cool, almost cold. Then she pulled her shoulder-length hair into a ponytail and set out to visit local shops and stroll through the park, seeing what other folks did on a Wednesday morning.

The first Spring vegetables showed off reds and greens in wooden wheelbarrows in front of mom-and-pop grocery stores, along with home canned jellies, jams, pickles, and relishes perched on shelves inside half-cut barrels. Ashleigh loved this aspect of mid-town.

She motioned to Mr. Harrison, "I'll wait to pick up some fresh vegetables on my way back to the apartment, so I don't have to carry them on my walk."

He waved and nodded. "I'll bag a few things for you."

She made the right decision. She felt so free being outside, breathing fresh air.

She wasn't in the mood for a run, but she could walk through the park. As she started on the path toward downtown, she was met with runners and fast walking men and women. Tomorrow she would dress for a run. She didn't want to miss any more of this beautiful weather being inside when she could be out in nature.

Her phone rang as soon as she stepped inside her apartment. She placed the bag of vegetables on the island. Should she answer it? If it was work, she didn't have anything to say to anyone there. If it was her parents, she didn't want to explain why she was at home. If it was JJ, she would leave a message on the answering machine.

She picked up the morning paper and stepped onto her balcony to enjoy the rest of the cool morning and read the news of the day. On the second page, there was a picture of a more dignified group of women being interviewed by a reporter on their part in the disruptive display on the courthouse steps Monday.

The article covered pictures and names of participants in the braless display. While their message was like Ashleigh's group, protesting unfair pay practices between men and women, their outrageous approach diluted the message. Their answers to the reporter did not promote changes for women. Ashleigh was irritated with the interview and felt it cemented the image of insurrection for both groups.

I wish I could do something to provide a logical, fair argument for women's rights. I wonder where the other members of my group stand with continuing our protest.

Her first call was to Saundra. "Hi, Saundra. I'm checking up on everyone to see how they fared after Monday. Any repercussions for you?"

"Very minor since our pictures showed us clothed. I'm so thankful. How about you?"

"Well, I was forced to quit because I would not promise to drop any future involvement in the cause."

"Why didn't you agree?"

"Because I want to continue bringing attention to the issue. Don't you?"

"Not if it ruins my career. Have you talked with anyone else?"

"No. You're the first. Have you?"

"Yes. I think you will find no one else wants to carry this banner forward."

"We can't just give up. That will make it worse. We will appear to be weak and insincere about our beliefs."

"I think each one of us must make a choice about how that issue really affects us. In my case, I don't think it is worth my time. It will take years to bring about real change. I need to spend those years developing my skills in my law practice."

"What about everyone else?"

"They can make their own decision. If it benefits them, they should pursue it. If not, it's up to the next generation to fight the establishment."

Ashleigh could not believe what she was hearing. She needed to call the other women to see if Saundra was correct.

Patricia wanted to continue with their efforts to bring about change. She wanted to do it differently. "Let's get together to see what other approach we can take. Have you talked with Martha?"

"Not yet. I don't think Saundra will meet with us. I'll call Martha and see if she will join us for dinner."

"Sounds good. How about next Tuesday? By the way, did you have any problem at work?"

"I resigned because I would not agree to drop the issue."

"Oh my, Ashleigh. I'm so sorry. We need to come up with a better plan. Before Tuesday night we should each make a list of the influential people we know who might get behind our effort."

"Good idea. I'll call Martha. If she agrees, we'll meet at Tanner's at six Tuesday night."

Ashleigh was busy the rest of the week. It was good she didn't have a job to interfere with her planning.

Chapter Six

Ashleigh smelled Tanner's Bar-b-cue a half mile before she pulled into the gravel parking lot. She wore old tennis shoes, jeans, and a heavy pink sweatshirt. Eating under a wooden canopy on tables resting on dirt and straw floors called for casual clothes, where heavenly sauce dripping from pork sandwiches could ruin a blouse, pants, or shoes.

She found a table in the corner of the L-shaped restaurant away from the local country singer and guitar. She placed folders filled with her research from newspaper articles, proposed law dismissals on fair wages, and lists of influential leaders in the community at the other three seats.

Saundra arrived before the other two women. "I agreed to come out of respect for you. I have no intention of keeping up this effort. I hope we can have a pleasant dinner despite my decision."

"I'm glad you came. It's okay to talk about issues without making commitments. I thought we would wait to order until everyone gets here. How was your week?"

"It was interesting. Two of the women in the other protest group had appointments with one of our partners. They want to file lawsuits against their companies for illegal firing after last Monday. I guess you were not the only one to pay for advocating change."

Patricia and Martha arrived together and slid into their seats as the waiter approached the table to take their orders.

The favorite barbecue sauce and southern sweet tea kept the women from having in-depth conversations until faces were wiped clean and banana pudding was consumed. They pushed away from the table with full stomachs. When Patricia opened her file folder, Saundra took leave of the group. Patricia spoke first. "Ashleigh you've put together a lot of work for a starting place. Why don't we take a few days for Martha and me to read and study everything and come up with suggestions for a next move. I'm too full to even think about anything this important tonight."

Martha closed her folder and began to rise. "I agree with Patricia. Let's meet somewhere closer to our apartments with light food, like maybe salads for next week."

"I do have one thing to share with you." Ashleigh cleared her throat. "Saundra didn't tell me this is confidential. Two of the women in the braless group approached a partner in her firm about filing a wrongful dismissal suit against their bosses. I don't know if the attorney accepted the cases, but that might be some-thing positive for us to use."

That news sent the group off with hopes of unlikely advocates.

The excitement of the evening's potential progress diminished as Ashleigh entered her sanctuary. She pulled off her tennis shoes caked in dirt and hay and headed for the laundry area. As she placed them on the edge of the sink, she felt a sense of emptiness.

She had just left her new friends, who returned to their homes and lives with husbands or boyfriends and fulfilling jobs. She had none of those things. She did have this new cause. It did not envelope her with hugs or joy. She walked to the living room and picked up the phone to call JJ. Her line was busy.

Okay, I need to knock off this pity-party and get back to a positive place. I'm doing the right thing. I need to release some of this frustration. It's too late for a run in the park. JJ is busy. Mom and dad are in Europe. Phillip is God knows where. God does know. God knows everything I'm going through.

God, I'm sorry I didn't come to you first. You know my heart. You know my needs. I asked for your guidance. I did what you led me to do. What is your plan for me now? I trust you and love you. I wait for your answer.

Peace filled her soul. She closed her eyes to enjoy its comfort.

What's that sound? Was I sleeping? Oh, the phone. What time is it?

"Hello. Phillip? Oh Phillip, I've been thinking about you. I'm so glad you called."

"Something nudged me to call you tonight. I'm sorry it's so late your time. It's early evening here."

"It was God. I was praying earlier. Do you have time for me to share what's going on with me?"

"I'm off duty for the rest of the night. Let me have it, Sis."

As she finished telling him about her work situation, she began to regret leaving her job.

"I worked hard for that job and earned the promotions I received. I loved being part of a mission larger than myself.

"I remember Saturdays growing up, when my friends and I would ride the bus downtown and spend the day window shopping."

Phillip laughed. "I remember you talking about some of those adventures. But I never hung out in Atlanta. I had sports activities on Saturday. I'm not sure I could remember the name of any streets in Atlanta back then."

"Well, I can. Davison's Department Store was on Peachtree Street. We walked from there to Rich's Department Store at the corner of Alabama and Broad Streets, stopping at Woolworth's lunch counter for a sandwich and milkshake in between.

"And while I was at Southeastern Tech, I worked at Five Points in the extraordinary triangular-shaped Hurt Building. It was bordered by three streets: Edgewood Ave on the North side, Ivy Street on the East, and Exchange Place on the South.

"I loved the old architecture of those buildings, but all the street names have changed. Atlanta is teasingly known for changing street names every five years. After graduating with my degree, I wanted to be part of the development and growth of the city, moving toward Buckhead in new, taller, sleek buildings. I dreamed of making that growth happen.

"I had that opportunity at Stockton & Associates. I threw it away."

Tears streamed down her face.

Phillip listened quietly through her telling and her sobs.

"Sis, you haven't thrown it away. You're making a statement that your work is valuable, and you are valuable. Your employer should honor that! Don't give up this easily. It's not like my headstrong, talented, capable sister. God will guide you. You probably will have to be patient, but He will work things out for you. You are going to make a difference for women. I'm so proud of you."

"I miss you."

"You, too. Look, I promise to call you every chance I get to see how you're doing. I don't know how often that will be. Just know that I'm thinking about you and saying prayers for you, too. Love you, Sis."

God answered her prayers with Phillip's call.

Chapter Seven

Heavy rain pelted the bedroom window, waking Ashleigh from a deep sleep. She rolled over to see the clock. Blurry eyed, she shot up when she saw it was nine o'clock.

I haven't slept this late in years. Guess there's no reason to hurry though. Rain is the one thing that keeps me from my morning run. I don't have a plan for today. The weeks have flown by even though I'm not working. I guess I really haven't made any attempt to look for a new job. I've spent Most of my time researching the history of women's issues. I need coffee.

She slid off the bed and found her fluffy bedroom slippers, heading to the kitchen to make coffee. The apartment's lack of window coverings showed the outside storm in full force. She cupped her hands around the steaming coffee cup. Snuggling in the corner of the deep-cushioned beige sofa gave her a direct view of the dark clouds rolling toward her building.

When I worked, I dreamed of having a day like today where the weather warned me to stay inside, and I could read a book or watch a movie. Now that I have that chance, it's the last thing I want to do.

The phone on the end table rang. Do I want to answer it? It's probably a salesperson, or wrong number. If I hesitate long enough the caller will hang up.

Wish I had answered. It would be nice to hear another voice this morning.

She grabbed some file folders, a pen and paper, preparing to make a list of things she could do today. Before she began, she bowed her head.

God bless this day. Thank you for the rain and all the wonderful things you give me each day. Guide me as I make some sense of what has happened and give me the wisdom to know your plans for me.

As she raised her head, the phone rang again. This time she answered without hesitation, "Hello."

"Ash, how are you? I've missed you at work. It's just not the same around her without you and your bubbly personality, and sarcasm."

"Jason. I'm so glad to hear your voice! How's the Deerfield project going?"

"The project has slowed down drastically since you left. Camden seems to be swimming up-stream. He's not pushing the design to us for our evaluation. We are looking for other work while waiting for him. I'm afraid we're going to lose the contract. Won't you come back?"

She squeezed the phone's receiver. "I think you're teasing because you know I can't come back. I won't ignore my principles."

"I understand. I miss you. Could we have dinner sometime?"

Hoping he would say soon, she answered. "Sure. Just let me know when."

"I'll be in touch. Have a good day."

"You, too."

News from Jason was upsetting. I didn't want my leaving to slow the progress of the biggest project the firm has. Camden needs to step up and keep the project going. I knew he depended on me for ideas and development, but I didn't realize he didn't have the talent or knowledge to do it himself. I thought he was just lazy.

It's not my problem any longer. It will be up to him to make it work.

Typical of the Atlanta weather, the rain subsided, and the sun peeked out from behind a dissolving cloud. She pulled on tights, a hooded sweatshirt and running shoes and found a scrunchy for her ponytail, and took the stairs down to the ground floor, rather than using the elevator. Everything was going to be physically active while she was unemployed.

The warm breeze invigorated her. Ashleigh ignored the wet sidewalks and smiled as she began a jog to the park. There, she moved into a full run for the first mile. She passed young moms with strollers jogging with their babies. She wondered what their lives were like. Were they able to stay home with their babies? Or did they have part-time jobs? There were so many choices women had, just not when it came to equal pay.

I have missed so much of real living the past eight years. School and work are requirements of adulthood, but why can't this free feeling be part of it too? Here I am again, back where life is taking me. What will my next steps be?

Chapter Eight

With a clear head, but no answers, Ashleigh picked up the morning newspaper from her mailbox on her way into the apartment. After making her usual two cups of coffee, she poured a cup and put the newspaper under her arm. She left the door to the patio open to fill her home with fresh air. Coffee and information in the paper prepared her for the rest of her day.

Nothing in today's paper inspired her into action about her situation, but an article about an approaching storm in the Atlantic Ocean caused her to calculate where her parents might be on their cruise. She worried that they might be heading into dangerous weather. Surely the captain of the ship will be wise enough to remain in port until the storm passes.

Hopefully, Mom will call and let me know their situation. However, it will be tonight before she calls. She thinks I'm at work. I can't spend my day needlessly worrying about them. I'm going to the archives of the local paper and research where the women's movement is going in the rest of the country. Maybe I can build a plan from what other states are doing.

She grabbed her briefcase and notepads as she left for the newspaper's archives, where she settled in with microfiche and a diet soft drink. She started her search in 1968 but looked back to 1964, when the Civil Rights Amendment was passed, protecting citizens against discrimination for their sex, race, or religion. She became enmeshed in the history of what she believed to be the feminism movement. She quickly learned that the fight for equality did not begin in 1968 with the protest at the Miss America Pageant. The first seeds of feminism began in 1848 as part of The Declaration of Sentiments, which outlined the need for equality among men and women, including voting rights.

She stumbled into an article about an organization called The National Grange of the Order of Patrons and Husbandry, who promotes the equal status of women. This early statement about equal status for women uplifted Ashleigh and supported her belief that her group could make a difference.

She read that the 14th Amendment was ratified on July 9, 1868. The First Article of the Amendment states, "No state shall deny to any person within its jurisdiction the equal protection of the laws." The suffrage movement used that wording to support women's rights to vote. Georgia ratified the amendment on July 21, 1868.

She found it interesting that the term 'feminism,' describing women's rights, came to the United States from France in 1910. The 'suffragettes' fought for women's right to vote. The 'feminist' included legal rights, financial independence, and the transformation of the relationship between the sexes. Following the 1920 ratification of the 19th Amendment, which granted women voting rights, feminism splintered from purely suffrage-oriented groups.

The Women's Liberation Movement of the late 1960s and '70s brought about women's desires to revolutionize the fundamental aspects of female life at that time: domesticity, employment, education, and sexuality.

Ashleigh couldn't believe that it had only been 17 years since the Equal Rights Amendment passed Congress in 1972.

She was not even a teenager. She did remember Ms Magazine from that time. Earlier magazines for women focused on domestic life, sewing, cooking, cleaning, and childcare. Ms Magazine focused on women's roles in business, their education and leadership. The magazine was owned and run by women. It promoted and supported the idea that women should be taken seriously and was the foundation for women's support and resources for the ground-roots movement for equality.

She gathered her research and drove home with a renewed desire to continue the fight. She hadn't felt this challenged since her last day in her job. But it was entirely different.

She had no control over this outcome. Her efforts could be in vain, but she had to try for her sake and every other woman's benefit.

The phone was ringing when she opened the door. Dropping some of her papers on the coffee table, she reached for the receiver.

"Hello."

"Hi, Sweetheart!"

"Mom! I'm so glad to hear from you. Hold on a second, I've got to get some files out of my arms."

"I'm surprised I caught you at home. I planned to leave a message on your answering machine. It's nice that you can work from home sometimes."

"Where are you? Are you in port somewhere? I've been so worried. I heard the weather report for Western Europe. I was worried."

"I was afraid you'd hear and be worried. We're in port and will stay here until the storms pass. However, we've decided we're tired of traveling. We're taking the next flight home, hopefully in a few days."

"I'll be so glad to see you. I've missed you so much."

"Why, honey? Is something wrong?"

"Oh, no. I just miss having my confidant nearby to indulge with scandalous tales about my salacious life."

"My crazy daughter! Love you. Hope to see you by next week's end."

Christine and Ashleigh had a special relationship, half-built on teasing and hyperbole and the other half on deep-seated love and respect. Ashleigh always felt better after hearing her mother's voice.

She felt confident Christine would support her decision, even though she would worry about her future. She moved the phone to her desk, placed the aloe plant on the end table by the glass sliding doors and rearranged her research in chronological order. She needed to have a plan in place before her mom got home. She didn't want Christine to worry about her.

As she organized her desk and phone for her project work, Ashleigh noticed the flickering message light on the phone. She pressed the button and heard JJ's voice. They hadn't talked in a few days. She assumed JJ was busy with an assignment.

"Ash, hate to leave a message, but I'm on my way out the door. I just got a prime assignment. It is a murder trial in South Georgia. The defendant is a wealthy beef farmer who is accused of killing his partner. Anyway, I'll be gone for a couple of weeks. The trial will go late into the evening, and I'll need to transcribe each night. I hate to run out on you, but this could be a career changing assignment for me. I'll call when I can. I'm praying for you to find a solution to the work situation. Love you."

Ashleigh was happy for JJ, who had struggled over the last year to find enough work to live comfortably. Maybe this would be a career boost for her.

She needed to focus on her own problems now. Her in-depth study of the 14th Amendment made her aware of the nuances it held for support of abortion legislation. She had never considered the connection that could be interpreted for it to support legislation to end lives of babies, while guaranteeing equal rights for women.

She had never given abortion a second thought. Her religious beliefs held all lives sacred, and she didn't know anyone who needed an abortion. Any consideration of abortion was beyond her reality. It was apparent she needed to understand more about the legal issue for women regarding their 'right' to an abortion and how that impacts equal rights for women in the workplace.

Chapter Nine

Several days of studying made her realize that she did not want to get in the middle of the abortion issue. She wanted to narrow its focus and pull-out points in the ERA to support equality in pay and position.

It's time to get the girls back together.

Patricia was her first call since she worked as a tax accountant and was not as busy after March 15th.

"Hi, Pat. Just wanted to follow-up on our group. Did you read the materials I gave you?"

"Yes, I read everything. I'm not sure how we make an action plan out of the material."

"That's why I'm calling. I want us to get together again and discuss some other issues that will affect how we approach our goal."

"I don't know about meeting, Ash. I have a lot going on."

"Isn't tax season over?"

"Yeah. I'm not as busy professionally. I've met someone and we are together most nights. I don't know how he would react to me being involved in a controversial issue. He's a councilman from my district."

"Oh. Are you bailing on me . . . us?"

"It's not about you, Ash. It's about having a life outside of work and work commitments."

"I didn't mean to sound so critical. I understand. Let me know when you have some time. I'm thinking we need to arrange a meeting with someone who can carry our concerns to the legislature. Oh, hey, could your guy . . . "

"Ash don't ask me to do that. This is a new, fragile relationship. I really like him and don't want him to think I'm using him."

"Gotcha. Okay. I'll talk with you later."

"Bye. Good luck."

Deflated, Ashleigh piled all the files in a stack. Was she going to be in this effort by herself? She walked to her patio and decided she could not stay inside. She needed fresh air and people. Since she was still in her jogging outfit, she grabbed a light jacket and headed to the local outside market. She missed having JJ to talk with.

I feel so alone, God. I know you're with me. That should be enough but having my best friend give me a hug and listen to my whining helped.

Wait a minute, she was telling God He was not enough. *You are enough for me, God. Please show me your path for my day.*

She realized it was a Friday morning, when she saw the swarm of folks hovering over fresh vegetables brought in today by local farmers. She gravitated to the tomatoes to make lunches of red-ripe tomatoes on fresh-baked bread with lots of mayonnaise and salt and pepper. On her way, she passed first-of-the-season cantaloupes. That would be a meal. Green beans, onions, blueberries, and local honey filled her reusable grocery bag.

What had started out to be a depressing day, turned pleasant. She bought wonderful treats from farms within a 20-mile radius from here.

Even though the bag was heavy, she took her time walking home on the short trail. Drawn to the sight of moms pushing baby carriages heading her way, she warmed to the sight of love surrounding each mother-child encounter and wondered if she would ever have a husband and children. She hoped so.

Her motherly instincts clicked-in for the first time.

Putting away her treasures, she realized her refrigerator needed a thorough cleaning. Then she noticed dark spots on the kitchen floor, and there was dust on the great room furniture.

She thought, It's a good day for cleaning. I'll reward myself with a tomato sandwich when I'm finished. I'll feel better in a clean home.

Thank you, God, for turning my self-pity into something positive. I am thankful for all your gifts. I need to stay busy to stay positive.

Just as she put the vacuum cleaner away, there was a knock at the door. Before she could close the closet door and walk the ten steps to the front door, the knock came again.

Who in the world? Impatient!

Looking through the peek-hole she saw yellow and white flowers, but no face.

"Hello."

"Are you Miss Ashleigh Justice?" The voice came from behind the spring bouquet.

"Yes."

"These are for you."

"I know that voice. Jason?"

"At your service." Jason lowered the flowers to show a smiling face and sparkling green eyes.

"It is so good to see you, Jason. Come in, please. I need a friend today." She opened the door and motioned him inside.

"Me too. Let's go out to lunch."

"I've just finished cleaning my apartment. Not dressed to go out, but I have fresh tomatoes and bread for a scrumptious sandwich. I can even slice a cantaloupe. I also have Southern Sweet Tea from the local tea house. What do you say?"

"How could I refuse? There's no better lunch than tomato sandwiches and cantaloupe, topped off with sweet tea."

"Tell me everything that's happening in your world."

"Okay, I can do that as we make those delicious sandwiches?"

Ashleigh retrieved the mayonnaise from the refrigerator. "Sure. I'm starving. I'm glad we seem to like the same simple things."

"Truthfully, I was relieved you didn't want to go out. I needed peace and friendly conversation for lunch. Didn't really want the noise and confinement of a restaurant."

"No noise here."

"Be thankful."

Ashleigh encouraged. "I am. Tell me what's going on."

Jason leaned forward, putting his elbows on his knees. "I mentioned Camden the last time we talked."

"Yeah. What's he doing now?"

"Nothing! That's the problem. He is doing nothing! And he is blaming the project's lack of progress on us, the engineering staff."

Ashleigh shrugged. "Sounds familiar."

"As the lead engineer I need to meet my team's timeframes, which I can't do without his input on design."

"I know it takes a long time to complete engineering estimates. Howard Stockton should realize that."

"He does, believe me. He has let two of our best draftsmen go because the workload has decreased. In their place, he bought a new software called AutoCad. It's a 2D and 3D computer desktop drafting program. He thinks it will save him money over the years, which it might. I don't like the idea that I won't have a person to discuss the output and see their changes as they are drawing them."

Her eyes lit up. "I remember something about that software being developed when I was a junior at Southeastern Tech. That's a big step. Who did he let go?"

"The two newest guys hired. I'm not sure about that decision. Those two employees were recent graduates and brought fresh ideas to the company."

"I'm sorry, Jason. I guess we all must adjust to changes we can't control. Let's go out on the patio and finish our tea, enjoy the weather, and continue our conversation. Do you have time?"

"Sure. I'm taking the afternoon off. Tell me what's going on with you."

She told him about her plans to pursue bringing a legal argument to congress that companies are not following the spirit of the Equal Rights Amendment and haven't been for years. She also shared that her protesting group was dissolving, and she was left alone to do whatever got done.

"I can't back out now. I lost my job over my beliefs. I need a new plan and a new job."

"I bet old man Stockton would hire you back."

She stood. "I've told you; I will not go back to that company with his beliefs about pay and women's value in their jobs."

Jason raised his hands in a defensive position, "Okay, okay. I give up."

"Let's go for a walk. Can you walk in those dress shoes?"

"No, but I keep jogging pants, t-shirts, and tennis shoes in my car. Give me a minute to grab them and I'll be ready."

Ashleigh put lunch items away while Jason was gone.

"Can I use your guest bathroom to change?"

"Sure. I'll get my walking shoes on while you change."

They began their afternoon walk by racing down the stairs to the ground floor. She pushed his shoulder aside and beat him to the bottom. He laughingly grabbed her around the waist and pulled her to him. They immediately withdrew from each other and began a stress-free afternoon on the longest trail in the park.

Dogwood and cherry trees lined the trail, reminding Ashleigh of her childhood belief that the dogwood's flowers of four petals with a slight brown shading in the middle, christened with holes in three of the four petals represented the cross. The blooms quickly deteriorated and fell to the ground soon after Easter. She felt God's presence with them as they gawked at the pink blooms of the cherry trees. The purple, white, red, and orange multi-colored pansies still in bloom from winter peeked out from wet brown leaves padding the path.

They didn't see many moms pushing babies in strollers this afternoon.

When they crashed on Ashleigh's sofa, they stretched out to rest their legs. "How is your family, Ash?"

"Mom called the other day. They cut their cruise short, after five weeks…I know, that's not short, but anyway they are flying home on the first direct flight they can get. They misjudged how restful a long cruise would be. They love home. I didn't tell her about losing my job. I look forward to seeing them but dread the telling part."

"But your mom is always supportive. She'll accept it was the right thing for you."

"I know, but she will be disappointed for my career. You're always so supportive, Jason. Thank you."

"You've backed me up many times this year. I believe in you. You can make anything work, Ash. I can't wait to see what you do with all this confusion and negativity."

Ashley touched his arm. "Me, too."

"Why don't we change into something more presentable and go to an expensive restaurant for dinner?"

She smiled at him. "Does it have to be expensive? How about something mouth-watering delicious?"

"Even better." Jason stood and smiled at her.

"I'll need a shower, so it will be a few minutes."

"Thank you! I didn't want to say anything." He backed away from her with his tease.

"You'd better watch it mister. You might lose your dinner date." She swiped at him as she walked to her bedroom.

"Oh, so, this is a date?"

"You know what I mean." She yelled from the bathroom door. "Now, leave me alone, or it will be breakfast time before I'm dressed."

He continued his banter. "I could go for that, too!"

"What's gotten into you, Jason? You've never said anything like that to me."

"I was just joking around. Don't overthink the remark. It will make this night uncomfortable."

"You're not getting out of it that easily. I'm ordering the most expensive item on the menu."

"Hey, I didn't say I was paying."

Ashleigh stuck her head out of the doorway, "But you are!"

Jason stepped into the hallway half-bath to sponge off and put his office shirt, pants and shoes back on.

"Want to go to the hang-out my friends and I go to when we want to chill out and see friends hanging out for a drink and light dinner? It's called The Brick House."

"You pick the place. I'm not familiar with this part of town. It has really upgraded in the past few years."

"There are several good restaurants. Are we going for food, or fun?"

"I'd say food!"

"Okay. We can walk to this place."

Their friendship kept the night casual and fun.

"Hey, have you asked Jolene out, yet?"

"What? Who?" He glared at her.

"You know the receptionist. She's had her eye on you since her first day at work."

"She's just a kid."

"She doesn't look like a kid. I see how she looks when you're around. She is love-struck."

"What are you talking about? No, I have not asked her out, and I will never ask her out. She is too young and not my type."

"Sorry. You don't have to get so huffy." She smiled as she took her last bite of steak.

He wiped his mouth. "That was the best steak I've had in a long time."

"My favorite too. I'm glad you like your steak medium rare. Can't think of drying out a piece of meat that tender."

He scanned the room. "Looks like the gang came earlier tonight but it's okay. I enjoyed your company."

"Me too."

He walked her to her door. "Well, since I'm a working man, I guess I need to head to my place. Thanks for the fun day and night, Ash." He leaned in for a hug.

Ashleigh put her hands on his shoulders and leaned to return his hug. His arms felt hard and shaped. She had never noticed his wide shoulders or tapered waist. In his t-shirt today she noticed how his stomach was ripped under his shirt. He is a good-looking guy.

"Stay in touch."

"I will. Sleep well."

She didn't sleep well. She realized how much she missed JJ and daily contact with people. Or was it daily contact with Jason she missed?

Chapter Ten

What is that noise? It's barely light. It keeps on and on. Is that the phone? Who is calling at the crack of dawn?

"Hello!"

"Good morning, sweetheart. I wanted to catch you before you left for work. Hope you weren't in the shower."

"Hi Mom. No, I was not in the shower."

"You sound grumpy. I thought you'd be glad to know dad and I are home."

"Yes. I'm delighted you're back on this continent all in one piece."

"Can you do lunch today?"

"Sure."

"I'll come by your office, and we'll go from there. Okay?"

"No, today is not a good day at work. Let's meet at Rudolph's. It's quiet and we can have a salad and visit. How about one o'clock?"

"That sounds fine. I'll see you there. Love you."

"You too, mom. And I am glad you are home."

Ashleigh looked in the mirror, steaming coffee in her hand. She needed a long shower, shampoo, and a business outfit for the meeting with Christine. Her mother would wear a cashmere sweater with pearls, pleated slacks, and high heels. The restaurant would be cool enough for a light-weight sweater. She needed to find something to wear to match Christine's casual business look.

After her shower, she pulled out all the documentation she put together for her attack on current ways of using females as second-class workers. The conversation about quitting her job would follow the confession of her participation in the protest rally. This would not be a pleasant home-coming lunch.

Arriving early to choose a table away from the crowd, Ashleigh watched the doorway for Christine. She unfolded the napkin and placed it in her lap and picked up the menu. She knew every item listed but she needed something to occupy her trembling hands until her mom arrived.

She heard Christine before she saw her. The maître de knew the family and led her to Ashleigh's table as she made polite conversation.

Ashleigh stood and embraced her mother. It felt good to see her again. Christine's presence always soothed her and gave her confidence to face any difficulty. It was no different today.

"Mom, you look wonderful! The trip must have been relaxing and enjoyable."

"Mostly, but I won't plan anything that dramatic anytime in the future. How are you, sweetheart? You look a little stressed."

How did she do that? One look at Ashleigh and Christine could read her daughter's demeanor and identify stress, sadness, frustration, and concern.

Today, all four were evident. "I'll tell you all about it after we eat, and you tell me about your trip."

"We'll have an in-depth show-and-tell after Carlton completes his slideshow. Tell me what you've been doing and what's a problem."

Ashleigh used the interruption by the waitress to stall. "I'll have the house salad with grilled shrimp."

While Christine was ordering, Ashleigh said a quick prayer for calmness and guidance. "Let me start by getting to the end."

Christine raised her eyebrows. "The end of what?"

"My job!"

"Oh, my. Sweetheart, what happened. I know they didn't let you go. They are far too fortunate to have you. What happened?"

Ashleigh relayed the whole incident, including her intentions, and showed her the newspaper coverage of the protest.

When Christine didn't respond immediately, Ashleigh told her about her conversations with her boss and her decision to quit rather than abandon her fight for equal pay for women.

"So, your name was never mentioned in the newspaper?"

"No, just a glimpse of me leaving the rally."

"I thought Howard Stockton had more courage than to be scared into letting his most promising architect leave because she would not be blackmailed into accepting a stance that dishonors her talent and achievements. He made a big mistake. Wait until I tell your dad!"

"No, Mom! I'm handling this. I don't want interference from you or dad. I made the decision to leave. I don't want you to 'fix' the repercussions for me. I'm an adult. I can live with the outcome."

"Honey, the value of having influential parents is to use their position when you need help."

"I don't need help. Let me handle this, please."

Chapter Eleven

Ashleigh plopped on the sofa and kicked off her shoes. The lunch had ended with hugs and tension. I knew she wanted to take over and solve my 'problem'. It's not a problem for me, yet. I know God has something greater for me. I'm okay waiting for his plan, while I continue putting together a group to work with the legal side for a solution.

She glanced at her answering machine as she walked to her bedroom to change clothes. The red light called her to stop and see who left a message.

"Ash, hey. It's me, Jason. I have an opportunity I want to share with you. Are you free for dinner? Call me and let me know. It's kind of important."

Intrigued, but needing to get out of dressy clothes, she pulled off her sweater as she continued into the bedroom. Pedal pushers and a t-shirt felt much better. She settled on the sofa and dialed Jason's number.

"Hi, Jason. I am free for dinner. Do you want to give me a hint about the opportunity you mentioned?"

"No, I don't. I'll come by at seven and pick you up. Hold on to your patience until then. Bye."

Well, that was strange. Usually, Jason couldn't keep important news to himself. This night might be interesting.

Jason was on time. "Come in. Would you like a soft drink before we go?"

"No. I have reservations at the Red Rock Restaurant."

"You aren't going to tell me your news before we get there?"

"Not a chance. I know you. We'll be here all night talking. We can talk at the restaurant. Ready?"

"Who are you? I've never seen you so pushy."

Jason laughed as he grabbed her arm and escorted her out the door.

They talked about Stockton & Associates on the drive. Jason was still concerned about Camden, but he had no control over the architect leading his project. They were peers.

"We have a presentation to Deerfield execs next week. I hope Mr. Stockton won't be surprised at the lack of progress. We're not going to ruin the evening by talking about my job. That's all I'm going to say on that subject."

"Okay. That's fine with me. Mom and dad came home, and she and I had lunch today. As expected, she wanted to take over and 'make everything all right' for me. I think I finally convinced her to leave it alone and let me handle it. I'm thankful you called. I need to get my mind off my parents' interference. I see the restaurant off to the right. I haven't been to this place in a long time. Are we dining at the lake?"

"Of course. No reason to come here, otherwise." Jason parked in a space near the front entrance to the ramp leading to the lakeside dining area.

"Sit here while I check-in."

Ashleigh was more than happy to sit quietly and look at the rippled water, silently kissing the bank. There was infrequent boat traffic this evening, which made the moon reflect undisturbed onto the water at the ramp's entrance. She was mesmerized. The lake had always been her place of joy and peace. She could sit here all night inhaling the fresh air and gentle breeze. Jason startled her when he opened the passenger side door.

"We're all good. You ready?"

Ashleigh jumped at his intrusion into her reverie. "Oh, sure."

"Did I scare you?"

"I was enjoying the peace and beauty."

"You'll have a better view when we are seated on the upper-level deck."

"You're joking. You must have made reservations a few days ago to get a table up there."

"Hey, I have connections too."

"No doubt."

He took her hand and helped her out of the car, keeping her hand in his as they climbed the stairs to the upper deck. She gasped at the beauty when she took the final step a story above the water.

"I've never seen the lake from this height. It is beyond anything I would have imagined. Thank you for bringing me here tonight."

"You're welcome. I thought it might be a treat. I've wanted to come here for a long time, but I haven't had anyone I wanted to bring here, until now."

Ashleigh's surprised look caught him off-guard. "Oh, I didn't mean anything by that. We just have a good friendship and I thought you might like a distraction tonight."

"That's for sure. However, I want to know about your intriguing message about something to share."

"Let's order our first course, then I'll tell you."

They both ordered salads with blue cheese dressing. "Okay. I have a buddy who works in an architectural firm that specializes in urban development. Their lead architect was just diagnosed with prostate cancer and will be out of work for the duration of his treatment, which could be up to a year. However, it is not guaranteed. They are desperate for someone who is creative, talented, experienced, and available for a few months. They are working on two buildings downtown that would mirror each other. The design has not been finalized or presented in any form to the developer. I told him about you. He went to the president of his firm and he wants to interview you for that position. He is in a bind and doesn't want to lose the contract, but he can't commit to a secure position long-term. When his lead man comes back to work, you will be let go."

Ashleigh bounced in her seat. "Are you kidding? That would be a perfect situation for me, for now. I don't want to give up my work on shoring-up legislation regarding women's issues, but I do need to have an income. Can you help me prepare for the interview?"

"Be happy to." Jason grinned at his friend. He looked happy about spending more time together.

They didn't rush dinner. They marveled at the beauty of the lake and talked about family and friends. As the restaurant began closing the lakeside dining, they reluctantly descended the stairs. Once again, Jason offered his hand to help her down the last step and did not let go as they walked to the car.

Chapter Twelve

Edward Northcutt greeted Ashleigh with an assuming air that he was doing her a favor.

"Miss Justice, have a seat. I understand you lost your last job suddenly and are looking for a position as lead architect. First, I must tell you I am not looking for a permanent employee at this time."

"I understand, Mr. Northcutt. I, too, am looking for a temporary position, while I work on a project near to my heart. That is the reason I quit my last job. I needed more freedom to move forward with my own goal."

"Are you telling me, you will not be one hundred percent committed to my company while I'm paying you?"

"Not at all. I will be committed during work hours, but I have a deadline on my other commitment that I will work on in my free time . . . If I'm hired."

"We also have a deadline on our mirror project. Dick Monroe is a talented, creative architect and had the beginnings of a dramatic solution to the development of the mirror buildings in downtown. Unfortunately, his illness has him unable to work now. He will return to pick up and finish the buildings when he recovers."

"I understand all of that. I researched Mr. Monroe and your firm and feel I can contribute moving his plans along until he returns."

"I, also, researched you and your work at Howard Stockton's firm. You seem to be a creative architect, unafraid to push the envelope with design. If I had a permanent position opening, I would consider hiring you. So, we have an understanding?"

"We do."

Ashleigh called Jason as soon as she closed the door to her apartment. "I got the job, Jason! Thank you so much for saving me. My bank account is dwindling."

"I knew you could pull it off. Congratulations! How about dinner to celebrate?"

"That sounds wonderful. I couldn't be productive today anyway. I've got to spend the afternoon getting things organized for my first day on the job, Monday."

After taking business clothes to the dry cleaners, she jogged the short trail back to her apartment. She vacuumed, scrubbed the bathroom, and put the kitchen in order. When she looked at the clock, she realized it was time to shower and dress for her dinner with Jason.

Jason seems to be near when I need a shoulder to lean on or a night to celebrate. He's a good friend. I need to do something nice for him.

She waited until they were settled in at the restaurant. "Jase, you've been so supportive. I want to cook dinner for you tomorrow night. Are you free?"

"Jase? Where did that come from?"

"Jason is so formal. I think we're closer than formalities. If it offends you…"

"No. I love it. I feel close to you too."

"I haven't had a close friend other than JJ in a long time, and she isn't here now. I appreciate you taking her place."

"Oh. Yeah. Of course."

When Jason walked her to her door, he made a quick exit.

"Won't you come in for a little while?"

"No. Thanks. I have a busy day tomorrow. I need to get a good night's sleep. See ya."

Well, that was abrupt. Something seemed different tonight. I guess he's thinking about whatever he's doing tomorrow.

Since it was early, she decided to call JJ. They had not talked in several weeks. Her phone rang several times and then the answering machine clicked in. Ashleigh left JJ a long message. She wanted to hear JJ's voice and tell her about the unusual situation with Jason.

Hoping JJ would call soon, she sat down at her computer. It was such a blessing to have a tool that allowed her to work seamlessly at home. Nineteen eighty-three had been a good year for IBM with an estimated ten million PCs in use. Now, in 1988 Ashleigh could access the Northcutt website and research Richard (Dick) Monroe. She wanted to know everything about him and his work product because she wanted to carry his dream forward until he could return to work. She began with a prayer.

Chapter Thirteen

Where is Jase? He's not answering his phone at home or at work. I didn't tell him what time I would have dinner ready. He never really said OK about tonight. Seven is normally when we get together. I'll plan for that time.

Seven came and went and no Jase. Ashleigh began to worry. At seven-thirty, she called his phone and left a message.

"Hi. Hope everything is okay. I have prime rib ready. Let me know if you're going to be later."

At nine o'clock she put everything away. She was worried about him. He always called her back. I hope he is all right. Maybe I should go to his apartment and check on him. No, I don't want to barge into his Saturday night, if he didn't really say he would be here.

Sunday morning the shrill of the phone woke her in a jerk. "Hello."

"Hi, Ashleigh. I got your message when I got in this morning. Sorry, there was a mix-up about dinner. I had other plans last night."

"Oh, hi. That's okay. You never said you would come over."

"Well, since I just got in, I need to get cleaned up for church. Have a good day. See ya'."

So, he didn't plan to see her today. Wonder who has his attention. I'm glad he has someone to spend time with. Oh, well, after church I have plenty of research to do anyway.

She slipped into the family pew just as the choir stood for the introit. Christine smiled at her daughter and slid her arm under Ashleigh's. Leaving the church took several minutes, as Carlton spoke with associates and long-term church members. Christine and Ashleigh smiled and waved at several couples but moved forward away from the crowd to have their own conversation.

"Are you joining us for lunch at the Club?"

"Not today, Mom."

"Oh. Do you have a date?"

"Yes. A date with my computer. I have research to do this afternoon."

"I'm planning a small dinner party Saturday night. Will you put that on your calendar? I want you to be there with us."

"Sure."

"You can bring a date."

"It will just be me, Mom."

"Okay. Good. We haven't had a dinner party in quite a while. I'm looking forward to this one."

"Here comes, dad. I need to get home after I get a hug from him."

The day seemed normal and familiar. She fell into the routine she had observed every Sunday since she graduated from college:

church, quite afternoon, preparation for work the next day. This Sunday she had prep to do for her first day at Northcutt & Associates.

She found out that Dick Monroe was married with two children, a six-year-old boy, Drew, and a four-year-old girl, Dillon. He was in-line to make partner when he was diagnosed with prostate cancer. His wife of 10 years was a stay-at-home mom, with a Master of Psychology Education. Before marriage, she worked as a teacher and counselor at a school for physically challenged children.

Dick seemed to be some-what of a star in the world of architecture. He won several awards for design while still a PhD student at Southeastern Tech. He and his family were members of a local church. He coached basketball at the YMCA every Saturday during summers. He was in a local running club and set aside time for his family.

Edward Northcutt hired him early in his career. He offered Dick a chance to help create a new skyline of Atlanta. Dick accepted immediately.

Wow, I have big shoes to fill; even though it's just for a few months.

God, I need you to give me wisdom, strength, and knowledge to be a voice for Dick during his absence.

Monday morning, Ashleigh arrived an hour early on the 12th floor, surprised to find the outside door locked. She was disappointed that she couldn't get a jump-start on the day. She retreated to the coffee-shop on the main floor of the building. It felt good to be in the hustle and bustle of professional folks visiting prior to getting to work. She was comfortable in this atmosphere.

As the coffee shop began to empty its customers, she followed along to the elevator. She entered the office to see a smiling face. Leslie Small stood and held out her hand, "Welcome Ashleigh. I'm Leslie Small and I'm glad you're here. I'm an architecture student and hope to be in your shoes someday."

"I'll try to be a good example for you Leslie."

"Mr. Northcutt is waiting for you in his office."

Ashleigh walked the short distance to the mahogany double doors of Mr. Northcutt's office. Before she could knock, he opened the double doors and invited her in.

"The first order of business is for you to meet the staff. We'll start that process now. You need to meet the rest of the team working on the twin project. There are three junior architects who support Dick. You will bring back recommendations from Dick to the rest of his team and assure they understand his directions for them. When you meet with Dick you will take the progress they have made and questions they may have back to Dick for his evaluation and input. Roger Langley is the most senior of the three support architects. You will probably work mostly with him.

Introductions took most of the morning, ending at Leslie's temporary desk. "I know you'll be working in Dick's office most of the time, but I wanted you to have a spot of your own to feel part of the company. Feel free to work where you need to each day."

Ashleigh thanked him, put her briefcase away in the desk drawer and walked into Dick's office. At first, she was overwhelmed at the disarray. Then she realized that many people had been in and out of his office, while he was recuperating. She began studying the stacks of files and drawings. By six o'clock she had things in an organized fashion to suit her style of working. She also realized she needed a more personal relationship with him to complete her assignment.

Edward Northcutt stuck his head in the door as he was headed home. "How was your first day? Do you need anything from me for tomorrow?"

"I would like your permission to check with Dick about visiting with him and his family. I'd like to get to know him and his style before I digest his drawings."

"Sure. I'll call now." He reached for the phone.

"Dick was excited that he would meet you to talk about his ideas. Tomorrow is fine."

When she got home, she dialed JJ's number. This is important. I need to talk with JJ to share my good news. Once again, there was no answer. This time the recording said the mailbox was full, please try again later.

Chapter Fourteen

Wow, here I am with nothing to work on tonight. But I do have something I should have done a week ago. I need to get the group together to plan our next steps.

She called Pat but got a message on her answering machine and got the same results from Saundra and Martha.

Leaving messages for them to meet at her apartment the following Wednesday at six p.m., she assumed they still wanted to support women. When they arrived, she would tell them it was a planning session.

Then she reached for her calendar to set hard dates for movement on their plans. She outlined what needed to be done and filled in names to take each part. Next, she checked the legislature's schedule for when they would be in-session over the next year. She wanted to have all the details ready for the group without having to research anything when they met.

She double-checked the representatives' names for federal, state, and local positions and started an in-depth search of their support on women's issues. She checked the docket to see what types of legislation each representative had authored or supported. Finally, she made a sheet for each of them to add names of representatives with whom they had any kind of relationship.

Tonight is a perfect night to do this prep. After I meet with Dick Monroe tomorrow, I'll be busy studying him and his work-flow. I wonder what Jase is doing tonight. I'd like to share my day with him. He was so supportive to put me in touch with Mr. Northcutt. After tomorrow, I may not have time to visit with him for a while. I'll be inundated with details, deadlines, and develop-ment of Dick's creation.

She looked at the clock and realized she had worked until midnight. It's time to get ready for bed. I can't sleep-in tomorrow. I've got to get used to my new routine.

***

Tuesday, she was awake before the alarm called her to attention. The early morning sun had not reached her bed when she slid her legs off its side and stood watching the day awaken. She didn't move for a few minutes, saying a prayer.

God thank you for putting me here in a challenging position where I can grow my talents along with a well-established, well-known architect. You know where I need to be, and you lead me there. Hold my hand as I start this journey and help me continue my search for someone to support equality in pay and position for all women.

She looked at the directions Leslie Small had given her for Dick's address. I think I can find his home easily enough. It is a little farther than I expected. He lives in a gated community on Lake Lanier. I think it's near a marina I've visited. At least it's off the same main road. I need to be on time. Just coffee and an apple this morning.

She pulled on professional slacks, a long-sleeved blouse topped with a blazer. As she slid under the steering wheel, she checked the gas gauge on her sports car. Traffic heading out of town shouldn't be as bad as heading into town, but she wanted to be sure she had enough gas for the return trip. She was excited to have a reason to leave the city and enjoy the early morning ride with the sunroof open and fewer gear shifts in the car's five-speed transmission. She rarely drove on the highway. Today's drive would free her from shifting gears every few blocks for red traffic lights. She eased out of her parking space and headed toward the Blue Ridge Mountains.

Leslie's directions easily led her to Dick's house. When she spotted the house number, she looked down at a winding driveway that sloped to the lake. Then she looked at the water beyond. For a moment, she held her breath. Sparkling waves of deep blue flowed toward the back of the house, lit by the sun's toying reflection. Across the cove, birch, oak, and maple trees cradled a gazebo with table and chairs at the water's edge.

She looked away from the view and slowly rolled down the driveway until she reached a large concrete pad.

I'm thankful I wore low-heeled shoes. The view is worth the walk.

Dick's wife, Marianne, welcomed her into a great room flowing toward the expansive lake view through glass sliding doors and floor to ceiling windows. She felt wrapped in the warmth emanating from Marianne and two well-behaved children.

Ashleigh paused for a moment to absorb the serenity she had entered. There seemed to be no separation from the comfort and flow of the entryway into the green and beige great room with fourteen-foot ceilings, hosting three dark beams pointing toward the deep blue water. An early morning sky of smoky blue opened the glass wall at the opposite side of the house. Trees as tall and straight as church steeples bordered the carpeted grass and pathway to the dock.

Marianne touched Ashley's arm. "Come in, Ashleigh. Dick is waiting for you in our bedroom. He is so excited to share with you his vision of the latest project Mr. Northcutt has undertaken."

"I'm excited to meet him. I've reviewed his work on the project, and it is one that will help bring the Atlanta skyline much praise and recognition."

Dick's warm smile and outstretched hand from the king-size bed drew her in to his courage and strength. "Ashleigh, come sit in the chair in front of the windows. Marianne has set up a chair and table where you can be comfortable. I can't get close to you because of the radiation but you will be safe sitting over there."

"Thank you for seeing me. I won't take too much of your time."

"It will probably be the other way around. I'm emersed in this project and hate it that I can't be in the office. I guess you know, I have prostate cancer. I am young enough to have the option of deciding between three options: doing nothing and wait to see if the cancer grows; have surgery to remove the prostate, which would mean a long recovery; or, have radiation pellets implanted to kill the cancer. I chose the latter, unknowing I would be unable to be around women of child-bearing age, young children or anyone with any condition that might be harmed by the radiation inside me."

"I'm sure that was a hard decision for you and your family."

"For sure. Marianne and I have two wonderful children and, knowing the radiation will kill any chances for me to father any other children, decided it was the best choice for us. However, I can't have the children in the room with me for long periods of time. I usually visit with them on one side of the great room and me on the other. It's not a perfect situation, but it's temporary.

"Now, tell me a little about you, before we begin work."

Dick had original drawings and detailed progress notes on his computer. They were able to make a good deal of headway. Ashleigh's preparation allowed her to follow his thoughts and comment or question here and there. They scheduled meetings twice a week for Ashleigh to bring her work and drawings to him.

Chapter Fifteen

Christine's dinner party was an obligation for Ashleigh. It was the least favorite way for her to spend time with her parents.

She wondered how many people would be invited to the dinner, and what level of importance they were to her mother's society. She chose her favorite black dress and sandals for tonight. Her diamond chip necklace was appropriate to give her just enough formality rather than highlighting the two and three carat necklaces her parents had given her for high school and master's degree achievements. She approved of the image in the mirror, showing the dress hanging loosely on her fit body and subtly emphasizing her femininity with spaghetti straps and skirt hitting mid-calf.

She parked in the back of her parents' home in front of the four-car garage and entered through the kitchen to slip into the crowd without making a noticeable entrance.

"Sweetheart, I didn't see you come in." Christine took her elbow and guided her around the room, making introductions to new invitees.

"That was the point, Mom." Ashleigh smiled and kissed her mom on the cheek.

"Where is Dad?"

"You didn't see him on the back patio?"

"I slipped in behind the shrubs."

"I hope you can stay after, so we can visit."

"It depends on the hour. I have a huge project with Mr. Northcutt's firm and need to be sharp in the morning."

"There's dad now." She slid her elbow from Christine's grasp and walked toward her father. He saw her heading his way and cut his conversation short, smiling with outstretched arms toward her.

"Dad, I always feel safe in your arms."

"I always love having you in my arms."

Christine asked the guests to bring their drinks into the dining room where dinner was waiting. When everyone was seated, Carlton stood.

"Dear Lord, bless this food to the nourishment of everyone here and remind us, where our blessings originate. We thank you for all your loving gifts. Amen"

Ashleigh felt comforted by her father's prayers. He never hesitated to acknowledge his faith and gladly shared with others the fruits of his labor.

Christine sat Ashleigh next to a young man who owned a successful brokerage firm. She hoped they would hit it off. He would make a perfect partner for Ashleigh. His parents were members of the country club and his father had business dealings with Carlton.

Ashleigh nodded to Ross as she sat down. He immediately rose and guided her chair under the table.

She smiled, "Thank you, Ross. I'm surprised we have never met."

"I went to military school and finished my education at a college in Macon. I never lived in mom and dad's home. They moved here from California while I was away at a military school. They wanted to be close enough to visit with me. Then I graduated and went to college, so they were still somewhat distant from me. I came home occasionally, but never got into the social scene. While at college, I became interested in investments and changed the focus of my education to investment banking."

"It's funny how our focus changes as we grow more aware of our world and the opportunities out there for us. I've always known that I wanted to be an architect. My uncle was a well-known architect and every time we visited, I spent all my time asking him questions and looking at the pictures of buildings he designed in Tampa. I had a razor focus on Southeastern Tech and worked hard to get accepted."

"That's a strange career for a woman, isn't it?"

"Maybe. But why should it be?"

"But you're working in a man's world."

Ashleigh took a moment to calm herself. "That's what needs to change. It shouldn't be a man's world. If I am smart enough to get through school taking the same courses men take, why shouldn't it be expected that I would become an architect, just like them? Have you heard of the Equal Rights Amendment?"

"Oh, I didn't mean anything disrespectful. Of course, I know what the ERA is. I have just never met anyone who is challenging it. I think it's great that you knew what you wanted and went after it. I'm sure it was much harder for you than typical female careers."

"I think we need to change the subject. Let's try to enjoy our dinner. Standing rib roast is one of mom's most popular dishes."

Ross looked away from Ashleigh, red-faced and quiet the rest of the dinner.

Ashleigh stayed through coffee and desert in the library but took leave as soon as the men started talking politics and the women moved to the formal living room.

"Thank you for a wonderful dinner, Mom. I've got a lot of work tonight. I'll call you in a few days. Ladies." She tipped her head in their direction and left through the kitchen the same way she had arrived.

Chapter Sixteen

Monday morning Ashleigh smiled as she dressed for her meeting with Dick.

Thank you, God, for leading me to this opportunity for me as well as for Dick. We work together as if we have been associates for years. His ideas mesh with my creative bents towards Atlanta's future skyline. Help me to represent his style in his project.

And help him recover from this surgery, where he can get back to work in the office. Bless his wife and children during this difficult time for their family."

The egg-yolk sun splattered across the passenger seat as she drove toward the lake home. She pulled into the driveway and parked in a spot facing the filtered sun through full-leafed maples. Marianne met her at the door with a cup of steaming coffee.

"You already know me pretty well." Ashleigh smiled as she took the morning mug of energy. "How is Dick this morning?"

"You can't imagine how much your coming here means to his progress. He wakes up ready to share ideas with you and has a purpose to his day."

"I hear you in there Ashleigh. I'm ready to get started."

"Guess I'll take my coffee and report in." Ashleigh bowed toward the door where Dick was sitting at his worktable, papers spread from one side to the other.

She placed her blueprints, files and computer on the desk facing him. "Where shall we start today?"

"The first item on the project plan is to motivate the civil engineers to complete the ground soil evaluation. Granite lies under much of the topsoil in the Atlanta area, even though Stone Mountain is twenty miles away. Granite is deep underground in this part of the state.

"The location of the buildings is technically in Sandy Springs, but they will overlook the Atlanta Perimeter and Georgia 400. We need to be sure granite is not in the area around either of the buildings in the twin development. I don't expect sandy soil like the beaches on the coast, because most of North Georgia is red clay but we must be sure whatever soil it has can support two thirty-two-floor buildings across from each other."

They called the engineering department and set up a meeting for Wednesday to talk about progress on their part of the project.

The rest of the day was spent going over Dick's project plan, dividing up the work he could do at home from the physical evaluation Ashleigh and the rest of the team must do at the site and in the office.

She left his home late in the afternoon and went directly to The Brick House. The girls agreed to meet here every Tuesday night to review their progress on getting support from a local representative in the state legislature.

She arrived early and secured a table for the group. She ordered sweet tea and settled in to listen to the local talent entertain the diners with soft piano music. Later, there would be a guitarist joining the pianist and rock music would override conversation.

It felt good to be in The Brick House. She hadn't been a regular for a while now. She settled in with her sweet tea, knowing the other women wouldn't be here for another half hour. She glanced around the room. There were a few tables close by with couples having a drink or an early dinner.

In the dark corner away from the main floor, she could see movement even though that table was rarely occupied. Then she saw the man stand up and pull the chair out for his companion. As they turned to exit the restaurant, she realized it was Jason with the receptionist, Jolene. They didn't see her. She didn't make a move that would attract their attention.

In the pit of her stomach, she felt a pinch of disappointment. That was foolish. Jason was free to see whomever he wanted. She had no hold on him. His overly firm rejection of dating Jolene had been a ruse. Or maybe her mentioning that Jolene was attracted to him made him want to pursue her. After all Jason was in his early thirties and had never been married. She wasn't even sure he had a long-term relationship since she knew him. He might be ready for a relationship with an attractive young woman.

They reached the door just as Pat opened it to enter. Jason recognized her and quickly looked around to see if Ashleigh was there. He saw her sitting by herself on the other side of the room, but he didn't acknowledge it. His hand was at Jolene's back, and he guided her out the door.

The night lost its energy for her. She smiled at Pat, as the other two women entered the restaurant and headed to the table. She couldn't muster enthusiasm for presenting her research, but when all three of them told her about their recent encounters at their jobs, the evening began to take on a different tone.

All three women tried to talk at one time. Pat secured the spot with her overly deep voice and no compunction to talk softly. "I'm definitely in for this crusade! This week a new client, wanted to transfer his account from a large firm whose accountant was a man with ten years' experience, equal to mine. As we talked and I told him my fee for the services he wanted, he puffed up and complained that my fee was the same as the firm he was leaving. He said he expected my fee to be lower than his previous firm.

"I told him that was the going rate for the work he asked me to do. I also suggested that we could cut the cost by deleting some of the services he wanted.

"He said, 'I am not prepared to pay a woman the same amount I pay a man!'

"I mentioned that I had the same training, CPA credential and experience as the previous accountant/CPA.

"He retorted, 'But you're a woman.'

"I said, yes…and? He had the audacity to say, 'You don't have a family to support.'

"I told him, "You aren't paying me for my family. You are paying for a service for you at a reasonable rate. It's for a service, not for the sex of the person.

"He said, 'You can't possibly be as qualified as a man and your once-a-month thing will make you irrational and irritable. I don't want to deal with that. I'll stay with my firm. Good luck to you finding any other male business."

"Ashleigh, I have got to work with you on this issue. This is the first client since Mr. Troutman's retirement, who has come to me with an attitude like that. It isn't right!"

Saundra spoke up. "I didn't want to be part of this issue, but it seems we are all connected in some way. I happened to be in the breakroom with Stanley Brickman when he received a phone call and had to go to his office to talk with the client. He inadvertently left his pay stub on the break table. I know it was wrong, but I couldn't resist looking at it. We started at the firm at the same time, with the same experience, but he is making Ten Thousand Dollars more than I am. I'm so angry it's hard for me to concentrate on my work. Ash, this just isn't right!"

Martha placed her napkin in her lap, indicating she was here for dinner and the team. "Ashleigh, I'm so glad you called me. I've been so frustrated this week. I met with the principal about renewing my contract. I overheard another advanced math teacher, a man, bragging about his contract to the other male teachers. Next year, he will make Five Thousand Dollars more than me because he has the credential to teach/coach volleyball. He will not have volleyball as an assignment, but his credential allowed the principal to give him the extra money. We are supposed to be on the same pay level. This bumps him to the next level. I'm so disheartened. I need to work with you to bring about equal pay for females."

"Sounds like we've got some momentum now. Has anyone made any headway with a local representative?"

"I have a friend whose next-door neighbor is a representative from our district. Let me talk with her to get some background on him." Saundra made herself a note.

Ashleigh looked at the other two women. They had no input. "Okay. Look at the information I gave you last time. I identified all the representatives, their political views and votes they've cast and what causes they seem to represent. Let's all research them thoroughly and decide who will approach each one of them about the ratification of the ERA. We can meet in two weeks to check on our progress. If anyone makes any progress or uncovers a greater issue we need to know about, we can meet sooner."

The meeting ended with the delivery of dinner to the table.

Chapter Seventeen

Tuesday mornings became routine for Ashleigh to meet with Roger Langley. She shared her meeting notes with Dick and reviewed the changes in the blueprints for his insertion in the master plan. Roger and Dick worked together for ten years before Dick was sidelined.

"How is Dick doing mentally as well as physically?"

"He seems to be fine. Marianne said he is gaining strength by working and having something to think about besides his cancer."

"He is a private man who doesn't show his deep feelings often. We've been friends for a long time. I still don't understand the depth of his caring and devotion to his family and work."

"I can already see that. He is hesitant to talk about personal things with me. Of course, he doesn't know me yet."

"I'm thankful you are here to be the go between for him and the rest of his team. I don't have time to travel to his home weekly. I have three other large projects I'm lead architect on. They are much smaller, two to three story buildings, or city-center plans for small cities. I'm juggling those as well as leading Dick's project until he gets back. I'll be glad for him to return to work for several reasons."

They worked the rest of the day sorting through changes and questions from Dick. Roger decided to bring in the two other architects to see how they worked with Ashleigh. He had a plan developing in his mind about the future for the twin project if things did not work out for Dick to return to work.

***

Ashleigh struggled with the front door lock and two bags of groceries. The pantry was empty, and she did not feel like going out for dinner. Suddenly, a hairy, muscular arm reached from behind her to turn the key and push the door open.

"Need help, little lady?"

"Jason! I'm so glad to see you. I've missed you so much!"

She practically threw the groceries on the kitchen counter and turned to give him a hug.

"Looks like you did miss me."

"I have so much to share with you. Can you stay a little while?"

"Sure. I thought we might grab a quick bite to eat."

"You don't have plans with Jolene tonight?"

"Jolene is taking night classes at Georgia State. She is working on a public relations degree."

"Wow. I'm proud of her for being pro-active in her career. Are you coaching her? Or just encouraging her with your wisdom and experience?"

"You are too funny. I'm not doing much, except advising her about her career choices."

"And her long-term social choices?"

"What are you getting at? I am not, I repeat, not dating her."

"Looked like it the night I saw you at The Brick House. You didn't come over to speak to me."

"No. Because I saw Pat and knew you were having a meeting. Also, Jolene needed to get to class."

"Oh. Well, that clears that up." She smiled her sideways tease at him.

"Change the subject. You want to grab a bite?"

"I didn't before, but now I feel like being in a crowd."

Ashleigh realized how much she missed him. It felt so good to walk down the street with Jason, his hand protectively on her elbow. With JJ absent, she needed a friend to hang out with.

When they got back to her apartment, Jason walked her to her door, but didn't go inside. "If you're like me, you have a busy day tomorrow. I enjoyed tonight. I'll see you soon."

He squeezed her arm and walked toward the elevator.

What did that mean? She closed the door and felt more alone than ever.

***

The pulsing light on the phone flashed red around the room and drew her attention. JJ had left a lengthy message. "Ash. Sorry I haven't been available. This trial has morphed into a major story and a very complicated trial. I've been working day and night. I'm exhausted.

"But I have been having some fun. The judge's clerk has been active in the courtroom. We had lunch together one day and I found out he was a law student preparing to take the bar exam this winter. He plans to move to Atlanta after he passes. We've squeezed in some nights to have dinner or walk on the courthouse grounds after the trial dismisses for the night.

"Oh, I haven't asked you about you! Stay home tomorrow night. I'll call you back to find out everything going on in your world. Love ya!"

The night could not have been better. She had heard from both of her good friends. She straightened the apartment, put on a load of clothes to wash and clicked on the television.

Sometime in the night she woke to a fuzzy screen and buzzing sounds. When she crawled into bed, sleep evaded her. She rolled out of bed, slipping her feet into soft bedroom shoes and wrapped herself in her favorite pink robe. She intended to look at her files from work but decided that she needed entertainment. Rummaging through her bookshelves she found an uncomplicated romance novel and curled up on the sofa to read.

The words sounded stilted and unrelatable. Life was not like the characters in the book. Everything did not have a happy ending. She hoped for a happy ending for herself, but there was no guarantee. She put the book down and focused on the Monroe family.

Dear Lord, please cover the Monroe family with your grace. Help them to endure the weeks or months Dick has until his cancer is gone and he can get back to his normal health. Grant him that future. Help me to be of some benefit to them. Give me the wisdom of what to say and how to respond to their needs. I love you, Lord. Amen

Sleep overtook her until the summer sun peeked over the horizon hitting her in the face. She jerked awake afraid she was late. The clock read six-twenty a.m. She had plenty of time. It was her day to visit Dick.

Chapter Eighteen

Several weeks passed before Ashleigh realized that summer was in full control, and she had taken no time off to relax. Every minute seemed to be taken with her work at Northcutt and group meetings to plan interventions in the local legislature's agendas, looking for someone to support ratification of the ERA.

Her routine split the week into Monday and Wednesday meetings with Dick. Tuesday, Thursday, and Friday she worked in the office with Roger.

One hectic Friday, Christine called her at work. "Sweetheart, I'm giving a dinner party tomorrow night. Is there any way you can clear your calendar to attend? I really need another female at the table."

Generally, Ashleigh would cringe at an invitation like this from her mother but today she needed a change in routine and upbeat, lively interactions with successful people. "I'd love to Mom. What's the dress and time?"

"That was so easy. I was prepared to beg and bribe you."

"No. I need a night of thoughtless conversation and casual visiting with new people."

"Great! If you wouldn't mind, could you be here at seven-thirty. Guests aren't expected until eight but I would like to have my own time with my daughter before they arrive."

"I'd like that too."

Saturday night she automatically pulled her standard spaghetti strap 'little black dress' out of the closet and accented it with the two-carat diamond drop necklace and half-carat earrings her parents had given her when she graduated from Southeastern Tech. Maybe a little showy, but the guest list included successful business executives in Atlanta.

She settled onto one of the island stools in the kitchen, while Christine arranged the catered dishes from Raphels.

"I'm getting a little lazy with some of these dinner parties. There was a time when I cooked everything I served. I almost feel guilty serving these delicious dishes in my China and silver."

"Mom, you deserve a break. You've been the queen of parties my whole life. It's time to change things up a little."

"You're right. Tell me about what's going on with you, your job and your project fighting non-compliance with the ERA."

"Love my job. It's challenging, but I'm not ultimately responsible for the success of the project. Roger Langley, who is a senior architect, is heading the twin project. I'm learning so much from Dick and Roger. I've never been involved in a thirty-two-story design project. It's valuable experience."

"I'm so happy you have this opportunity. Now, tell me about the progress of the personal project you champion."

"Everyone is on-board now and working hard to find a sup-porter of the ERA in the local legislature. We're hoping that we might get a representative or senator behind the effort to ratify it. If we can start conversations about ratification, we're hoping to force companies to adhere to it. For now, we have not found a legislator who is sympathetic to the cause. We need a female in the Georgia legislature. She could make some noise that might get the ball rolling. For now, we're putting together a committee to encourage the only woman who is thinking about running in November."

"Sounds like you are making some progress. How does your salary at Northcutt measure up to the male architects?"

"Oh, Mom. I'm not concerned about that now. I'm just glad to have a job."

"Wait a minute. You either support 'equal pay for equal work' or you don't. You can't validate it in one situation and deny it in another. Stand up for your beliefs."

"But Mom. This is a whole different situation. I took the job because I was desperate but now, I'm happy I have a nice salary for the months I'll be there. My career is not at Northcutt. And I want to help Dick and Marianne Monroe. His situation is so sad."

"All well and good. That should not immune you from asking what you're worth."

"Let's not talk about it anymore tonight. This is supposed to be a chance for me to forget work and 'the project.' Who's on the guest list?"

Ashleigh didn't recognize any of the names Christine mentioned. When she looked at the place cards, she saw she was seated next to a man without a female name card on his other side. I guess this is a set-up for me.

Carlton came into the room and put his arm around her shoulder.

"How's my girl?"

"I'm okay, Dad. Tired and glad to have a night out with new faces and stories."

"I want to tell you how proud I am of the work your lady's group is doing on that ERA discrepancy. You have always had a cause to fight for. I guess you didn't lose that as an adult. This is important stuff."

"Do you pay your female investment brokers the same as the male investment brokers?"

"It's a little different in financial situations. Yes, they work off the same scale and pay ranges. But their main income develops from the investments they make for their clients. We are a fiduciary firm. If the clients do well, the advisor does well, whether they are male or female. If the advisor makes bad recommendations for their clients and the client loses money, the advisor/broker doesn't make money. I would never think to tell a woman she must have a lower percentage of profit than her male counterparts."

"I didn't think so, Dad. Just had to be sure."

"Cagey young lady, aren't you? I wouldn't have it any other way. So, who is this young man sitting next to you? Are you familiar with his name."

"No. I know the Richmond name. I wonder if he is part of that family?"

Christine entered the dining room and took Carlton's arm.

"We need to head to the living room to be ready to greet our guests."

Ashleigh watched her parents become one as they walked toward the front of the house. She hoped that one day she would find that perfect fit for herself. She wouldn't settle for anything less than what her parents have.

She treasured this room, so familiar to her. She couldn't even image how many dinner parties she had attended here. The large Georgian table and chairs could seat twenty people. There were always flowers on each end of the table.

Mother had them delivered twice a week, so they would be fresh for an impromptu party. The mammoth hutch sat on one wall normally filled with China and crystal from great-grandmother's collection. Sterling silver trays, pitchers and serving cradles adorned the top shelves and filled the shelves behind the bottom doors.

The whimsical pink, yellow and green floral wallpaper contrasted sharply with the baroque furniture but gave the room warmth and charm. A twelve-foot sideboard sat opposite the hutch, laden with trays hosting every hors d'oeuvres imaginable. As guests arrived, she would take the trays into the library where wine and liquor would be served.

Place settings were alternated between modern American porcelain China and cherished antique dishes made in China in a much clearer fragile porcelain. Ashleigh was terrified of breaking one of these dishes, but Christine said they had no value if they weren't enjoyed.

For tonight's guests, Christine hired a college student to serve the dishes from the kitchen and clear the table after each course. She wanted to be at the table during the entire meal. She was eager to watch Ashleigh and Scott Richmond III get to know each other. She felt they could make the perfect couple.

Carlton kept his eye on the couple too. He respected Scott's father, whose family was one of two families who could trace their ancestry back to the seventeenth century and were founding fathers in this suburb of Atlanta. They developed the business district and started the country club in the area. They were the backbone of social life. Ashleigh would do well to make a connection with Scott.

Ashleigh was delighted with her dinner partner. He was intelligent, funny, and engaging. They talked through the entire dinner and walked to the library together. Dessert was served and wine and liquor topped off the evening.

"Ashleigh, I'm so glad to meet you. I don't know why we haven't run into each other. I would have remembered you."

"I lived on campus at Southeastern Tech. As an architecture major, I needed to be close to all the support I could get from the library, study groups and upper classmen and women. I've always lived in this house, but I never got into the social scene. I was just focused on my career."

"That's amazing for a beautiful young woman like you to know exactly what she wanted and to go for it. I bet your parents are proud of you."

"We are. She is one of a kind." Caroline and Carlton approached the couple to see how the two were getting along.

"I guess it's time for me to head home. I would like to see you again, Ashleigh. Is it okay if I call you?"

"Certainly. I'll get a business card for you. Both of my numbers are on the card. You can reach me either place."

"Good. I look forward to seeing you again."

Christine and Carlton smiled at each other as Ashleigh walked Scott to the door.

"He would make such a suitable husband for her."

"Let's don't get ahead of ourselves, Carlton. They just met."

"I know. I can hope."

Chapter Nineteen

Ashleigh and Scott soon were together two or three nights a week. She took him to The Brick House for an introduction to life in Midtown. He took her to the Country Club for dinner to acquaint her with his lifestyle.

A couple of weeks into their relationship they went to The Brick House to hear the new act playing in the restaurant. "This is fun. It's a neat place and the food is good. I understand why you enjoy coming here. However, there isn't much chance for conversation over the music."

"We can go back to my apartment if you like."

"That would be nice."

Scott picked up the check and they headed for the door. While he was paying for their dinner, the door opened, and Jason and

Joline entered. Ashleigh was so happy to see Jason she reached out and grabbed him in a hug.

"Hey Jase. I've missed you."

Jason was startled but smiled at her. Jolene glared in her direction and Scott stepped up and took her arm.

"Who are these folks, Ashleigh?"

"They work at the firm where I worked. This is Jason and she is Jolene. Guys, this is Scott."

The men nodded but didn't speak. Scott took Ashleigh's arm and ushered her out the door.

"What was that about, Scott. I didn't get to speak to Jason. He is a good friend, and I haven't seen him in a while."

"You said hello with a hug. That should have been enough."

Ashleigh looked at him unnerved by his comment. When they got to her door, she was not going to ask him in, but he took her key, unlocked the door, and stepped inside.

"I'm sorry Ashleigh. I overreacted. Of course, you should have had time to visit with your friends. Maybe you can hook up with them tomorrow."

She looked at his contrite countenance and decided to forgive him. They sat on the sofa facing each other. She told him about her 'project' and the problems they were having with getting the attention of any representative.

"I don't want to give up. I can't give up. Women have a right to be paid what their jobs pay men. I don't know where we should go from here."

"Can you get off work for a while tomorrow?

"I guess so. It's Thursday and I'm in the office. Why?"

"I have an idea. I can take you down to the Capitol and introduce you to the people I know. That should give you an audience for a few minutes. Maybe that would help."

"Scott, that would be wonderful! It's the first positive idea we've had. Yes, let's do it. Can we go during my lunch break? I will ask to get it extended."

"Why do you have to ask? Do the other architects ask to leave the office?"

"I don't think so, but I'm a temp."

"What's that got to do with it? You're getting paid to do a job. As long as you're doing that job you shouldn't have to count minutes or hours in the office. If you want equality with men, Ashleigh, you need to think equal with men."

"You're right. I still have the mentality of an hourly employee."

"It appears that way. Grow up and get some courage to demand what you have earned."

"Okay. I'll do it. What time can we meet?"

"We're not meeting. I'm coming to your office and picking you up."

"Everyone will know I'm leaving on personal business."

"That's the point. Start acting like an important part of the team and a professional architect."

She loved him for the protective way he was treating her. He was right about her actions. She needed to be more assertive.

When Scott showed up to take her to the Capitol, she grabbed her briefcase and told Leslie she would be back in a couple of hours. She started to say where she was going but Scott grabbed her arm and led her to the elevator.

She was almost dancing when they reached the sidewalk. "That was so cool, Scott."

"No. That was so natural. Do that from now on."

"Yes, sir." She knew it had been easy because he was there with her.

Chapter Twenty

They parked in the underground lot, using Scott's pass, and rode the elevator to the second floor. Ashleigh was impressed that he had a pass for parking and knew exactly where to go to meet legislators.

The first office they approached was dark. Scott continued down the corridor to another door. He opened it and smiled at the young woman at the first desk. "Hi, Jennifer. Is he in?"

"Hi, Scott. He is, but he's on the phone. Can you wait a few minutes?"

"Sure. I want you to meet Ashleigh Justice. She is here to present a request for his help on a project. You just might be seeing her around."

"Hi, Ashleigh. I hope Thomas can help you with your request. I'm sure he will, at least, listen."

"Me too. I'll be happy for him to listen."

Jennifer took a call and Scott leaned in. "Don't be apologetic to her or him. They are representing you and your wishes and needs. You have a right to ask for their help."

Ashleigh sighed. She had so much to learn.

Jennifer buzzed Thomas' office when he hung up from the call. "Thomas, I have Scott Redmond and Ashleigh Justice here to see you. Got a minute?"

Thomas opened the door with a big smile for Scott, He grabbed his hand and man-hugged him. "So good to see you man. What's up?"

"I've brought Ashleigh Justice, a very good friend, to talk with you about an issue she has with the ERA not being ratified by Georgia. Can you listen to her for a minute?"

"Sure. That's my job. Come in the office."

Ashleigh gave him a bird's eye summary of the group's issues with the lack of equity in pay for women. She asked if he would meet with the entire group to hear from each woman what had happened to her. He agreed and promised to have other representatives join them for the meeting.

She was beside herself as they exited the Capitol building. "Scott. How did you make that happen?"

"Honey, these guys are just people like us. They are us. Don't feel any awe of them. They are doing a job just like we are. The difference is they must get elected, and we pay their salaries. They work for us."

When Ashleigh got back to the office, she could hardly sit the rest of the day. Scott had a late business meeting, so she had her night free. She got on the phone with the rest of the group and wanted to set up a meeting for the next night.

"I know you're excited. I think it's great that you've contacted someone who might help us but tomorrow night is Friday night, a date night for me."

Pat put a damper on Ashleigh's excitement.

Saundra and Martha said the same thing.

"I guess it can wait until Tuesday night, when we usually meet. Okay, I'll see you at The Brick House at seven, Saundra."

She didn't know if she could wait until Tuesday to share her news. I'll call Mom and Dad. They will be happy for me.

They didn't answer their phone.

She called JJ. No answer.

Is everyone busy, but me? I know who will be happy to hear the news. Jason. He might be on a date with Jolene. I'll call and check.

He picked up on the second ring. "Hello."

"Jason. How are you? Are you busy?"

"No. Just got home from work. What's up?"

"I'm so excited. I know you'll be happy for me."

"Happy for you? About what?"

"I saw Thomas Worthington today, our state representative. And he agreed to meet with the whole group to discuss our thoughts on the ERA."

"That's great, Ash. How did you manage an appointment with him?"

"Scott took me to the Capitol and introduced me."

"Oh, Scott."

"Yes. He knows everyone in the state government. He was a big help."

"Good. I'm happy for you, Ash. Maybe you can make headway now with Scott opening doors for you."

"I miss you, Jason. Are you busy? Could you come over?"

"Not a good idea, Ash. Your boyfriend seems a little protective. He wouldn't like it."

"I don't care. If you are free, I'd like to see you."

"I guess I'm not free. See you around, Ash."

Well, God. I guess it's me and You. I have good news to share and no one to share it with. Is this part of me taking control of my life?

Chapter Twenty-One

Scott seems to be around all the time. When he is not working or attending a business function, he's here, or wants me to go to his place. I miss the solitude of my apartment. I'm feeling confined.

Amid her thoughts, she heard a loud, insistent knock at her door. She wanted to ignore it. It had to be Scott. The knock came again. She put her book down and hesitantly shuffled to the door. In the peephole she saw Scott's irritated face.

Unlatching the door, she could hear his sigh. "Ashleigh, it's time for me to have a key to your apartment. I feel foolish standing out here knocking when you are just inside the door."

"Scott, I had dozed off." She lied. *Sorry, God.*

"That's the point. Why should I stand out here waiting for you to wake up, just to let me in. I could already be inside."

"I don't have an extra key."

"Well, give me your key, and we'll have one made."

Trying to change the subject, "What's up so early on a Saturday? We didn't have plans for today."

"We don't need plans to see each other, do we?"

"No. I guess we don't."

"What's wrong with you today? Aren't you glad to see me?"

"Sure. I was enjoying a lazy morning to have a third cup of coffee and look at the view."

"Well, I have a full day planned. You won't have to think at all. Just dress in something casual to wear to the lake and bring your swimsuit."

"We're going to the lake?"

"Isn't that what I just said? Are you on something this morning?"

"Just tired."

"You don't want to go?"

"It sounds like fun." *Not exactly a lie, God.*

"Well, hurry up. I've got the top down on the Mercedes, and a picnic basket and wine in the backseat."

It was a done deal. She went to her bedroom, found her swimsuit, threw it in a beach bag and grabbed shorts and a T-shirt. As she locked the bathroom door and turned on the shower, Scott called out, "and bring a change of clothes. We may spend the night."

The remark glued her to the floor. How? Where? No! She showered and dressed quickly. While she was brushing her hair, he tried to open the bathroom door.

"Scott, I'm not ready yet."

"But why do you have the door locked? Aren't we passed that in our relationship? I want to see your body."

"You can see it when we're married, if that is in our future."

"Whoa! You're assuming a lot. I haven't said I love you."

She opened the door, fully dress with her mane of sun-streaked hair in full bloom. "Exactly."

"You don't have sex with your boyfriends?"

"No! I will have sex with my husband when that day comes."

"Oh, okay. Well, let's go. Our friends are waiting."

The rest of the day was tainted by the bathroom conversation. Scott attempted casual conversation with her, but it was strained. He focused on the other two couples, their "friends" that she had only met that morning.

The other two couples were staying over in Scott's parents' cabin, but Ashleigh asked to go home. Scott didn't hesitate to help her gather her beach bag.

The thirty-minute drive to her apartment was the longest ride Ashleigh had ever experienced. Scott didn't get out to open her door or walk her to her front door.

"See you around, Ashleigh."

When she closed the door to her sanctuary, she felt a wave of relief. She dropped her bag and crashed on the sofa. She was bone tired and heart weary.

Sunday morning greeted her with summer blue skies and a happy sun. I'm so thankful I can go to church, see my parents, and forget about yesterday.

"Hello, sweetheart! You look tired today. Are you alright?"

"I'll tell you about it at lunch."

"Okay. We'll be at our regular table at the Club."

Ashleigh listened to the sermon with half her mind on her stance with Scott. They had not talked about sex. He had never made an inappropriate move toward her. Hugs and kisses were all they had shared. Why the big jump? She couldn't understand men.

At lunch, dad was visiting here and there with business associates and friends, which was his usual way to work the room until his standard Sunday fare of porterhouse steak was set at his place.

While he was away from the table, Christine looked at Ashleigh. "Is everything okay, honey?"

"I don't know mother. Scott and I went to the lake yesterday with some of his friends and he wanted to spend the night. I could have thought of it as a casual 'girls in one room and boys in the other' but before we left the apartment, he said to me that he wanted to see my body! I was apoplectic! I told him that would only happen when we were married. He was freaked out! The day was ruined. He didn't even walk me to the door or open my car door when we got to my apartment."

"I guess that was something you would expect from a young man as long as you have been dating. However, he was crude in the way he approached it."

"Are you saying that it's time for us to have sex?"

"No. Not at all. I'm saying that it isn't unusual for a healthy young man to want sex. You both handled the situation poorly."

"Well, you may not see him with me any longer. He was pretty upset."

"I hope that is not the case. He is a perfect match for you. I hope you two work it out."

Carlton reached the table just as the steak was set on the crisp white tablecloth.

"How is Scott, Ashleigh?"

Chapter Twenty-Two

The weeks since the incident with Scott passed quickly. Ashleigh missed him, but she was busy preparing for the presentation to Rep. Thomas Worthington and the group of representatives. There were going to be six legislators in the presentation.

Work with Dick and Roger from the Northcutt firm moved along smoothly. Roger counted on Ashleigh's input from Dick as much as Dick counted on her reports back from Roger. She thought about what Scott had advised her about asking for more money for her job but was not eager to broach the subject.

JJ called her every week to check on her mental health and to share her relationship with her new-found boyfriend. Ashleigh wondered if she would ever come back to Atlanta.

This Sunday afternoon, she was proofing her presentation, preparing for her meeting with the group Monday night.

She absentmindedly picked up the phone on its first ring.

"Ash, this is Jason. How are you?"

"Jason! I'm so happy to hear your voice."

"Do you have company?"

"No. I'm working on a presentation to some legislators tomorrow."

"Oh, okay. I won't bother you."

"Don't you dare hang up. I want to talk with you. How have you been. How is Jolene?"

"Quit asking me about her. I don't have a relationship with her. I'm just an older man who is giving her some guidance in her studies."

"Okay, won't mention it again. So, how are you?"

"Pretty worn out. Dealing with Camden is a daily battle. Howard doesn't see it though. We're barely hanging on to the Deerfield project. It's a good thing they have had some financial setbacks and are okay with our slow response for now."

"I'm happy to hear that. Anything exciting in the rest of your world?"

"No. Sounds like you've got a full plate, though."

"That's an understatement! I'm happy."

"So, things with you and Scott are going well?"

"Not so sure of that! We haven't talked in a few weeks."

"Sorry to hear that. That is, if you're sorry."

"I really haven't had time to dwell on it. I miss him, but not excruciatingly. I try not to think about it."

"Well, I miss your voice and our time talking. Just wanted to say hello."

"Do you have to hang up?"

"You're busy."

"I've almost finished with my proofing. Can we meet somewhere for dinner? My treat."

"I'd love to have dinner with you, but I'm paying. The Brick House at seven?"

"Perfect."

Ashleigh closed her presentation, stacked folders, and put them in her briefcase. She was ready. Ready to meet with Dick in the morning. Ready to make the presentation tomorrow evening to the group. But most of all, ready to see her old friend, Jason.

She hadn't realized how much she missed him. It was different from the way she missed Scott. That relationship was more electric. Her relationship with Jason was comfortable.

Looking through her closet, she needed to choose something for the ninety-degree weather in August in Atlanta. However, The Brick House was air conditioned.

Why is it taking me so long to decide on what to wear? It's just The Brick House, where customers were jeans or shorts or business clothes. And it's only Jason, who doesn't care what I wear.

But she cared.

At seven o'clock she entered The Brick House with a bright pink, spaghetti-strapped dress fitted at the bodice with a flowing skirt. Her pink sandals highlighted her light tan and hot pink toe-nails. She carried a white shrug to ward off the air conditioning.

As her eyes adjusted to the darkened interior, Jason touched her arm and pulled her to him in a warm hug.

"I have a table over in the corner. Is that okay?"

"Yes. I'm in no hurry to get home. We'll have privacy back there."

"I ordered for us. Filet medium rare and house salad with pears. Okay?"

"You remembered." She stepped ahead of him and made her way to the corner. She didn't look around at the crowd. She was eager to get Jason alone.

"Of course, I remembered. We like the same things. Don't you remember?"

They sat facing each other, enjoying the view. "You look beautiful, Ashleigh."

"Thank you, sir. You don't look so bad yourself."

"I've missed you."

"Me too." And she had. She had missed his soft, strong voice; his muscular hands holding hers when they walked; his warm smile that always felt like he knew something she didn't; and his presence. Just being with him felt good.

They dived into the steaks and salads and still managed snippets of conversation. When they laid their napkins on the table, Ashleigh felt someone coming up behind her.

"Well, I see you didn't waste time getting a new beau?" Scott scowled at her, never acknowledging Jason.

"Hey Scott. You remember my friend, Jason."

"Not really. Have a happy life, Ashleigh."

Her shocked face froze for just a moment. "Jason, I'm so sorry. I've never seen him act that way."

"Sounds like jealousy to me. Do you want to go after him?"

"Certainly, not. I was not sure where our relationship stood. Now, it is clear."

"Okay...dessert?"

"Why not!"

The ruined joyfulness called for the night to end.

"Did you drive?"

"I walked."

"I'll drive you home."

"Thank you, but no. I need the fresh air. It was a lovely evening, until..."

She left as he paid the bill. Outside, she stood for a minute to acclimate herself to the noise of cars, buses and conversations as couples passed by. Each step confused her more. I don't know what Scott is thinking. Did he ever care about me? Was he drunk tonight?

She opened the door to her apartment and stepped inside to flick the light on. Suddenly a hand pushed her forward. She fell on the sofa and screamed. The door was already closed.

Chapter Twenty-Three

Holding Ashleigh's shrug that she had left on the back of her chair, Jason put his wallet back in his pants pocket and looked toward the door where she had slipped into the night. He started to follow her, but he knew she wanted to be alone.

"Hey, Jason."

He turned to see the waving hand across the room. It was a friend from his previous employer.

"Come have a drink with us. I haven't seen you in forever."

Jason looked toward the door again but, wanting to visit with an old friend, headed toward his table.

"Are you starting a new style with the dainty sweater?"

Blushing, he explained his date had left it on the table. He met his friend's wife, drank a beer, and enjoyed their company. When he looked at his watch, an hour later, he said his goodbyes and headed out of the restaurant. He got in his car and turned toward his apartment. Something nudged him to circle the block and check on Ashleigh. He could use her abandoned sweater as an excuse.

He rang the bell to a quiet interior. He stood there a minute and turned to leave when the door opened just enough for him to see her face.

Every damning emotion rushed through his mind in a split second. He pushed on the door to open it enough for his broad shoulders to squeeze in. Grabbing her in his arms, tears pouring down his face, he picked her up and laid her gently on the sofa.

His heart was racing. His head was spinning. He didn't want to let her go, but he needed to close the door. He looked outside but saw no evidence of who or what had attacked the love of his life.

He went to the bathroom and wet a washcloth with warm water. When he returned to her side, he gently wiped her face and pushed the hair out of her eyes. He saw terror there. He had so many questions but calming her was the most important move now.

He pulled the throw from the back of the sofa and covered her half-naked body and then pulled her into his arms. He couldn't let her go.

Eventually she calmed enough to sit up and pull the throw closer, wrapping her sinful nakedness.

"Jason, my other half. I shouldn't have left you tonight. I should have let you bring me home! I am so prideful that I can handle everything. I'm not sure I can handle this."

"Do you want to talk about what happened?"

"It was Scott. But it wasn't Scott. There was a demon inside that person who attacked me, and…and raped me."

She fell into Jason's arms. "He took the most delicate part of me. He took something I was saving for my husband. I'm a tainted woman."

"You are not tainted. You are a survivor. You are strong and as perfect now as you were before this attack. Do I need to take you to the hospital?"

"No, no, no. I don't want a record of this."

"We need a record of this. He committed a crime."

"No, Jason. I can't have everyone knowing."

"You will have bruises you'll need to explain."

"No. The bruises are not visible. They are hidden deep inside me. He didn't hit me. He just surprised and overpowered me. He was hiding in my apartment. I don't know how he got in. I did not give him a key."

"Did you accidently leave the door unlocked?"

"No. He asked me for a key a few weeks ago. I told him I didn't think that was necessary. He must have copied it when he drove my car to get gas for me one night."

"That bastard!"

"I had never seen him the way he was tonight."

"I want to tear him to pieces."

"No. You don't need to get involved. I think this evening will make him stay away from me. That's all I want."

"Ashleigh, there is so much more to it than that. Is he a danger to other women? The police need to put him on their radar."

"Don't ask me to do that. His family has a lot of power in this town. No one will believe me. Even my parents would have a hard time believing that he would do this. They have known him and his family for years.

"I can't go through that. Please, just stay here while I shower. By the way, why are you here?"

"I brought your sweater. You left it on the chair. I could kick myself. I could have prevented this. I was headed this way when a friend called me over to his table. I visited with them for an hour! Oh, Ashleigh...I could have caught him before..."

"Don't you dare take this on as your fault. You are my savior. You're here with me now." She squeezed his arm and stood shakily.

He helped her walk to her bedroom and closed the door for her privacy.

While Ashleigh showered, he paced. He cried. He pounded on the kitchen counter. He prayed.

"Will you stay overnight with me. I'll get sheets for the sofa."

"I wouldn't leave you, but I don't need sheets. I'll be on watch."

"You are always here for me. I love you for that." She kissed him on the cheek before slipping under her covers, knowing she would not sleep.

Chapter Twenty-Four

Jason was dozing when Ashleigh came into the living room. She wanted to touch his face and thank him for everything he gave her.

He awoke and reached for her. Ashleigh took his hand and snuggled next to him. She wanted to stay there for the whole day, but she had to be at church at eleven like nothing was wrong. After a few minutes, she rose and smiled at him.

"Thank you for last night. I'll always remember your protection of me. I am blessed that you are in my life. Right now, I need to shower and dress for church. I hope I didn't make you late for your church."

"No. I'm good. I don't want to leave you. What if he comes back?"

"I think I'm rid of him. He wants to maintain his elite position in the community. He won't bother me again. Last night never happened."

"Is that something you can do?"

"I must. I don't have a choice."

"You do have a choice and I can back you up."

"Not really. You didn't see him here. You just saw me after an attack."

"Ash don't do this! At some point you will have to face it. You'll relive it. It could haunt you for the rest of your life. You may not be able to have a normal relationship with your husband."

"Don't talk about all that with me now. I must do this my way. I need to be in control of this situation."

"I don't understand but I accept your decision. Call me if you need me."

The apartment was so empty when he left. She had almost called him back, but that would only delay her moving on.

In the shower she looked at her body and took in the full acceptance of what had been done to her. She had lost the one valuable part of her that would be treasured by her husband. Could she ever give what was left to another man? She stood there, scalding water cascading down from her head to her feet, tears joining the flow of the stream.

When the water turned cold, she shut off the waterfall and stepped out of the shower. In the mirror she saw a hollow woman looking back at her. Dead eyes with no promise of returning to vitality, hope, or joy.

Jason was her only connection to her former self. She didn't want to lose him, but she couldn't do what he asked. No one could know.

Chapter Twenty-Five

The sun was shining but she felt drab. She found her brown mid-calf dress from years ago and dark brown Mary Janes. The only jewelry she wore was a gold choker necklace with one small diamond in the center.

Since she was running late, Christine wouldn't have a chance to question her choice of winter dull colors, rather than lightweight summer yellow, Ashleigh's favorite color.

"Hello, sweetheart. You're running late." Christine slid over to make room for Ashleigh to sit at the aisle. This was not her usual spot. She was supposed to sit between her mother and father. Not here on the aisle, exposed to everyone walking past. She felt vulnerable. She couldn't sit any longer. She stood just as the Doxology began and the congregation stood. She squeezed in front of her mother and stepped back between her parents, grabbing her father's arm.

Christine and Carlton looked at each other with raised eyebrows over Ashleigh's head.

Ashleigh rushed up the aisle as soon as the minister finished his closing prayer, not looking or speaking to anyone. Outside, she stopped only when she reached the parking area. She waited until Christine and Carlton caught up with her.

"I can't have lunch with you today. I've got a ton of work to do for both Northcutt and for my group. I'll call you later in the week."

She raised on tiptoes to kiss her father on the cheek and hugged Christine. Then she was gone.

At home she was jittery and could not sit down. She walked the floor, turning on her computer and avoiding it afterwards. She went out to her patio and sat. As soon as she looked out over the city, tears streamed down her face. She got up and went to the bedroom to change clothes. What should she wear?

She stood in the middle of her closet unable to decide why she was there. As she scanned the racks, her eyes locked on her running clothes. She grabbed them. Changed quickly and within five minutes was on the stairs heading to the hiking trails across the street.

It felt good to move, the wind pulling her hair up and back felt as if she were lifted above the evil of last night. She breathed in freedom. She knew deep inside that she could overcome the tragedy of her lost virginity. She knew she could with God's help. She wanted to ask God where he had been last night? Why hadn't he saved her? But she knew those were fruitless questions. She had to face it and get stronger.

Instead, she prayed, *"God, help me understand that what happened last night was not my fault. Guide me through the next days and weeks. Be by my side. Renew in me a forgiving spirit and give me wisdom to prevent anything like this from happening again. Amen"*

Ending her run at the starting point, she felt stronger. It was late afternoon. She had made it through the day by herself. That was a good first step.

She pulled leftovers from the refrigerator and heated them in the oven, while she reviewed the information she had prepared for the group's next meeting. With her first bite she realized she was starving. That was good. She ate, cleaned up the kitchen, did a load of laundry and stacked the packets for tomorrow's meeting next to her briefcase.

When she checked the front door to be sure the deadbolt was on, she realized that when she left the apartment, it was not protected from a key in the wrong hands. The deadbolt would be off when she came home Tuesday night. She broke out in a cold sweat.

She called Jason. He did not answer. She left a message asking him to meet her at The Brick House on Tuesday night around nine o'clock so he could be with her when she entered her apartment.

With every noise, she got up and checked the door's slip-lock. It was only when the early dawn arrived that she was able to sleep.

Chapter Twenty-Six

She dressed in bright colors for her visit with Dick. On the way to Monroe's house, she spotted a local donut shop and decided she would take a treat to the family. The gesture encouraged her to be positive about the day. Marianne opened the door before Ashleigh could touch the doorbell.

"Come in. Everyone's still asleep. Dick had a rough night. He needs to sleep. What's wrong. You don't look like yourself."

"I'm not."

"Thanks for the donuts. Let's get some coffee and head to the patio. Drew and Dillon will find us when they wake up."

Relieved she wouldn't have to see Dick looking like she felt, Ashleigh followed Marianne to the patio. The morning air was refreshing. The sound of the water caressing the shore was relaxing. They sat near each other to talk softly, even though with doors closed the patio voices could not be heard from inside.

"Now. Tell me what's going on."

"Scott raped me!"

"Scott? The young man you've been seeing for a few months?"

"Yes. He was enraged when he saw me having dinner with my friend, Jason. He was in my apartment when I got home. I guess he copied my door key."

She stopped for a few minutes, trying to gain control, shaking, and trying to stem the flood of tears bursting from her eyes.

Marianne pulled her into a hug. "Oh, sweetheart. I'm so sorry."

"He had been sulking since he wanted me to spend the night with him and a two other couples at his cabin on the lake and I told him I was waiting for marriage before having sex."

"Did you call the police?"

"No!"

"Does anyone else know?"

"Jason came by the apartment to bring my shrug I had left at the restaurant. He got there shortly after Scott left. He was a comfort to me, but he's not a woman. He couldn't understand the devastation I felt. Thank you for listening."

"When are you going to tell your mother?"

"I'm not."

"I have gotten to know you enough to know you can't keep something this important from your mom."

"She and dad are friends with Scott's parents."

"So. Even more reason to tell them."

"She would want me to press charges."

"Yes. Good."

"No. You know how that kind of thing goes. Lots of publicity and shame and the guy goes free, because his family is a prestigious family in town and the woman is always at fault."

"Ashleigh, you're a strong young woman. You've proven that in your work on the ERA. You can handle it."

"This is entirely different. No. I can't say anything. Please don't tell anyone."

"I wouldn't betray your confidence. I still think it is the wrong thing to do."

"Thank you. You're a good friend. I'll be okay." She wiped her eyes and smiled at Marianne.

"Listen, since Dick had a bad night and the kids are sleeping in, why don't you go home for the morning. You need some time to put this whole thing in perspective and decide how you can manage the next few days. You can work with Dick next week. I'll call Edward and tell him Dick isn't able to work anymore this week."

"That would be wonderful. I do need to be alone today. Thank you, Marianne. You're so understanding. I'll see you next week."

"Take care of yourself. You feel like a little sister to me. I want you to be safe."

"I will be."

"Drew and Dillon will enjoy the donuts. Thank you. Call me if you need me."

Relief flowed over her as she drove home. She needed to be busy. But she couldn't be around people today.

Chapter Twenty-Seven

She needed to get control over her emotions. She picked up her Bible and sank into the security of her sofa. *God, lead me to a passage to help me today. I'm shaky and ashamed. I need your comfort.*

The cool morning called to her from the open patio door. She quickly changed into running shorts, t-shirt and running shoes and was at the entrance to the trail before she could change her mind. An hour later, her tired muscles refused to carry her farther. She walked back to the street and stopped at the fruit stand for bananas and blueberries. A smoothie would cool her down and give her energy to work in the afternoon.

The blinking red light greeted her as she stepped out of her running shoes. She ignored it until she had a shower and dressed in comfortable work clothes. Jason's voice was controlled but she could hear the worry in his tone.

"Just checking on you. I'm going to stop by after work if it's okay. If you want to be alone, buzz me back."

The rest of the afternoon a calmness rested on her body and in her mind. Jason would be here soon.

At six o'clock Jason rang her doorbell. She looked through the peephole to be sure it was him and opened the door to a handsome chiseled face and two hands filled with bags of heavenly smelling food.

"Dinner?"

"Didn't think you'd want to go out."

"You're right. You always are."

She took some of the bags and sat them on the kitchen counter. As he unwrapped the contents, she lifted two plates from the cabinet. It felt so natural with Jason here. He fit her apartment and life so comfortably. He was like a warm blanket. He was a good friend.

"Did you see David today?"

"No. I went to the house, but Marianne said he had a rough night. Since he was sleeping, she wanted to leave him alone. We visited for a little while. When I came home, I couldn't settle down to work, so I went for a run. That cleared my mind, and I could work some this afternoon."

"How was your day?"

"Not good. Camden is driving us all crazy. I'm not sure how long I can tolerate this work atmosphere."

"You can't leave. You're the backbone of the Deerfield project."

"It's not much of a project now. I've been doing some rain-making and have been talking with a new prospect in Mississippi. I'm flying out there next Monday to see if I can work out a deal with them. It would be a new account without Camden as the architect."

"That would be terrific. Maybe your job could get back to where it was before Camden."

She bumped his shoulder as she filled her plate with more rice and sweet and sour chicken.

"I can't believe you can eat so much. You're so tiny, but you eat like an elephant!"

"Hey. You're supposed to be cheering me up, not bringing me down."

By the time Jason left, she felt in control of herself. One day at a time, that's what 'they' say. She was working on it.

She locked the door, slid the deadbolt in place and watched through the peephole as Jason headed for the stairs.

Just as he stepped into the stairwell, another figure appeared in her view. Scott exited the elevator and headed toward her door. She quickly checked the lock again and ran for the bedroom, dragging the phone's long cord with her. She could hear a key trying to fit into the lock's chamber. She knew it wouldn't work, but she held her breath until it stopped.

There was no other sound for over an hour. When she checked the door and looked through the peephole the hallway was clear.

All the progress she had made vanished with Scott's appearance. When will this be over?

Chapter Twenty-Eight

The next week she went through the motions at work. She hid in Dick's office, head down so no one would approach her. Roger stuck his head in the door a few times to get an update on her progress without Dick's input.

Since Jason was in Mississippi and JJ was in South Georgia, Ashleigh spent her evenings working on her plan with the ERA group and congressmen. She was beginning to feel confident about the presentation but was anxious to hear about a date to make it.

Jason called on Wednesday night to check on her and told her he was getting good vibes from the group in Mississippi. His good news gave her a reason to be positive. She wanted good things for her friend.

"Ash, they have asked me to stay over the weekend to view the site and discuss dates. I'm sorry I won't be there for you this weekend."

"Jason don't worry about me. This is your future. You need to be totally absorbed with this company and see where it takes you. I know you're thinking about me, and I am totally safe. Scott has not tried to contact me. I'm busy at work. I've got my project proposal to work on. I'm fine. I love you for worrying, but don't."

She had dinner at the Club with her parents after church on Sunday.

"Ashleigh, come by the house and visit for a while." Christine took her arm as they left the country club.

Her first reaction was to say 'no'. Realizing she would be alone for the afternoon, she agreed.

"I haven't been home for a while. It will be nice to have some time with my parents."

Entering her childhood home always brought happy memories to her. She and Phillip enjoyed being together. He was a special 'big brother.' Neither one gave their parents any reason to worry. They were brought up with a stable, Christian life.

They settled in the overstuffed chairs in the library. Carlton picked up the weekend newspaper, intending to read it from cover to cover, as he did every Sunday afternoon.

Realizing he wouldn't join their conversation, the women moved to the sunroom, after stopping in the kitchen for lemonade. Christine looked at Ashleigh.

"Honey, is anything wrong? You look strained and worn-out."

"No, Mom. I've been working long hours lately. I'm just tired. I'll be fine."

"Are you sure? There's something in your demeanor that is off-center."

"My whole life is off-center. It will get better, when we make the presentation to the representatives about correcting pay practices for women and when I find a long-term job."

"I can loan you some money to carry you through this time."

"I don't need the money. I'm being paid better at Northcutt's than I was at Stockton's."

"Well, that's good to know. I don't want you doing without anything."

"I'm fine, Mom. The garden is beautiful. Did you change gardeners?"

"I decided to let Thomas make the decisions about plants this year. He did an excellent job. I think that made him happy."

"I definitely agree."

Ashleigh left for her apartment around dusk with a basketful of meats, salads, and fruit to keep her from cooking for the next few days. She unloaded the goodies, her purse and briefcase and practiced a balancing act all the way to her front door.

She struggled to unlock the door without putting anything on the floor of the hallway. With her last effort the door swung open, and she was shoved into the room with such force she dropped her basket and food spilled across the floor. She screamed, but no one was around to hear her. She knew before she looked that it was Scott.

"What are you doing? You have some nerve showing up here!"

He glared at her with such hate she could feel the heat from his body. "I have plenty to say. If you tell anyone about what happened between us, I'll make sure you'll never find a job in this town."

"Scott what is going on with you? Who are you? The polite, gentle, kind man I dated seems to be somewhere else."

"You're driving me crazy. All I wanted was for you to show me some affection and respect. You think you are too good for that." He advanced toward her.

She backed away, bumping into the sofa. "That's not true. I have different values from you. I don't sleep around. It has nothing to do with you. It has been my decision since I was fourteen years old. I value my virtue."

He leered at her. "Well, you don't have it anymore."

"I am shamefully aware of that. Does that make you feel powerful?"

Scott turned away from her. "No. I didn't want to make love to you that way."

"That was not making love."

"It's the only way I could get it from you."

"So, that should take care of the situation. You got what you wanted." Gaining courage, she sat up straight on the sofa.

"No, I didn't. I wanted you to want me, too."

"We can't go backward. You did what you did, and I feel the way I feel. Unchanged."

"Can't I fix it?"

"The way you came in here tonight? No. Now, I need you to leave and never come back."

"Did you call the police?"

"Do you think you would be standing here if I had?"

"No. I guess not. I'm sorry, Ashleigh."

"Goodbye, Scott. You can tell people you broke up with me."

"Okay."

She started shaking as she closed and locked the door. Fortunately, the food containers stayed closed and none of the food was spilled. After putting everything away she jerked on pajamas and covered up in bed. It was still early, but she couldn't calm herself enough to do any work or watch television. Bed was the safest place for her.

Chapter Twenty-Nine

There was no sun to brighten her Monday morning. Clouds hung low and gray matching her mood. She thought about the Monroes and how close she had become to them. Marianne seemed like a big sister and Drew and Dillon would be special to an aunt.

"I'm thankful to be heading to work with Dick today and to visit with Marianne for a little while. I'd love to be the children's adopted aunt."

When she left the bedroom, last night's encounter haunted the great room. She quickly made a cup of coffee and grabbed a banana to eat on the drive. She wished for a magic potion she could spray in the room to cleanse it of Scott's ruthless aura.

God, release me from his evil nature and return my apartment back to my refuge. I will try to forgive him, but I will need your hand and strength to show me how. I lean on you for my strength for today.

She poured her thoughts into loading the car and turning onto the highway toward Dick and Marianne's home. The drive could be cool and refreshing in sharp contrast to the heat and hatred she left in her apartment. She couldn't wait to see them again. When she arrived, Marianne opened the door with red eyes, still in her housecoat.

Ashleigh grabbed her in a hug. "What's wrong?"

"Dick got some bad news yesterday. His pain was getting worse, so we called the doctor to get some stronger pain pills. He told us to go straight to the ER at the local hospital. They kept him overnight. I'm trying to get ready to go get him. I took the children to my mom's house yesterday for a visit and to give me and Dick some alone time. I haven't picked them up yet. They wouldn't let me stay with him."

"I'm so sorry. What can I do?"

"When I left him, he asked me to give you the files and blueprints he worked on. They are on his desk in the bedroom. Do you mind getting them while I shower? I'm afraid to be away from the phone. Can you stay until I get dressed?"

"Certainly. I thought he was progressing in his recovery."

"We did too. I'll find out today what caused the pain and see what they can do to ease it. He can't stand what he went through yesterday. It crushed him."

"I'll stay here as long as you need me. Take your time dressing."

She retrieved the files and blueprints and ran out to the car to put them in the trunk. She was afraid she might forget them if she didn't do it immediately.

Marianne showered and dressed quickly. "I'll call you at the office when I know something."

"And if you can think of anything I can do, please let me know."

They left simultaneously, both heading into the city. Each with worries and frail emotions. Neither one being prepared for the next few days.

Ashleigh shared with Edward Northcutt the news about Dick. He was worried and went to the hospital to see Dick and Marianne. Ashleigh laid out the work on the drafting table but couldn't look at Dick's notations or instructions. Roger noticed her frozen at the table and came up to her.

"You okay, Ashleigh?"

"Not really. They took Dick back to the hospital last night. Marianne said he was in excruciating pain. I don't know what's going on. Edward went to the hospital. Hopefully, he'll have better news when he returns."

Everything seemed to move in slow-motion. Ashleigh's emotions were on edge. She told Roger she had to go out for a few minutes.

"Will you man the phone while I'm gone? I don't want to miss a call from Marianne, but there's something I must do."

"Sure. Go do what you need to do. I'll listen for the phone."

Ashleigh grabbed her purse and headed for the key shop. She asked about getting a new lock and key and wanted to know how long it would take to change the lock.

"I've just hired a temporary employee to make house calls. He can do it now if you like."

It was a Godsend. "Yes. Can he follow me home?"

She called Roger and told him she would not be back today. He had no news from Marianne.

The employee was efficient and friendly. He had the lock installed within an hour, leaving her plenty of time to get to The Brick House for her meeting.

***

She was early, the group was late. She had two glasses of tea before they arrived.

Pat and Martha entered together. By the time they ordered their drinks Saundra showed up.

They ordered salads and started reviewing Ashleigh's work. In principle they all agreed. Saundra frowned at Ashleigh.

"Why didn't you put anything in here about abortion rights? Women have been fighting for those rights since before 1910, when doctors were the only official voice on that issue and the only group that could approve an abortion, and then only if it was deemed to save the mother's life."

"Roe v Wade covered that in 1973, assuring that the 'due process clause of the 14th Amendment' protects the right to abortion."

"There has been nothing but controversy since then. The Hyde Amendment prevents Federal dollars from going to any governmental insurance program like Medicaid, except for rape or life-threatening risk to the pregnant woman."

Ashleigh questioned, "Is that really part of the 'equal pay' issue. That's what we're fighting for now."

"Why is that all we're fighting for. Equal rights should cover every aspect of a woman's life."

"That would be a very hard argument at this time." Pat spoke up with a wavering voice.

Martha looked at each woman. "I don't want to get that broad with our demands. We might be able to get some support for Georgia to ratify the Equal Rights Amendment, which would be a step in the right direction for the pay issue. If we make our proposal all encompassing, we might not get any action for years. And I really don't know how I stand on the abortion issue."

Ashleigh spoke up, "Maybe fight one issue at a time."

Everyone nodded and discussion continued on who would present what part of the proposal to the congressmen when they met.

Ashleigh promised to get a meeting date in the next few days. They relaxed and enjoyed their time visiting while they ate.

Jason walked up to the table at nine o'clock. At first Ashleigh was startled, then she realized she left a message for him to meet her here to take her home safely. He put his hand on her shoulder and smiled at the group.

"Good evening, ladies. If you have finished with your business and dinner, I would like to take this lady home."

Smirks circled the table. "By all means, Jason. She's all yours."

There was no point in trying to explain a lie. She merely stood, said goodnight, and walked out of The Brick House with her protector.

"Jase, I forgot you were coming. I'm sorry. I had an opportunity this afternoon to get a new door locking system installed with an outside key for the dead bolt. There was no need for you to come pick me up."

"I'm glad you did that. I'm also glad I get to take you home."

She smiled and grabbed his arm, balancing her briefcase and purse with the other.

Chapter Thirty

When they got to her door, Ashleigh handed Jason a key. He turned the lock and pushed the door open, returning the key.

"That is yours."

"Mine. You're giving me a key to your apartment?"

"Yes. You are the only one I trust with it. If I'm ever in trouble again, you can get in to save me."

"I pray that won't happen again."

"Me too. Just in case."

He checked the bedroom and bathrooms. Everything was clear.

"Looks good for tonight."

"I would ask you to stay for a visit, but I have a backlog of work to do for Dick. He's not doing well. They took him to the hospital in a great deal of pain. I'm hoping they gave him some medicine and let him go home. I'm going up there tomorrow just to check.

"Marianne needs someone right now. She is scared and worn out."

"You're doing a good thing. I'll check on you tomorrow night."

"Thanks, Jase."

He leaned in and kissed her cheek. "Goodnight."

She really didn't have the energy to work tonight, but she pulled the files out anyway. She looked down at her sofa and re-lived the incident with Scott. She ran to her bedroom and closed the door. After a few minutes she realized she had not set the deadbolt.

When she reached the door, she remembered there was an automatic lock as the door closed. She was safe. Thank God.

She set the alarm for an early morning wakeup and changed into winter pajamas so her body would not be exposed.

Wednesday morning, she called Marianne to check on Dick.

"They kept him overnight, Ashleigh. Thanks for calling. I'm heading to the hospital now. Mom came over to keep the children. I'll let you know as soon as I know something."

"You sound stronger today. That's good."

"I prayed all night. God is with me today. I can face anything with Him by my side."

"Amen. I look forward to your call. My prayer is for both of you to be back home."

She stuffed her files in her briefcase and headed for the office.

Chapter Thirty-One

The office was buzzing with activity, exactly what she needed. Roger greeted her as she put the files on her desk.

"I heard about Dick. Looks like he might be out longer than we planned. I've talked with Edward. He wants to see you first thing. I think he's available now."

Fear struck her. What if he needed to hire a full-time regular architect to take Dick's place? What if he is unhappy with her work? She worried all the way to Mr. Northcutt's office.

"Ashleigh, come in. I'm glad you're here early. We can take care of this before you get involved in anything today."

Here it comes.

"We are so thankful for the work you have done over the weeks you've been on the job. Your relationships with Dick and

Roger have enabled the project to progress nicely. I'm afraid we need to make a more permanent change now."

"I understand, Mr. Northcutt. I have enjoyed working here, even under the circumstances we faced. I've learned so much. Thank you for giving me that opportunity."

"You're quite welcome. I hope that means you are open to a change in your job. I know I promised you a temporary position, so you could have time to spend on your special project. I'm sorry to say I haven't kept up with your progress on that project.

"My needs now…the company's needs require a full-time commitment from an architect in a full-time position as co-lead architect with Roger. Of course, that position comes with significantly more pay and executive benefits. Are you open to accepting that position now?"

"Me? Now? I thought I was being replaced."

"No way I'm going to let someone with your talent and abilities get away from this firm. I've checked your total years' experience and the major projects you've led. I would make you lead architect on a new project, but I don't want to take that position away from Dick. When he returns, he will be able to smoothly take lead again."

"I'm thankful you're holding his position until he can return. He is a special person and an inspirational architect. I can learn so much from him. And yes, I accept your offer."

"I haven't told you the pay yet."

"Okay."

"I hope it is acceptable to you. You'll start at Sixty-five Thousand dollars with a raise in six months. Is that fair?"

Ashleigh could hardly speak. "That is more than fair."

"We have a very structured pay scale. Hiring pay starts with job title, it increases with number of years' experience and next, level of position at previous jobs. The starting rate begins there. Yearly increases are based on quality of work, meeting or exceeding project deadlines, rainmaking, and creativity of project goals. Gender plays no part in any of these steps.

Ashley was shocked and excited. "Thank you for giving me a chance. I won't let you down."

"You've already proven yourself. We are fortunate to have you join our company."

She got up and shook his hand.

Walking out of Mr. Northcutt's office in a daze, she almost ran into Roger. He stuck his hand out to shake her hand, grinning like he had found a treasure.

"Congratulations, Ashleigh!"

"How did you know?"

"Northcutt and I have been discussing you and your work since the day you came to the firm. We've been amazed how easily you picked up on the project and helped me move it forward. I've missed Dick, but you have his talent. We will make a great team."

"Thank you for accepting me, Roger."

"Okay, partner, let's get to work!"

Partner, that sounded wonderful. Sounded like an equal to him. Roger had been pleasant to work with. She could look forward to continuing this project together.

Thank you, God, for putting me in this position. You had something more than I expected waiting for me here.

Chapter Thirty-Two

Roger and Ashleigh coordinated a new plan for her participation in the project. She spent the day updating Dick's last
changes and was ready to shut down for the day when Mr.
Northcutt called her and Roger into his office.

"I just heard from Marianne. Dick is going to be in the hospital
for several days. The doctors have decided to remove the pellets
because they have severely damaged his bladder. He will need
close supervision for a few days. After they clear him of all traces
of radiation, he will undergo surgery to remove the prostate. His
recovery time will be lengthy, and he will be unavailable for any
work for at least a month.

"We all need to pray for him. Which means Ashleigh, you and
Roger will be co-leaders on the project now. When Dick is able,
he will review everything you've done. If he agrees, you will

continue with that plan. If he wants to make changes, you will accommodate them, unless you have resounding reasons to disagree. Understood?"

"Yes sir." Ashleigh and Roger answered at the same time.

Leaving Mr. Northcutt's office, Roger spoke up, "That was a lot to take in. Can we wait until tomorrow to discuss how to proceed from here?"

Ashleigh was as shocked as Roger, "Yes. Definitely. I certainly need the night to get my thoughts together. See you tomorrow."

She was heartbroken for Dick and Marianne. She wanted to stop by the hospital on her way home, but she wasn't sure Marianne would want to see anyone.

She parked close to the entrance to the seven-story imposing structure. Even the parking lot gave her a feeling of sadness. She stopped at the information desk and asked for Dick's room number.

When she got to the fifth floor, she looked in the waiting room for Marianne. She saw her staring out the window facing Atlanta's skyline. As she got closer, she spoke her name, not wanting to startle her. "Marianne?"

Marianne turned and fell into Ashleigh's arms. "I'm so thankful you're here. I feel so alone. Mom is with the kids, and I don't have anyone else to be with me. Thank you for coming."

"I'm so sorry about Dick's situation. I know it will put a strain on you and the kids."

"I feel so helpless. We thought we had a good plan. Of course, we knew that anything could happen. We just didn't plan for it."

"Is there anything I can do? Will your mom be able to keep the kids while you're here?"

"Yes. She lives close by. Since dad passed away, she has been lost. This will give her a purpose for a while. I really want her to move in with us, but she wants to keep her home and her independence."

"It's something everyone will face. Have they operated yet?"

"No. They are removing the pellets now. He will need a few days to recover from that operation before they take the prostate out."

"Why can't they just remove the prostate with the pellets in it?"

"I'm not clear on that. I think they need to have a closed environment to remove the pellets and put them where they don't harm anyone. There are two different surgeons and operating staff for those procedures."

"That makes sense. Just sorry you must hang out for each one. I wish I could stay with you, but we've got to keep Dick's project moving."

"Mr. Northcutt is so wonderful. He has supported Dick from day one. His salary is continuing, and insurance is still effective. I don't know what we would do without his support!"

"He does seem to be an unusually supportive boss for his employees. I'm thankful to be working with him, Dick, and Roger."

"Roger is a real support to us too. Dick hired him about six years ago. They have become good friends."

The doctor came out from the bowels of the operating rooms. "Marianne, everything went well with the surgical removal of the pellets. You can see Dick now."

"Thank you so much, doctor. Ashleigh thank you for coming by. It means so much to have you in our lives. I'll keep you up to date for the next few days."

Ashleigh gave her a hug, "Tell Dick I'm praying for him and you and the kids."

She left feeling hopeful for Dick's recovery, knowing she had become part of a special family.

Chapter Thirty-Three

The weeks flew by. Ashleigh handled her functions as a lead architect, which was her comfort zone. She and Roger worked well together and settled small differences with professionalism and respect.

Ashleigh made headway with one of the local representatives, who promised to give her a date to appear in the legislature's subcommittee meeting the next month. The group had dinner once a week and became good friends.

Pat and her boyfriend were moving slowly with their relationship. He was divorced with two children and wanted to give the girls time to feel comfortable with Pat being around them. She was happy with taking it slow, too, and used some of her free time to spend with the group.

Martha's husband didn't involve himself in her social issues, which were many. He was accustomed to her being gone at night several times a week. He had his television sports games.

"I sponsor Girl Scouts and have a Cadet troupe of my own. We meet every week after school to work on badges and occasionally take overnight trips. I wish I had been able to be a scout leader when my girls were young. I'm making up for lost time. These get togethers are my adult projects."

Saundra was quiet for most of the dinner. They all looked at her concerned; something was awry with her job or dating. Since she was usually the outspoken one in the group, no one wanted to be the first to approach her. Finally, Pat touched her arm.

"Are you okay, Saundra? You've been so quiet tonight. We're worried about you."

"I didn't want to talk about this, but you are my only true friends. I'm afraid I'm pregnant. I've been seeing another attorney in the firm and thought we were being careful, but I'm having morning nausea and have missed my last period."

They reached out to her with sympathy.

"It's okay. If I am pregnant, I'll take care of it. Sydney isn't serious about our relationship. He wouldn't want a child."

"What would you do? Can you stay in your job?"

"I'm not at that point yet. I'll wait a couple of weeks before I make my decision. Abortion is legal. I'll just have to find the right doctor."

The conversation ended and the group began to separate and excuse themselves to head home. Ashleigh stayed.

"What can I do Saundra? I'll stay as long as you need someone tonight. You can spend the night with me if you want."

"You're too kind, Ashleigh. I'm okay. I have a lot to consider."

"I understand. Call me if you change your mind."

"I appreciate you staying."

"No one should be alone when they need comfort and support."

"Not everyone feels that way. You are a special friend, Ashleigh."

As she walked home, Ashleigh felt Saundra's pain. There had been no one for her to talk with about Scott's attack, except Jason. Sweet Jason. What would she do without him?

I haven't heard from him all week. Hope he's okay. When she got home, she picked up the phone and dialed his number.

No answer.

She left a message. "Hi Jason. Just wanted to check on you. Miss seeing you this week. Hope you're okay."

Chapter Thirty-Four

She slipped on pj's, grabbed a coke, and opened the door to the balcony. The evening sparkled with streetlights, which seemed to meld with the starlit night.

Thank you, God, for this beautiful night. I'm alone, but I don't feel lonely. I even feel safe. Thank you for that.

The phone's ringing brought her thoughts earthward. It was a wrong number. Holding the phone in her hand, she thought of Jason and dialed his number.

"Hello. Hi, Jason. Are you home, or out of town? They must be really interested in you and your project proposal. No, I'm good. Just wanted to talk to my friend tonight. Enjoy your dinner. I'll see you when you get back. Good night."

Now, she felt lonely.

She never knew that a friendship could be so compelling. She hadn't realized how important Jason was to her everyday life until he wasn't around every day. Even her friendship with JJ was not this powerful and she truly loved JJ. What was this feeling for Jason? Could she be in love with him?

She wished this call had been on her answering machine. Then she could play it over again and listen to the soft tones of his voice, the strength of his words and the caring he conveyed.

Trying to clear her head, she turned on the television to hear the evening news. It didn't help. She did some isometric exercises to no avail. She dusted the furniture. She scrubbed the bathroom. Finally, she crawled into bed and prayed.

God, please help me understand these feelings for Jason. I've always thought of him as a good friend. Something is different. My feelings are stronger. I miss him. I miss everything about him. I know he sees me as a friend. I would be broken hearted if he falls in love with someone else. I need your wisdom and strength. Amen

***

The week seemed to drag by. Dick was scheduled for his prostate removal surgery on Thursday. The whole office held its breath. Ashleigh and Roger went to the hospital to be with Marianne.

After Dick was taken into the operating room, Ashleigh tried to distract Marianne with conversation about her children.

"How is your mother doing with the kids?"

"Fine."

"Are they enjoying school?"

"Yes."

It was apparent Marianne wanted to be left alone with her thoughts. Ashleigh sat quietly. After an hour, the nurse came out and told Marianne that everything was moving along as expected.

Roger went to the nearest phone and called Edward Northcutt.

"Thank you for letting me know, Roger. I'll tell the rest of the office."

The nurse said, "I'll be back in about another hour to update you."

"It will take another hour?"

"Yes. This is a complicated surgery. I thought you knew the doctor planned about four hours to do the surgery."

"Maybe I did. I don't know." Tears streamed down Marianne's cheeks.

Ashleigh put her arms around her. "Let's get some lunch. They won't be back for an hour. You need to get some lunch and some fresh air."

Roger chimed in, "I'm starved."

Hesitating slightly, Marianne agreed.

It was afternoon when they got the news that the surgery was over, and Dick was doing extremely well.

Marianne rushed to his room. Ashleigh and Roger left the hospital and headed to the office.

Dick needed two weeks of complete rest before Ashleigh could continue with their work. She and Roger were ready to present him with a full project plan.

The following Monday morning Roger caught Ashleigh as she entered the office.

"Hey, Ash...do you mind if I call you that? It seems less formal."

"That's what all my friends call me. It suits us."

"We're at a point where we need to go to the site and meet the engineers. Want to go with me?"

"I'd love to. That visit is what really brings the project to life for me. I've missed doing that since I left Stockton & Associates. You going this morning?"

"Yeah."

"I'm ready."

They headed out to the worksite eager to get the feel of the project at ground level. The visit validated their project plan.

Roger took Ashleigh's arm, "We're ready for Dick to see our work. Hopefully, we can meet with him next week."

"He will be so excited. Marianne said he's so bored with his recovery. He's ready to get back to work."

"Let's celebrate. Can you have dinner with me tonight?"

Without thinking that Jason would be back in town this afternoon, she answered, "Sure. That will solidify our teamwork."

Dinner was easy because they had gotten to know each other over the months. They lingered over dessert and when she got in her car it was close to eleven o'clock. She unlocked her apartment door and realized the light was on. She never left the lights on when she went to work.

She backed out of the door and hesitated. There was no way Scott could be there. He didn't have a new key and the door had not been damaged. She wanted to call Jason, but he was out of town. He would know what she should do.

She dialed his phone and heard it ringing in the phone and somewhere within her apartment.

"Hel...lo. Hello."

"Jason?"

"Yeah. It's me, Ash. Where are you? I fell asleep on your sofa."

"Is it you in my house?"

"Yes. I came straight here when I got in town this afternoon. You didn't come to the door, so I knew you weren't here. I came in to wait. I guess I fell asleep. I was so tired from the drive."

"You drove from Mississippi?"

"Yes. I couldn't wait to see you. I missed you so much. I couldn't get a flight out today. So, I rented a car and drove."

She was smiling as she walked into her living room. Jason was standing in front of the sofa, looking out at Atlanta's skyline.

"Where are you? When are you coming home?"

"Right now. I'm here."

He turned and saw her grinning at him. "How am I talking with you when you are on your home phone?"

He threw his phone down and picked her up in a bear hug that took her breath away.

When he set her back on the floor, she pointed to the phone, "What is that? And how did you get it?"

"It's one of Motorola's latest developments. It's a mobile phone. It accesses my home phone calls remotely."

"It's kinda big,"

"Yeah, but it's great. I don't have to be at home to get my calls."

"You techie guys. Always have a new toy." She plopped on the sofa and pulled him with her.

"I've missed you."

"Me, too."

"How are things going?"

"Dick's surgery went well. Roger and I are presenting new project plans to him next week. Mr. Northcutt hired me full-time at an unbelievable salary. Mom and dad are fine. Scott has left me alone. I told him he could tell folks he broke up with me. And…I have an appointment… the group has an appointment with the legislative subcommittee on women's rights next month. How's that for a good report?"

"That's wonderful."

She sat on the sofa and patted the spot next to her. "Now, tell me about you and your job."

"The Mississippi commissioners have hired me as their structural engineer under Stockton's firm."

"Are you moving to Mississippi?"

"No. But I will be working there a good bit over the next year."

She didn't want her disappointment to show. "That's exciting for you."

"It's a positive change. At least I won't be around Camden every day."

"He's really gotten to you."

"You could say that. I need a change of pace. A fresh atmosphere and a challenging project. I think I'll have it in Mississippi."

"I'm happy for you, Jase. You deserve to be happy."

"I didn't say this change will make me happy. It will just give me a breather."

"When will you leave?"

"I'm going there in a couple of weeks to set everything up with the other engineers and the architect. Then I'll be back for a week. After that I'm not sure."

"I'd love to see you again before you go."

"Sure. Let's have dinner tomorrow night. I'm sorry I intruded tonight. You must have been on a date."

"Not really a date. Roger and I went to dinner to celebrate Dick's successful surgery and our progress on Dick's project."

"Oh, Roger. Well, can you go to dinner tomorrow night?"

"Of course."

"Okay, I'll be here at our regular time, seven. I'll let you get to bed."

She walked him to the door. He lingered a moment to look at her and then he turned and left.

The night had been a roller coaster. First Roger and then Jase waiting on her in her apartment. She wasn't sure she would sleep at all.

Chapter Thirty-Five

Dinner was only the beginning. Jase took her to the Red Rock Restaurant at the lake.

"I feel this is our place. Is that okay?"

"Of course. I love it. I'm interested to hear about your job."

"Ash, it is so different from the hustle and bustle of Atlanta. It's a small town about five miles off of I-20. At one time, it was a growing town with every kind of service business on the business strip. Life moved at a slower pace. People were thankful for what they had. They welcomed folks who would stop to take a break and have lunch or dinner, including a walk to the gift shops, when traveling toward Texas. It spurred growth in the town.

"When the expressway was built, it diverted traffic away from downtown. The businesses began to see a decline in sales and eventually saw very few tourists stop over. Finally, the town council brought together the business owners and investors to solve their problem. They need something to attract travelers. A reason for out-of-towners to stop and enjoy the town, the river and good food.

"That's when they got in touch with Howard Stockton to offer our help in urban development for their town. I fell in love with the town the way it is, but it can be better. We can create a destination for travelers. I'm excited to be a part of that."

Ashleigh hung on every word Jase said. She could picture the town. She heard the excitement in his voice and knew he had made a good decision.

They saw each other every night until Jason left for Mississippi. Having so much time with him and then none was hard for Ashleigh to accept. He promised to call every night. They set ten o'clock for their phone visits, which meant it was nine o'clock in Mississippi.

When Jase left, Ashleigh filled her nights reviewing every-thing she could find about the women's movement. She wanted to be able to answer questions that might be asked at their meeting with the legislative subcommittee. At the next group meeting she carried copies of all her research so they would all be prepared for questions at the meeting.

As usual, Ashleigh was the first to enter the restaurant. Their waitress expected them every Tuesday night and had their table ready in the corner, away from traffic flow inside the restaurant to give them privacy. She smiled as Ashleigh headed toward the table and immediately brought her lemonade.

By the time she distributed the information to each seat, Saundra entered the restaurant. Ashleigh noticed an unexpected glow about her tonight.

"You seem happy. Do you have good news?"

"I do. I'll share when everyone gets here.

"Okay. Can't wait."

Pat and Martha were both late, making it hard for Ashleigh to carry on casual conversation with Saundra.

Finally, the other two women arrived and took their seats at the table. Saundra spoke up.

"I've made Ashleigh wait until you two arrived to tell you my good news."

They all spoke at the same time. "Tell us. What is it?"

"I am not pregnant. I guess I was under stress from my relationship, not knowing what Sydney wanted. I don't have to worry anymore."

She held out her left hand and showed them a brilliant diamond ring on her finger. Everyone jumped up and hugged her.

Ashleigh squeezed her shoulder. "I'm so happy for you, Saundra. When you do get pregnant there won't be any decision to make. You both will welcome a little one into your lives."

She gave a silent prayer of thanks for God's intervention in Saundra's decision.

Pat asked, "Saundra, what would you have done if you had been pregnant, and Sydney didn't propose?"

"I can't answer honestly. I'm afraid I would have had an abortion because I could not raise a child by myself and hold down a full-time job. Then I would have carried the guilt the rest of my life. I'm thankful I didn't have to make that decision."

Ashleigh tried to bring the group back to a celebration. "We can talk about our appointment with the subcommittee next week. This is a night to celebrate."

When she opened the door at nine-thirty, the red flashing light on her phone drew her attention. She was hoping it was Jason. The voice was JJ's.

"Hi, Ash. I'm heading home tomorrow. The trial is finally over. Save me tomorrow night for us to visit. I've missed you. I should be there around seven thirty. Okay. See you tomorrow."

More good news. Even though it wasn't Jason, JJ's message was the next best thing.

At exactly ten o'clock Jason called.

Chapter Thirty-Six

Roger approached her first thing the next morning. "Are you free for dinner tonight?"

"Good morning, Roger. No, I'm sorry I'm not available tonight. My long-time friend, who has been out of town on a job for several months, is back in town. We're having dinner tonight to get caught up. I'll take a raincheck though."

"Disappointed, but I'll take it. Are you going to Dick's this week? Edward said he called last week and is ready to get back to work."

"Edward asked me to wait until next week. He's afraid Dick is rushing things. He thinks Dick needs another week of rest."

It was hard for Ashleigh to keep her mind on her work. She couldn't wait to see JJ. The months apart made their friendship dearer to her. At four thirty she couldn't wait any longer, closed her files for the day and rushed out before anyone could catch her with questions or problems.

JJ was at the restaurant when she arrived. "You must be hungry. Or you couldn't wait to see me."

"I missed you so much, Ash."

"Not so much to come home."

"I did have to work every night and weekends. Well, at first, I did that. But the last couple of months I was busy with Rodney, Rodney Stephens Murray."

"Yes, and?"

"And we're in love." She raised her left hand where an antique gold band hosted a small carat diamond.

"JJ. What? You're getting married and I haven't even met the guy." She jumped up and hugged JJ.

"I know. It's unbelievable. He's the bailiff I told you about. He took the bar while I was there, passed and was offered a job with the largest firm in Warner Robbins. We celebrated together and then he asked me to marry him.

"Ash, I'm so in love. I never knew it would be this way. Our wedding will be around Thanksgiving. The only negative thing about my happiness is that I will live three hours away from you."

Ashleigh had listened quietly while JJ talked and saw the sparkle in her eyes and heard the love in her voice for Rodney. "JJ we're all on different paths. I'm so happy for you. We can deal with three hours. You've found your guy! We will always be close."

"I knew you'd be happy for me, Ash. Will you be my maid of honor?"

"Of course. Just pick dresses we can wear later, okay?"

"Got it."

They talked until the restaurant closed. "I'm going to spend the day with Mom tomorrow and need to see the rest of the family with my news. It might be Friday before I'm free again."

"I understand. You have my number and know where I live. Any time you're free just show up, after work hours, or call. I should be free. Jase is in Mississippi on a job, so my nights are free, unless I go out with Roger. Oh, and Tuesday nights are saved for meeting with the group working on the ERA issue."

"We didn't even talk about that, and I forgot to ask you about your relationship with Jason. I'm sorry. I made tonight all about me."

"As it should have been. Not much to tell about my life. We'll catch up next time. Love you JJ."

"You, too. See you soon."

***

Closing the door to her apartment, Ashleigh realized she was starting a new season of her life. *I'm so happy for JJ but I know things will be drastically different in our relationship. Jase may decide he loves Mississippi and move there. I'm in a new job without close friends, except Roger. The ERA group is taking up most of my leisure time. This is not what I expected my life to be. Worst of all, I am a damaged woman for any man who would want to marry me.*

God, thank you for your love, a love I can always count on. You are the one constant in my life now. Your presence is stronger than my parents'. You're with me one hundred percent of the time. You hold my right hand.

She undressed and slipped into cool sheets and peaceful dreams.

Chapter Thirty-Seven

Dick was excited to see Ashleigh and her project progress. He was sitting in the great room with a small desk in front of him. Marianne let Ashleigh in with a hug.

"Don't keep her to yourself, sweetheart. I need to see this wonder woman. I've heard about all the work she and Roger have done. Edward couldn't stop ranting on and on about them. Young lady, don't even think for a minute you're going to take my job."

Ashleigh smiled and gave Dick the first hug she had been able to give him. "There is no one who could take your place, Mr. Monroe, architect extraordinaire!"

"You and Roger are saving my bacon."

"There would be no bacon if you hadn't developed it."

"Okay, enough of this. Show me…"

They worked until the sun started its descent behind the fall kaleidoscope of reds, yellows, and oranges pushing out the green leaves of birch, maple, oaks, and falling pine needles. Ashleigh looked up to see evening beginning to settle over the cove pulling her into its beauty but pushing her to make her exit before it got dark. The road leading to Dick's home was snake-like and narrow. She didn't want to leave in the dark.

She promised to come back on Thursday after she and Roger took Dick's input and integrated it into the plan.

The drive home felt like an awakening to the realization of what she wanted out of her life. She thought about the fittings for her dress for JJ's wedding. She wanted a wedding in her future but she, also, wanted to advance in her job, and she wanted to finish her quest to help all women get paid appropriately for their work.

Can you give me all that, God? Am I asking too much? I know I'm not worthy of it.

She needed to get her mind on plans for the group meeting tomorrow night at The Brick House. Their presentation to the subcommittee was coming up.

***

The meeting was raucous. Everyone wanted to talk at once. They had reviewed Ashleigh's material and looked up additional points of reference they each wanted to highlight.

Ashleigh had been thinking about each of the women addressing the subcommittee. None of them had fought for their beliefs. They demonstrated one day and then hid in their current situation without speaking out for themselves. She hated to squash the celebratory mood, but she felt they needed to have credence in their requests. What were they willing to sacrifice to get the legislature to listen?

"Ladies, I think we all need to be prepared to have our own

story to tell the subcommittee. They will want to hear some evidence of how we have been rebuffed ignoring the equal pay issue. Identifying our slight is one thing. Actively seeking justice and a change in our position will solidify our request.

"Just think about it over the next few days and decide what action you can take."

When the manager started turning out lights, they realized they needed to wrap it up and head home.

Ashleigh was exhausted and exuberant. Then she realized she had missed Jase's call. He had not been home since he left for Mississippi. She hurt thinking about him. Was he seeing someone else? He never mentioned anyone when they talked. He seemed glad to talk with her, but he missed his nightly calls several times. It probably wasn't important to him. He thought of her as a good friend, nothing more.

The phone message light was on. She listened to his voice. "Hey, Ash. Sorry I missed you. Guess you're out with Roger. I'll try to call again tomorrow night. Bye."

Out with Roger! What was he saying. Did he think she and Roger had a 'thing'? That was crazy. She and Roger had been to dinner several times, but he had never come to her apartment and never asked her to come to his. Their time together was spent talking about work. However, he did regularly grab her hand when he walked her to her car. No. That meant nothing. He was not interested in her in a romantic way.

She never thought of him on a social basis. He was a good-looking man, several years older than herself. His blonde hair, cut in the professional comb to the left, made him appear safe and settled. His hazel eyes lit up when he smiled. He was taller than her by eight or nine inches, but she had never been close enough to him to feel his muscular chest or arms.

Deflated she went straight to bed without unpacking her briefcase, turning on the news or taking a shower.

Chapter Thirty-Eight

September days eased their way toward October. The sub-committee meeting was scheduled for next week. Ashleigh talked with Thomas Worthington on Friday morning to confirm they were still on the agenda for the Wednesday meeting. She told Edward Northcutt she needed to be off the entire day. He had no problem with it.

Nerves were getting the better of her. She called Christine.

"Mom, are you free tomorrow?"

"Sure, honey. What's up?"

"I haven't really visited with you and dad much lately. I thought we might spend the day together. I can come over and we can shop and then cook out."

"You mean we get you the whole day?"

"If you don't have other plans."

"That sounds wonderful. Come at nine and we'll start with breakfast."

Ashleigh surprised herself at how excited she was to spend the day with her parents. Carlton would play golf after breakfast, but she and Christine would go downtown and shop. It would be like old times.

When she arrived, she was greeted with her mother's delicious crepes with fresh strawberries, bacon and crowned with caramel flan. Christine ground her own beans to make the smoothest coffee Ashleigh ever drank. She was aware how easy it would be to move back home. She wouldn't be alone at night. Mom's cooking was enough to entice her, but the idea that she would also face daily suggestions about her life and introductions to available young men at weekly dinner parties brought her back to reality. The price was too steep.

"Ashleigh, dear, I'm having a dinner party next Saturday night. Could you come and be my female balance?"

"I don't know mother. I have a lot to do in preparation for our meeting with the legislative subcommittee next week."

"I know this is a burden to you. Somehow, I miscalculated the number of females. You know how I pride myself on having pairs of guests. I would really appreciate it if you would take a few hours off, have a delicious dinner (Francis will be the chef for the evening) and relax for a change. I can have Carlton call someone in the legislature for you. Then you won't have to worry about a presentation."

"No Mother. I do not want Dad to intervene. I've got control of this."

Not wanting to ruin the day because of a disagreement, she softened her voice and acquiesced to attend.

***

The week flew by. When Saturday arrived, she picked out a yellow knee-length jersey dress with three-quarter length sleeves and a fitted skirt, adding sandal heels for the dinner. She wanted her mom to be proud of her and she was okay to attend the dinner to keep her social life active.

It appeared she was early because there were only two cars in the circular drive. She parked in the back in her usual space. She tried to slip in through the kitchen, but the door was locked. That was weird. That door was only locked when no one was home. Shrugging, she headed to the front door.

Mom opened the door and gave her a full-on hug, rather than the lean-in, cheek kissing welcome that had become natural for them. Ashleigh immediately became suspicious.

"Mother, have you invited a potential suitor for me to this intimate dinner."

"Why Ashleigh. What makes you think this is an intimate dinner?"

"I see only six place settings."

"One of the couples cancelled at the last minute."

Ashleigh raised her eyebrows but decided to let it slide.

"Francis will have dinner in about twenty minutes. Let's have a glass of wine while we wait."

She led the way to the great room and handed Ashleigh a glass of white wine. They sat on the Duncan Fife sofa facing the floor-to-ceiling windows overlooking the pool. Ashleigh feigned a taste or two of the wine, because it was the proper way to visit prior to dinner. The doorbell rang and Christine jumped up to answer it. Ashleigh walked around her favorite room in the house, touching all the precious antique pieces handed down from great-grandmother-to-grandmother and finally to her mother. One day they would be hers.

Susan and Paul Duncan appeared in the doorway before Christine. Ashleigh rushed over to them, surprised and excited to see these long-time friends of her parents.

"I can't believe you're here. I haven't seen you in ages. How long will you be in town?"

"We've made reservations for a week. I don't know if we can manage to stay that long. We'll see." Susan held Ashleigh's hand.

Catherine smiled at the surprise for Ashleigh. Susan and Paul were like second parents to her and Phillip.

"Let's go ahead and be seated for dinner." Christine guided them to the dining room table.

"Mom. Shouldn't we wait for the other guest?"

"He'll be here in a few minutes. I don't want to hold up dinner for him."

That was not at all like her mother. Ashleigh raised her eyebrows but followed along to the dining room. The other guests paused and allowed Ashleigh to enter first.

She stepped around the doorframe and stopped for a second. When she realized who was sitting at the table, she ran to Phillip sitting next to her seat at the table. "Phillip, Phillip. When did you get in? How long can you stay?"

She was spewing questions as she fell into his arms.

"This is the best surprise I've ever had. Mom, you outdid yourself."

"Thank you, sweetheart. He got in this afternoon. He will be here for a week. He can tell you the rest of his orders after dinner."

Phillip answered questions more than he ate during the meal.

***

Ashleigh did not want to go home after dinner. When Susan and Paul left, she snuggled up to Phillip like a child needing protection. She felt precious and loved by his side. She realized how much she missed him, but she knew this visit wouldn't last long enough for her to get her fill of him.

They made plans to go to The Brick House for dinner Monday night. She didn't want to leave, but she needed her sleep to manage her work and review the presentation. She hugged her family and left the comfort and security of her childhood home.

Once again, she had missed Jase's call. Was this an omen about their relationship?

***

The comfort of her bed was not enough to encourage sleep. She was tired, excited, and happy until she thought of Jase. She wanted him to be part of the reunion with Phillip. She wanted the three men in her life to know each other. Maybe Jase could come home before Phillip had to leave.

She would call him tomorrow.

She dozed as the horizon splayed pink striations of sun rays filtered through grey cotton clouds. The alarm brought her to full awareness. Her bones ached with relentless throbs as she stumbled to the shower. A sleepless night was no way to start a stressful week tinged with happy moments with Phillip and, hopefully, Jase.

Chapter Thirty-Nine

Jase answered on the first ring.

"Everything alright, Ash?"

"Yes, it is. It will be perfect if you can come home over the weekend and spend time with me and my family. Phillip is home and I want you to meet him."

"Phillip? Wow. Definitely. I'll leave early Friday morning and be there by Friday night, late."

"Can't you come Thursday, so we will have the whole weekend with Phillip?"

"Ash, that might be difficult. Let me see how I can rearrange meetings this week. Maybe I can make it work. I'll call you tonight."

"Perfect. Thank you, Jase. You will love Phillip. He's a lot like you."

"Not sure that is a good recommendation."

"It's a perfect recommendation. Talk with you tonight."

That's a better way to start the day. She picked up her brief-case, an apple and her first cup of coffee. Balancing the coffee in her left hand holding the briefcase, she locked the door and listened for the deadbolt's click. Everyday routines carried a couple of extra steps since Scott.

***

Roger was ready when she got to the office. They loaded up files, blueprints, and Roger's AutoCad computer. This was going to be an important day for Dick, and they wanted everything to work smoothly.

Ashleigh had a secondary wish for the day to go smoothly. She was excited to have dinner with Phillip tonight. He would be all hers for the evening. Mom and dad had another engagement, which was typical for Carlton. Christine had been with Phillip all day. Allowing Ashleigh to have time with her brother was important to Christine.

The power-point presentation seemed to design itself. Dick began with his ideas and Ashleigh and Roger fell into his vision easily. They took turns tweaking the presentation and printing new blueprints. Dick became tired around three o'clock. Ashleigh and Roger packed up and headed back to the office with feelings that the day was successful. Their meeting with the developer could be scheduled. Mr. Northcutt was happy to hear that good news. Roger and Ashleigh would present the plans jointly.

It was the perfect day to leave early, giving her time to change into casual clothes for dinner with Phillip.

There was a moment when Ashleigh felt a little unsteady, unsure of what her body was telling her. I hope I'm not getting sick. I don't want to give Phillip anything that could compromise his next mission. I wish he could tell me what it will be.

The nausea passed and she was ready much earlier than expected. She had time to call Jase. She didn't want to miss his call tonight but she didn't want to cut the evening short with Phillip.

"Jase, I hope I'm not disturbing you. I had a few minutes before I meet Phillip for dinner. I thought I'd check to see if you can come home Thursday. Are you in the office?"

The mobile phone was charging in the car while Jase was on a tour of the town in Mississippi.

"Well, okay. Leave me a message when you call tonight. I will be at dinner with Phillip and may not be home early."

She drove to her parents' home to meet Phillip. Since he did not have a car in town, she would drive them to the restaurant. She had not seen Phillip in street clothes in a long time. He looked relaxed and fit in his v-neck brown cashmere sweater over a button-down collar blue and brown plaid shirt and pleated khaki pants. His thick blond hair was military buzzed but still prominent around his forehead.

"Hi, sis." He reached over to kiss her on the cheek.

"I'm going to treat you to a special dinner tonight. We'll save The Brick House for another time. We're doing steak at the lake."

"Okay. I'm certainly ready for that. I've had a long day."

The dinner atmosphere was the same as the night Jase brought her here but felt different with Phillip. She wanted her attention to be on Phillip's face. She needed to savor every smile, twitch, frown, and attentive solemn look he displayed. They never knew how long his next assignment might be. It could be months or years before she saw him again.

He asked her questions about her work, social life and love life. She teared up when she told him about Scott. She had no plans to tell him, but he could always get the deep-down issues bothering her. His face turned blood red. He pushed back from the table and demanded they leave so he could confront Scott.

"Phillip. We can't do that. No one knows about the rape except Jason. He came by the apartment a few minutes after Scott left. He helped me through the night and has been my rock since then."

"What did the police say? Is Scott in jail?"

"I didn't call the police."

"The hospital is supposed to notify the police in a rape situation."

"I didn't go to the hospital."

"What. What's wrong with this Jason person? Why didn't he take you to the hospital?"

"I would not go. I didn't want to admit anything had happened. Scott's parents are business associates of dads, and they are in the same social organizations as mom and dad. I didn't want dad to cause friction between their businesses."

"Friction? I'd say rape caused the friction."

"Phillip. Please. I've had to rein Jason in about this too. He wanted to find Scott and expose him, after he gave him a few bruises and bloody nose.

"I don't want this to get out. I'm ashamed. I am now a tainted woman."

"You are not tainted. Scott is the one who is tainted, messed up and criminally guilty. He should be in jail."

"Well, that won't happen. It would be my word against his. I didn't call the police and I didn't go to the hospital to have a rape kit prepared. That was my decision. Please honor my wishes."

"I can't believe mom is allowing you to do this."

"Mom doesn't know. Dad doesn't know. Jason is the only one who knows, and he wouldn't know if he hadn't come by my apartment to bring me my sweater that I left at The Brick House when we had dinner. I insisted on walking home alone. He saw the sweater after I left and brought it to me. He has been so supportive, even though he doesn't agree with my decision about keeping the situation quiet."

"I hear what you're saying, but this is not right! You're letting a rapist go free. What if he rapes another young woman?"

"I don't know. I didn't think about that. I was just so shocked and damaged. I couldn't think about anyone else. I know I should have. God would have wanted me to. I just couldn't. Don't judge me, Phillip. It would kill me if you are disappointed in me."

"Sis. I could never be disappointed in you. I'm furious for you. I want to hit or kick something. Let's skip desert. I can't sit any longer."

"I ruined our dinner. I'm so sorry. You know, I can't keep anything from you."

"You didn't ruin anything. You've survived something unspeakable that happened to you. Something that took away a very special part of you. Something no one had the right to take. It was you who should have been able to give it to your husband. I hurt for you."

"Promise you won't tell mom or dad."

"If that's your wish. I won't. I think they need to know but I'm not here to help them and you work through the devastation that would cause everyone concerned. I'll leave that decision up to you. I love you, Sis."

Chapter Forty

Tuesday night the group met at Ashleigh's apartment for a final run-through of their presentation to the legislative subcommittee on Wednesday. Everyone had come through with a highlight of their own efforts to promote equal pay for women.

Wednesday morning Thomas Worthington greeted them outside the subcommittee meeting room. He escorted them to a small office off the main hallway in the capitol legislative offices.

"Thank you, ladies, for coming today. Are you prepared to make your argument to the session?"

Ashleigh spoke up. "We are. We have an overall presentation with facts and figures and we each have examples of our own struggles being subjected to unfair pay practices. Finally, we will give examples of how we have tried to support other women in their jobs.

"In order to assure women of equal pay for equal work, we feel that it is necessary for Georgia to ratify the Equal Rights Amendment in order to provide just cause for claims against employers who practice unfair pay practices."

"That sounds great. Facts and figures are what they are looking for. Social ideology is a waste of time, so keep those comments out of your presentation if you want to garner support. Okay. I will come back and get you when we are ready for you. We've allowed an hour-and-a-half for you to make your case. Good luck."

He opened the door to the hallway. They could hear the legislators moving about and entering the meeting room across the hall. Ashleigh was tempted to open the door and get a peek at the representatives.

It was two hours later when Tom knocked on the door. "We're ready for you now. A few of the members had to step away for other meetings or to get a break. Don't be disappointed about the number of folks waiting to hear your presentation."

The 160-seat room held four legislators spread out in seats across the auditorium. Ashleigh's heart sank. They had to make a splash to get attention from the four men to move their proposal forward. Noticeably, there were no women in attendance.

The ride from the Capitol to mid-town was deadly quiet. When she stopped in the parking lot at The Brick House, everyone chose to go home rather than have the celebratory dinner they had planned.

Ashley's mind was spinning. That was a disappointment, but we did get in front of four lawmakers. What is our next move? We have our materials prepared. We only need an audience.

She entered her apartment with an armful of information in presentation form. Where can I take that information next? I'll find a list of women's organizations in town and national women's business organizations. There has to be a plethora of women's groups that might be interested in hearing what we've discovered.

I'll start with local groups.

As evening approached, she looked at her watch. Where has the time gone? I'm going to be late for dinner with the family.

I'll freshen up my makeup and change into casual pants and blouse. No time for a shower.

She parked in her usual place in front of the garage in the back, where she could look through the floor to ceiling windows in the back of the house. The dining room was lit with soft light. Christine had set the table with her best pottery dishes, used for casual dining. Ashleigh smiled. Oh good, a true family dinner tonight. She opened the back door to the smell of braised pork.

Phillip grabbed her in a bear hug and kissed her on the cheek. She was home.

Chapter Forty-One

Phillip entertained them with a catalogue of stories about places he had been without disclosing the locations. He had always been an entertaining storyteller. It didn't matter if the stories were true or not. His animated telling kept them entranced. After performing for an hour, he looked at Ashleigh.

"Hey, you had an important day today. Tell us about it."

"It bombed. None of the legislators were interested in hearing our presentation. Only four remained to listen to us. I don't know if we made enough of an impact to get some attention of the full legislative body."

"That's too bad, sweetheart." Christine's attempt to be empathetic fell flat. She didn't seem to understand Ashleigh's insistence on taking this route with her cause.

Carlton spoke up, "You should let me get in touch with some of my business associates. We can make some noise up there in the legislature. It would save you a lot of time and heartache. Men are not going to listen to a small group of women complaining about pay issues."

"That's the problem, Dad. We are not just doing this for our own pay. We want all women to have the opportunities that men have in their jobs. None of your colleagues can speak to that issue with passion."

"You've always had to take charge of your goals. I respect that. I hate to see you charging full force into disappointment."

"You can't own it, if you are not in charge of it, Dad. I do feel like I'm trying to control one of those huge hot air balloons. I'm filling it with ideas and good folks, but it wants to drift off in the wrong direction. I don't know how to control that part. I can make it go up with more air and make it descend with less air. The actual movement toward getting anywhere is beyond my control right now. You understand how that frustrates me."

"End of subject. This is a happy time. Game time in the great room." Christine ended the serious talk demanding they get on with their favorite activity.

Ashleigh noticed Phillip kept looking at his watch with a concerned look on his face.

"Anything wrong?"

"I was hoping to hear from one of my buddies. They were on a critical mission tonight. I want to be sure everyone is okay".

Ashleigh suddenly realized the danger implicit in Phillip's assignments. His safety had never been at issue before. She had thought of him in an office, somewhere far away from danger. Had his mission changed? Or had she blocked out his vulnerability?

She tried to concentrate on having fun with the game but an image of him in combat kept interrupting her thoughts.

The night ended with Phillip challenging Dad with the final moves in the game.

"Morning comes too soon for me. Sorry guys, I need to head home. Wish I could take off a few days while you're here Phillip. Our visits are so short."

"Hey, I understand. If you popped in to one of my missions, I probably wouldn't be able to take any time to visit. We still have dinner tomorrow night and all-day Saturday. We'll make the most of it."

She grabbed her hero and didn't want to let go. A tingling feeling of doom flowed down from her head to her feet. She shook it off and smiled goodnight to everyone.

Chapter Forty-Two

Jase's message flashed red on her answering machine. She needed to hear his voice tonight. It was too late to call him back.

Thankfully, he will be here late tomorrow night. I hope he calls when he gets in.

I feel unusually tired tonight. The stress of the presentation to the legislature and the excitement of Phillip being home must have drained me of all energy.

She took a quick shower and put on flannel pajamas. Fall's night air was beginning to cool things quickly. She snuggled under grandmother's fan quilt and fell asleep easily. In the middle of the night, she woke with a start.

Something has happened. I feel it. What's wrong? Who do I call? It is too late to double check with family. I know someone would call me if anyone is hurt. It feels so real.

She rolled over. *God, please protect my family and Jase. If anyone is in danger, I can't protect them. I'm not in control of what happens with them. You can stretch your hand over them and bring them through any danger. Thank you for bringing Phillip home and for all my blessings. Amen*

Morning burst into the room with authority and determination. The day was moving on with or without her. She raised her head and looked straight into the fireball of light. It can't be morning already. I'm exhausted. She eased her feet over the side of the bed, slowly sat up and immediately felt sick. She made it to the toilet before the eruption inside her could materialize onto the floor.

1 can't be sick. I haven't been around anyone who was sick. I have too much to do and Jase is coming home tonight. The waves inside her weren't subsiding. She curled up on the side of the bed with the bathroom trashcan within reach on the floor.

After twenty or thirty minutes she felt stable enough to get some orange juice. Within an hour she was dressed and heading out the door for work.

***

She met with Roger in the drafting room to continue making changes Dick had requested. They planned to meet with him next Tuesday with the changes completed. Unexpectedly a wave of nausea flowed over her and caused her to fall into a chair beside the drafting table. Roger looked at her and immediately took her arm to steady her on the chair.

"Ashleigh, your face has lost all its color. Are you okay?"

"No, Roger. I'm not. Can you help me to the restroom? My legs are shaky. I don't think I can walk but I need to throw up."

He lifted her by her arm and put his arm around her to steady her walk. He waited outside the restroom door. He was afraid she was seriously ill by the noises he heard inside the room.

When she opened the door, he helped her to her office. "What can I get you? Do I need to take you home?"

"No. I feel better now. I could use a coke to settle my stomach."

"Coming right up."

The coke seemed to revive her, and they finished the morning's work. "Could you eat anything? I'll go get something and we can eat here in your office."

They kept the door closed all afternoon, which was unusual for coworkers to do. When they reached a stopping point, Ashleigh felt much better.

"I'm going home. We have a family dinner tonight. My brother, Phillip, is in town and I don't want to take the chance of getting sick again. Thank you for your help today, Roger."

She reached over and kissed him on the cheek just as someone opened the door.

The office gossip grinned.

"Sorry about that."

"I guess we will be the topic of office gossip tomorrow." She smiled as she grabbed her briefcase and left for the day.

Chapter Forty-Three

She closed the makeup drawer just as she heard Jase's voice. "Anyone home?"

She opened the bedroom door and rushed into his arms. He pulled her closer.

"I love that greeting!"

"I've missed you so much."

"Me too. I came early so we would have some time to talk before we join your family."

"I'm so glad you did. I hope I don't give you my germs. I've thrown up two mornings in a row. I don't know what I have. As far as I know, I haven't been around anyone sick."

"It's probably stress from everything you've been dealing with."

"I hope that's it. Let's sit. Tell me how everything is with you."

"I love what I'm doing and best of all Camden is not around. The folks I'm working with are accommodating and professional. They may use us for other projects when this one is finished. The other two architects keep me in the loop for any design changes they make. The rest of the staff is welcoming as if I were one of their employees."

"Jase, do you think you'll be there for months?"

"On the current project, I'm at a point where I can visit every other week for a few days. If we sign up for other projects, I don't know. I love the small town, but I don't want to live in Mississippi."

"Thank goodness. I miss you when you're not around bugging me." She bumped his shoulder and grinned.

"I'm excited to meet your brother. He seems like a stand-up guy."

"He's more than that. He's perfect."

"Perfect?"

"Well, as perfect as any man can be."

"And he is your brother."

"Yes, he is. I can't explain how empty a part of my heart is when he's gone but this career is his choice. He is good at it and it's his life. I can't deny that."

"Maybe I can fill some of that emptiness in your heart."

"You already have."

She wanted him to kiss her. She wanted to feel his strength and the comfort of his embrace. He simply grabbed her hand and squeezed it.

"I guess we'd better head over to my parent's house. I don't want to miss another minute with Phillip."

Introductions were easy and Jason was engulfed with love from the Justice family. Conversation with their friend, Paul Duncan, came naturally.

Susan nodded toward them as she touched Christine's arm. "He is a nice young man. And a good-looking guy, too. Is this serious between Ashleigh and him?"

Christine looked at him and over at Ashleigh, who was feigning conversation with her dad and Phillip, but she was focused on Jason.

"I don't know. She has kept this part of her life separate from us. I can see love in her face tonight as she looks at him."

Francis came to the doorway and announced that dinner was ready to be served.

Chapter Forty-Four

After dinner, the Duncans offered their lake house for the next day as a send-off for Phillip and a remembrance of all the summer days their families spent on the lake together. On this visit, they closed the house's sale, severing their final physical connection to the town.

Walking to Jase's car after the emotional dinner, Ashleigh hugged herself and leaned on Jason. "Everything is changing in my life. Phillip is leaving again, and we don't know how long he will be gone. Susan and Paul will not come around as much since they won't have a home base. You're moving on with your career and may not come back to live here."

"Whoa. Hold on. I am not thinking about moving permanently. This is my home and, besides that, you're here."

"Thank you for saying that but I know how things can change for you."

"Let's don't start making assumptions. By the way, am I invited to the lake with you tomorrow?"

"Of course. Susan gave you a personal invitation."

"That's right. They are fine folks."

"Don't be upset if I spend a lot of time with Phillip tomorrow. He's leaving Sunday morning. He must be back on base by midnight, or he is considered AWOL. Could you spend Sunday afternoon with me?"

"Yes. I would love to. I'm working in the office here Monday, flying out Tuesday morning."

***

Saturday pretended to be a happy occasion. The group water-skied, swam, floated on innertubes, and ate off-and-on all day. In the afternoon, Ashleigh went to the house when no one was inside, to throw up for the third time, leaving Jase floating on an innertube.

When she came outside, she saw Jason and Phillip floating beside each other, deep in conversation. How do they have anything serious to talk about? They just met last night. As she looked at two of the men she loved, she felt the warmth of family and wanted the day to last forever.

She grabbed a coke and sat on the Adirondack chair at the water's edge, trying to ease the ebb and flow of her stomach.

"Sweetheart, you haven't eaten much today. Are you okay? Being around the water usually makes you ravenous, like the rest of us."

"I've just eaten a lot in the last few days. I need to cut back to maintain my 'girlish' figure."

"You don't have a problem with that, but you do look like you've gained a few pounds. It looks good on you."

Christine had a way of making a derogatory remark seem like a compliment. It didn't work today. Ashleigh had noticed that some of her clothes were beginning to be a little tight.

After Jase and Phillip drifted back to shore, she grabbed Phillip and led him off to the swing under the canopy of the aged Oak. She needed alone time with him before the days end.

"Sis, you look a little peaked. Are you okay?"

"I don't know Phillip. I've been sick every morning and some days, all day. I throw up several times a day. I'm always queasy. Phillip, do you think I could be pregnant?"

"Have you been intimate with Jason?"

"No! You know I wouldn't do that. I've only had one experience and it was Scott. I can't be pregnant with his baby. I can't be pregnant at all. That is not in my plans. Even if it was Jason's baby, I would not be ready for it."

"Have you done a pregnancy test?"

"No. I'm afraid."

"Not knowing doesn't make it go away."

"I know. I don't want to face it."

"Maybe you aren't pregnant. Maybe it's the flu. Maybe you're worrying for nothing. Take a test. Do it today. Do it with Jason."

"What? Do it with Jason?"

"Yes. He's your best friend besides JJ and she isn't here. You need someone to lean on if you are pregnant, until you tell mom and dad."

"I can't even think about that. They would be horrified."

"You might be surprised. If you tell them about the rape, they will understand your situation. They will be your rock if you are. And, I would like to know before I leave in the morning. Please do it today."

Tears ran down her face. "Phillip. I'm so afraid."

"I know, sis. I wish you had told mom and dad when it happened. It would be easier for you now. But all we can do is move forward with what your reality is."

"Okay. I'll do it. I'll call you after."

Christine walked toward the swing and sat on the other side of Phillip. "My two children saying their goodbyes?"

"Yes, Mom."

"May I join you? I want every minute with my son I can get today."

"I'm sorry, Mom. I didn't mean to hog Phillip."

"I understand. You have always been close. I hope you stay that way for the rest of your lives. It will be comforting for me in my old age, when I get to my old age, to know you have each other."

The three stayed on the swing talking about old times until the sun began its slide behind the trees across the lake, sending dappled sunrays on the water and shoreline.

Carlton ambled toward them, taking his usual part in their threesome as the steady patriarch but the consummate outsider.

"I think Paul and Susan want some alone time to say goodbye to their home. You ready to go?"

Goodbyes were sad but filled with expectation that they would always remain friends and stay in touch.

Chapter Forty-Five

Ashleigh spotted a drugstore about a mile down the road from the lake.

"Jase, I need to pick up something from the drugstore. Will you stop at this independent store?"

"We're not far from our neighborhood store. Can you wait until then."

"No, not really."

"Is it an emergency?"

"Frustrated that he questioned her she raised her voice. "Jase, please just stop."

"Okay. I'm pulling in right now."

"I'll only be a minute."

Tears were waterfalling down her cheeks when she opened the door and got inside.

"Ash. What's wrong? Did I say something wrong? I didn't mean to argue about stopping. It's no big deal."

"It's not that, Jase. I bought a pregnancy test and didn't want anyone we know to see me buy it."

"What? Ash, do you think…"

"I don't know, Jase. My early morning sickness and me gaining a few pounds makes me wonder."

He reached over to grab her hand. "You want me to be with you when you do the test?"

"Would you?"

"Of course. You shouldn't be alone when you do it."

"You are too kind, Jason. You've always looked out for me."

"And I always will if you let me. You know, you're very independent." He smiled as he started the car.

She squeezed the brown paper bag, dreading the unveiling.

They held hands as they took the stairs to the fourth floor. She hesitated at her door. "I really don't want to do this."

"I know, sweetheart. It's best to know, rather than guess."

"That's what Phillip said. He wants me to tell him the results before he leaves in the morning."

"Phillip knows, but not your parents?"

"Yes, he has always been the cushion between me and our parents. My strong will hasn't been understood by them. He guides them to an understanding of my choices and helps them accept my actions. I tell him everything."

"He knows about the rape?"

"Yes, I told him one night right after it happened when he called me. He was angry that I had not called the police or gone to the hospital, until I told him you were with me."

"He didn't mention it today."

"He wouldn't. It was confidential between us."

"He's some kind of brother."

"Yes, he is. He was my rock until you came along."

"Me? I didn't know you saw me that way."

"Well, I do. This will be your greatest test."

She lifted the brown bag and, closing the door to her bedroom and bathroom, went into her bathroom. She undressed and put on a short robe and soft slippers. She sat on the end of the bed looking at the bathroom door. She felt immobilized. She didn't know how long she had been sitting, when she heard a soft knock on the door.

"Ash. Are you okay? Did you do the test?"

"No. Not yet."

"You want me to come in?"

"If you want."

He slowly opened the door and saw the image of a defeated woman. Someone he did not know. It shook him to his core.

"Ash, honey. It will be okay."

"Will it? What if I am pregnant? What will I do? I wouldn't marry Scott if he wanted to, which he would not. I can't have a baby as an unmarried woman. It would ruin my parents' image in the community and my career. I guess I could have an abortion, but I'm not sure I could do that. It is completely outside my beliefs."

"Let's not get ahead of ourselves. Do the test, then we'll see where we are."

"Where 'we' are?"

"Yes."

"Jase. This is not your problem."

"It could be my solution."

"No. There is no way I would tie you to something like this. If it were your child, I could consider it. But no. Not with someone else's…"

"Just go take the test. I'll be sitting right here to wait with you for the result."

Halting steps felt like it took forever for her to reach the bathroom ten steps from her bed. She closed the door. When she came out five minutes later, she was shaking. They slid down to the floor, their backs resting on the foot of the bed, eyes downcast looking at his watch.

"Time's up. Let's look together."

An injured cry erupted from the depths of her soul. "No. No. No. No. It can't be."

Jason grabbed her and held her tightly until the shaking and sobs subsided.

"Come. Let's sit on the sofa. I'll get you some water."

She followed his instructions without question. She needed someone else to make all the decisions for her tonight. She trusted Jase. He was here. She would lean on him.

Chapter Forty-Six

They woke up at the same time. He was stretched out on the sofa with her head on his right shoulder. His left hand held her tightly.

Neither one spoke. She walked to the bathroom and started the shower. He went to the kitchen and made a pot of coffee. They drank coffee in silence. When she stood to enter the bedroom to finish dressing, she spoke for the first time.

"You don't need to stay, Jason. I know you've got to get ready to return to Juliet tomorrow. Thank you for being with me last night."

"I'll take you to say goodbye to Phillip and spend the afternoon with you as we talked about last night."

"Everything has changed since last night. I can't involve you in my problem. It could ruin your career."

"I'm already involved. I'm not worried about my career."

"Mr. Stockton wouldn't be so accepting of you and the image you would bring to his company."

"I don't care about Stockton. I could get a job easily if he let me go."

"Thank you, Jason, but the next few days and weeks will be difficult for me. I won't be much fun or company for you."

"Do you think that's what I'm looking for from you? Ashleigh, I want to be with you no matter what's going on. I want to spend my life with you. I love you. Can't you see that?"

"You're such a good man, Jase. I appreciate you saying those things, but if they were true, you would have told me before this."

"That's not true. I was waiting for a sign from you that you felt the same way about me."

"Jase, I adore you. I respect you. I do love you, therefore, I will not put this burden on you."

"Ashley Justice, it is not a burden. It's what I've been waiting for. I can love this child if you can."

"I don't know if I can, Jase. That's just it. I don't know if I can. I don't know what I'm going to do right now. I need some time. Go to Mississippi and work. When I decide, I'll let you know."

"That's not the way it works between people who love each other. They share in decisions, especially decisions of this proportion."

"Married people share in decisions. Single people get to make independent decisions."

"I want to marry you."

"You just think that now. Think about what life would be like as newlyweds, not with freedoms but with chains, starting out our lives together. Responsibilities, maybe some legal issues with Scott."

"You're not going to tell him, are you?"

"He has a right to know."

"No, he doesn't. He only thinks about himself and his parent's reputation."

"What if a baby would change him?"

"Are you saying you want to be with him?"

"Never, but if he wanted to be part of a child's life, I would agree to it."

"You're not thinking straight."

"I know I'm not. That's why you need to go. I need to deal with mom and dad today. It will be difficult for them. I will consider their advice before I make a decision."

Jason stood.

Ashleigh squeezed his arm and kissed his cheek. "Goodbye for now Jason. Go and see what else is out there for you…a new job; a girlfriend; a new city. You can go anywhere you're called. You're free. I'm not."

***

Ashleigh parked in the front circular drive, knowing that the family would be in the great room at the front of the house. She opened the front door and walked through the foyer locking eyes with Phillip. As she got closer, she couldn't control herself and ran into his arms.

Catherine stepped forward, "Oh, Ashleigh, don't do that. I've been holding back all morning. I don't want Phillip to leave us with ugly faces from crying."

"Mom, I don't think she's crying over my leaving."

"What do you mean?"

"Let's sit down. Ashleigh, I'll start. Okay?"

Ashleigh could only shake her head yes.

"Mom, Dad, I call Ashleigh from the field when I can, just like I do you two. One night I caught her at a vulnerable time. She was crying and confided in me about a tragic event that happened to her. She needed to talk with someone about it and I was available. She didn't want to burden you with it. So, I honored her request to keep quiet. She felt the situation would resolve itself and there would be no need for you to know.

"By her emotions tonight, I assume the issue is not resolved.

"Ashleigh, do you want to pick up here?"

She did not want to pick up here. She wanted Phillip to tell her parents of her dishonor and shame, but she knew she had to take responsibility and tell them.

"You know I dated Scott Richmond for a while. I met him at one of your dinner's here at the house."

"Yes, Ashleigh. I'm not senile. I remember. I wanted you to meet a nice, respectable, young man. He is from a fine family. I assume you two didn't get along, even though you dated for a couple of months."

"We had different values and goals. He was fun but was becoming controlling and aggressive. One weekend we went to the lake with two other couples. They were planning to spend the night. I didn't know about that. When I realized he expected me to sleep with him, I told him I needed to go home. He became angry but he took me home, complaining about how I had led him on and how I was ruining his weekend. I told him I was a virgin and would only sleep with my husband. He became outraged. After cursing at me, he left. I thought it was over.

"About a week later, I was having dinner with Jason at The Brick House. Scott came up to the table and yelled at us and caused a scene and then left. I was upset. I told Jase I wanted to walk home to calm myself. When I opened the door to my apartment, Scott came up behind me and pushed me into the room and down on the sofa. He held me down and raped me."

Christine screamed. "No, not my baby."

She rushed over to Ashleigh and held her in her arms. They both cried until Carlton spoke up. "So, what did the police do?"

Ashleigh looked toward Phillip. "I didn't call the police."

"Ashleigh, you're a smart young woman. You knew you should have reported the incident."

"It wasn't 'an incident' Dad. It was my virginity. It was my gift to my husband that I can never give now. He took a part of me that no one can give back to me."

"I know, honey. But didn't the hospital call the police?"

"I didn't go to the hospital. I wasn't able to think or move until Jason came by to bring my sweater I had left at the restaurant. He found me inconsolable. He tried to get me to call the police and go to the hospital. I couldn't. I needed to heal. I didn't want you to find out and be ashamed of me. I knew you would confront Mr. Richmond and it would ruin your work relationship. Anyway, no one would believe me."

Carlton stood and started pacing.

"I don't give a damn about my work relationship with Richmond. I want that bastard held accountable. He needs to be off the streets, behind bars."

"There's more to it, Dad. Tonight, I tested positive for pregnancy. I've had morning sickness for a few days. Phillip and Jase convinced me that I needed to know for sure."

"You knew all about this Phillip and didn't tell us." Carlton and Catherine were getting angry and frustrated.

"Don't blame anything on Phillip. I made him and Jason promise to keep my secret. Let's don't make this about anyone beyond Scott."

Christine looked over at Ashleigh.

"She's right. She has a good friend in Jason and a respectful brother in Phillip. We know how strong-willed she is. I'm glad she had the two of you to support her. What is next Ashleigh."

"I don't know. I just need you to know and support the decision I make."

Carlton clinched his fist.

"I can talk with Thurston Richmond."

"No, Dad. I am going to tell Scott when the time is right. I don't want anything from him, but I think he has a right to know he will have a child, if I decide to have the baby."

Christine looked at Ashleigh and then Carlton.

"What do you mean?" Christine's eyes began to tear.

"Abortions are legal now."

Carlton walked toward her.

"Don't even go there. If this is real, you have a little person inside you. To kill a person is a sin unless it is self-defense."

"Dad, I know that but what about the rest of my life? What about my career. God forgives sins."

"Can you forgive yourself?"

"I don't know."

"There is always the option for adoption."

"That means I would have to carry the baby, and everyone would know. They would think I slept around. My reputation would be ruined."

"I know, honey. You should not be in this position. We need to bring charges against Scott. Then folks will know he raped you and you are not promiscuous."

"Let's not talk about this anymore now. We need to focus on Phillip."

"You're right. Phillip, tell us what you know about where you'll be and what you will be working on."

Phillip put his arm around Ashleigh and hugged her to him. "My thoughts will be with my little sister. I pray that she will decide about this baby that she can live with peacefully the rest of her life."

Ashleigh hugged him back.

"You're still my hero and protector. I love you. Take care of yourself wherever you are. I pray for God to take care of you too. You will be in my heart and mind until I see you again.

"If it's okay with you, I will not accompany you to the airport. That can be a time for you, Mom and Dad to have together. Besides, I'm afraid I wouldn't make it there and back without throwing up again. Safe travels."

She left before them, so she wouldn't have to see them drive Phillip away. She wasn't eager to go back to her empty apartment, but she had told Jase to stay away. She needed to plan what she would do next.

Chapter Forty-Seven

I would normally be in church at this time. Mom and dad would also be in church. Today is the first day of the rest of my life. People used that phrase for so many different reasons, for happy futures, for brokenhearted futures, and for unknown futures. I'm not in church, but I can still reach out to God for guidance and counsel.

Her patio called her. She made her third cup of coffee, which was beyond what she normally drank. Nothing was going to be 'normal' in her immediate future.

I wish Jase were here. I want his comfort, but I need to be guided by God, not any man, for this decision. Sitting in the indirect sun, the perfect fall coolness soothed her frayed nerves. She sipped her coffee.

God, please take charge of my life and show me what you want me to do.

There were no immediate answers. She didn't expect them. God works at his own pace. By late afternoon she realized she was hungry. Her refrigerator was empty of nourishing food. I need to start eating healthy for this baby's development. I'll run down to the fresh market to see what's left in today's picks.

She changed into comfortable clothes and carefully stepped down the stairs to the street. The market was still open with a variety of vegetables. She was looking over the greens for salads when someone touched her arm. She jerked around to look into the face of the man she loved.

"Jase, what are you doing in this part of town?"

"I was hoping to see you before I leave tomorrow."

"But . . . "

"I know you told me to stay away. That's like telling a starving man to stay away from the feast on the table. I won't talk about anything. I just want to be with you for a little while."

She looked into his loving eyes. She wanted this man in her life. She longed for his touch, his soft voice and the safety and security he made her feel when he was near.

"I'll walk with you while you pick out your groceries and I'll carry them to your apartment. That's all I'm asking."

She couldn't refuse this lifeline.

"Okay. I'm glad you came. I missed you last night."

He reached for her basket and cupped her elbow in his strong hand. She relaxed in his protection.

"How was Phillip this morning?"

"I think he was ready to get back to his life. He was a big help with mom and dad last night. He was impressed with you."

"I have that effect on people." He grinned as he feigned a haughty pose.

"I know. You've always impressed me."

"I have? Didn't know that."

"Don't go getting the big head."

She picked romaine, iceberg lettuce, spinach, and other greens. Tomatoes, apples, bananas, and peaches filled the rest of the basket.

"If you keep going, we'll need another basket."

"I'm done. I can carry these to my apartment."

"The deal was that I would carry the basket to your apartment. We're taking no chances on you stumbling and falling."

She gave in to his nudging, loving him more for his insistence. He placed the basket on the kitchen counter. She began unloading the contents. Suddenly she stopped.

"What am I doing? I'm acting like I plan to carry this baby. I'm buying groceries to have a healthy pregnancy. I haven't decided that I'm keeping a pregnancy yet. I may decide to have an abortion. No one would ever know. I could go on with my life like I choose.

"If I decide to put it up for adoption, I want to deliver a healthy baby. How do I decide when what I'm doing is making decisions by the actions I'm taking. So, I have no control over this decision either. Is there any part of my life I control?"

"Look at it this way. You want to eat healthily whether you're pregnant or not. What you buy to eat does not commit you to action either way."

"True. Thank you, Jase, for thinking clearly for me."

"Do you still plan to tell Scott?"

"Don't you think he has a right to know?"

"I would want to know, but I'm not sure Scott can handle the truth."

"I'm not asking anything from him. It's my decision what I do because it is my body."

"Agreed."

"We weren't going to talk about this today."

"You're right. I need to go anyway. I have to pack for an early flight. Call me if you need me. Okay?"

"You sure?"

"I'm positive . . ."

He kissed her on the cheek and left.

The afternoon and night stretched before her taunting her to decide about the baby.

No. I'm waiting for God to direct me.

She put together a large salad with items from her grocery shopping trip, added a boiled egg and a handful of blueberries and sunflower seeds. As she cleaned the kitchen, she decided she would approach Scott tomorrow. With one decision made, she slept soundly.

Chapter Forty-Eight

She called Scott's office and made an appointment with his secretary to meet him at eleven thirty, before he could get away at lunch.

Everything in the office looked the way it had when they were dating. She had second thoughts about telling him here but felt it was the safest place. He wouldn't get out of control at work, where other employees could hear.

The receptionist sent her back to his office at eleven thirty sharp. His door was open, and his secretary closed it as she guided her inside. Scott was not there.

"Please have a seat. Mr. Richmond will be in shortly."

It was eleven-forty-five when he finally appeared from a door behind his desk.

"Well. What a surprise. What do you want? I'm very busy."

"It won't take long. I thought you should know I am pregnant from your raping me."

Blood rushed to his face. "You're crazy. I never raped you."

"I'm not here to debate it. I am merely giving you respect by telling you. I don't know what I'm going to do yet. I may carry the baby and offer it for adoption. I may have an abortion. I want nothing from you, and I certainly want no additional contact with you. Goodbye, Scott."

"Wait just a minute. Don't go out telling everyone the baby is mine. I'll deny it."

"I have no intention of telling anyone it is yours. I don't want anyone to know that we were ever intimate, even if it was rape."

"If you go to the police, I'll deny it to them. You can't prove it's mine. In fact, you don't know it's mine. You and that Jason guy have been pretty cozy this year."

"I told you I was a virgin when you raped me. It is your baby. Goodbye."

Getting that 'truth' out to Scott, released the tension she carried for the past two months. She hoped he did nothing with the information. He wouldn't want his name mentioned in any conversation about getting her pregnant. She hoped his self-centeredness would keep his mouth closed and him away from her.

She left his office and went to her job eager to lose herself in her work.

Roger greeted her with warmth and concern. "You okay to-day?"

"I am okay. That's about as good as it's going to get for a while."

"Can we talk?"

"Sure. My office or yours?"

"Let's go in yours."

He closed the door as she sat at her desk. "What's going on Roger?"

"Don't think I'm being too personal, but…"

"What?"

"I have three sisters who have all had babies. The glow beside the morning sickness is very similar to your looks and nausea over the past weeks."

"I would deny it with anyone else, Roger. But I trust you. Yes, I'm pregnant. I was raped by a man I was dating. That one time was enough for me to get pregnant. I wanted to be a virgin on my wedding night, but he took that away from me. I did not call the police and I did not go to the hospital for a rape case. So, it is my word against his. I don't plan to have him arrested or take anything from him. I don't want to ever see him again, but that is going to be difficult because his father and my father are in the same professional organizations.

"I don't know if I'm going to put the baby up for adoption or have an abortion. I do not want to keep it. It would be hard to love a baby created out of rape."

"I'm so sorry, Ash. What can I do to help?"

"Try to keep the gossip mongers away until I decide what to do. I need to tell Mr. Northcutt. I'm beginning to gain weight. He will notice soon."

Roger walked around her desk and hugged her as she stood. At that moment, Leslie Small knocked and opened the door at the same time and saw Roger's hug.

"Um, sorry. Ashleigh, Mr. Northcutt wants to see you."

Red faced Roger looked straight ahead as he exited Ashleigh's office.

She knocked on Mr. Northcutt's office door. "Come in, Ashleigh. Have a seat. I'm worried about you. I heard you left the other day after being sick in the bathroom. Are you okay?"

"Yes. I'm better. I do have something to tell you, though."

"I hope you're not quitting."

"No. Nothing like that. I hope you won't fire me when you hear what I have to say."

"Don't be absurd. It would take a lot for me to fire you."

She told him her story from beginning to end. He sat quietly, face turning angrier as she shared her feelings of helplessness, violation, fear, and then nothingness. Now she feared condemnation, firing and loss of her career because she was pregnant.

He said nothing for a long time, until she saw tears slipping down his cheeks.

"I will share something with you that no one else in this firm knows, except Richard Monroe. I trust you will keep it confidential as I will keep your trust. My youngest daughter was a beautiful, bright, exuberant young woman. She was a talented designer and we had started her business here after she finished her master's degree. She had a bright future ahead of her. One of her clients met her at his bachelor apartment for advice on decorating each room. It amounted to a nice contract, and she was eager to get started. They met after work for her to measure the rooms and get a feel for a design style for him.

"She was open and trusted everyone. He interpreted her friendliness as a 'come-on' and began making advances toward her. She tried to brush it off, but he was determined to do what was on his mind. She was a virgin. His rape was so rough and forceful that she can no longer have children. He was never charged for the rape even though there was clear evidence for the police to offer for prosecution. His father is a well-known, well-respected businessman and political supporter of the mayor.

"My daughter gave up her business and is afraid to be alone with any man. Her life was raped out of her that evening. I understand your situation. Do not worry about your job. Just take care of yourself and do what you can for now."

"You are too kind, Mr. Northcutt. I'm so sorry about your daughter. I will pray for her."

"Thank you, Ashleigh. I appreciate that. Can you work the rest of the day?"

"Yes sir. Roger and I plan to go to Dick's house tomorrow to work with him. I need to finish my part of the design work."

How can I be so blessed to work for a man as giving and supportive as Edward Northcutt?

Thank you, God, for placing me in this job.

Chapter Forty-Nine

When she arrived in the office the next morning, several employees were crowded around the coffee bar. Conversation stopped as she walked through the room smiling and speaking to them. She felt a tinge of ostracization but decided she was being too sensitive.

Roger met her in her office, and they gathered the materials for the meeting with Dick.

Ashleigh reached to close the door. "Roger, I want to tell you something."

He pulled her into the room. "Okay, but don't close the door."

"It's private."

"Tell me on the way to Dick's."

"Okay. Why are you being so strange?"

"Let's go."

He would not talk until they got in his truck. "I heard some gossip when I passed two employees this morning. They were talking about us. They think we're having an affair."

"What? Why?"

"Because they saw me kiss you on the cheek and we close the door a lot when we work."

"You're kidding."

"No. We need to be careful. Some people have a need to gossip. It can lead to damaging misconceptions."

"Wow. Don't people have better things to talk about?"

"Obviously, not."

"Edward told me about his daughter."

"Of course. That experience was enough to destroy most women. You are very strong to handle it the way you are. I'm proud to work with you."

Chapter Fifty

Tuesday night dinners with the ERA group had become more about personal lives than planning next moves.

"It's good to see each of you. Sorry for my absence from the last two dinners. I have brought a list of women's organizations that might be supportive of our efforts and work with us in the future. I've printed out a page for each of us. Look it over this week and decide which ones you will contact and tell them about us. It would be a boost to our chances of legislative support if we have a list of women's organizations that will back us and stand with us for changes.

"Before we eat, I need you to know, but to keep confidential, the issue I have been struggling with. Three months ago, I was raped. I chose not to report it to the police or to go to the hospital.

Therefore, I have no proof I was raped. Last week I did a pregnancy test, and I am pregnant."

When the women recovered from her news, they surrounded her with hugs and assurances that they supported her.

"I have not decided about the outcome of the pregnancy yet. I don't know if I can love a baby born out of an act of violence. I am praying whether to have an abortion or to put the baby up for adoption. I would appreciate your advice about including abortion rights in our future presentations.

"When we get together next week, let's finalize which groups you will assume responsibility for contacting. For now, let's eat."

Her cavalier display did not represent her feelings. She wanted to scream, to cry, to blame Scott but she maintained control. She did have control over her actions, if not her life.

She held her tears until she locked the door to her apartment and headed for the shower. She examined her nakedness. There was a new fullness in her stomach and waist. Her breasts looked a little firmer and her buttocks a little wider. But her skin felt softer, and her eyes sparkled.

Seeing changes in her body made her realize the finality of her situation. She would never be the same young woman she had been before the rape.

"How can I offer this tainted body to another man, to Jase. He would be repulsed to see the changes, even though he never saw the pure me. He would feel cheated. I need to move on and not try to hold on to him. He deserves a virgin when he marries. I can't give him that."

Negative thoughts haunted her into the morning light.

Chapter Fifty-One

The trees in the courtyard of her apartment building competed for attention with yellows and reds finally overtaking green leaves. From her vantage point, a patchwork of colors fought the morning's sun for attention. It almost made Ashleigh feel better.

The call from JJ at seven-thirty accomplished the feat.

"Ash, how are you? I'm so sorry I haven't checked on you. Everything is crazy here. Mom came down to help decide on the venue for the wedding, the venue for the rehearsal dinner and the reception after the wedding. She didn't try to plan the honeymoon. Thank goodness."

"Hello my long-lost friend. It has been a rough time for me, but we need to talk about dresses for your attendants. Have you found a bridal shop yet?"

"I think I'm going to come to Atlanta to have more choices. I'm thinking about this weekend. Would that work for you?"

"Sure. I could use some JJ time."

"Is everything with Jason okay?"

"He is still working in Mississippi. I've decided to end our relationship, whatever it is, or was."

"Ash, why? He's in love with you."

"I can't give him what I wanted to give him."

"That won't matter to him."

"It matters to me. Anyway, let's not have this conversation on the phone. Will you be here Friday night, or Saturday morning?"

"I'm coming Friday morning. I'll spend the day with Mom and Saturday I'll spend with you."

Ashleigh needed her friend more than she would let her know. She hated to lean on anyone, and this was supposed to be a happy time for JJ. She dreaded telling JJ about the pregnancy. It would be emotional for both of them.

I'm thankful we haven't already ordered my maid-of-honor dress. It would need to be a different style, especially by Thanksgiving.

Looking forward to seeing JJ on Saturday helped the time pass until the weekend.

***

Catherine called on Thursday morning.

"How are you feeling sweetheart? Still having morning sickness?"

"Not much, Mom. I'm glad you called. I'm looking for women's organizations that would be willing to hear a presentation on what the ERA group and I are doing and offer their support by encouraging their state representatives to back our platform."

"That's a new approach. Do you mean the Women's Service League?"

"Yes, and any other organizations you feel would be open to the idea."

"I'll think about it and get you a list of the organizations, contact person's name and address. Have you been thinking about what you're going to do with the pregnancy?"

"I've been thinking, but no decision yet. I've decided to break off my relationship with Jason."

"That makes no sense. I'm sorry; I'm not judging. Are you sure? He is your main support outside family now that JJ isn't close by."

"That's why he needs to move on. He doesn't need to be caught up in my problems."

"I don't think he would feel that way."

"Mom, here you go again. You can't control this situation. I can't even control this situation. Now, let's talk about something else. Have you heard from Phillip?"

"We received a short note saying he had arrived at his new location, and he will get in touch with us when he is able."

"I hate that he is so far away. I guess he's far away. Anyway, we can't get to him unless we have a serious family issue."

"Life seems to throw curve balls."

"Curve balls? Mom, why are you using that vernacular? It's out of character for you."

"Your dad has been glued to the television watching the Atlanta Braves. We've gotten invested in their games. It's fun."

"I'm so glad you have something other than 'high society' interest."

"Our life is not what we expected at this age either, sweetheart."

"I know, Mom. I'm sorry."

"You have nothing to be sorry for. Get that out of your head. You are the perfect young woman we knew you would be. We're very proud of you."

"Perfect? I think not. Complicated. Yes. Unsure of myself? Definitely."

"I love you. You will work it out with God's help. I'm sure of that. See you Sunday?"

"Probably. JJ is coming this weekend. If I come to church, I'll bring her."

The phone call from Catherine pulled Ashleigh back to her center. Family.

Chapter Fifty-Two

Saturday morning, JJ knocked at her door at seven o'clock. Ashleigh opened it with a flourish of smiles and hugs. She pulled her into the kitchen, where she had a plate piled high with crisp bacon, a basket with apple fritters, peach fried pies and dough-nuts, and a pot of steaming coffee.

"You remembered all my favorite breakfast foods."

"How could I forget? I'm not missing a chance for me to have an excuse to indulge in these treats."

"I'm not going to be your excuse for gaining a few pounds."

After the first cup of black coffee and an apple fritter, Ashleigh looked at her best friend with a serious expression.

"JJ, I need to tell you something. I have a huge decision to make. I need your advice."

"What is it, Ashleigh? You look like someone died."

"In a sense they did. Me."

"Are you sick?"

"No. Yes. I'm pregnant."

"By Jason? Not pregnant? Oh no, Ash. The rape?"

Crumbling into herself, "Yes. The rape was not enough. Now, I must decide whether to carry this devil's child or kill it."

"Honey, I'm so sorry. I'm so sorry." JJ pulled her into her arms and held her shaking body until she could gain control of herself.

"That means I'll need a special type of dress for your wedding, unless I decide on an abortion."

"Are you seriously considering an abortion?"

"Yes. Carrying a rape baby would kill my career and going through an adoption would kill me."

"What about your faith?"

"Are you judging me?"

"No, no. You know I'm not. I'm just trying to walk through your thought process with you. I want you to come out of this with a healthy mind and body."

"I knew I needed you here. I don't know what to do. If I have an abortion, I need to do it soon. I'm not ready yet."

"Okay. The ugly is on the table. Now, let's get out of here and go look at dresses. Get our mind on something of less gravity. Let's walk the streets of Atlanta and look in windows and try on dresses and have lunch and come back here and crash with left-over peach turnovers and cokes."

"Sounds wonderful. I have you for the whole day. Can you stay over and go to church with me tomorrow?"

"Sure. You see that huge bag I brought. It has my necessities in it, and I can borrow an outfit from you for church."

Chapter Fifty-Three

Carlton and Christine were happy to see JJ. It was like old times when she spent the night with Ashleigh almost every Saturday night and tagged along for church Sunday morning.

"Will you come for brunch with us?"

"Wish I could, but I promised my mom I would spend the afternoon with her. We'll be seeing each other over the next weeks as I prepare for the wedding, have showers (hint, hint Ashleigh) and shop for my trousseau."

She leaned over to give Christine a kiss on the cheek as they walked out of the church.

"Take care of Ashleigh. She's pretending, but she is very fragile. She needs lots of family time."

"Okay, what's all the whispering about?" Ashleigh caught up with them.

"Nothing. Just sweet goodbyes." JJ smiled at Christine.

Carlton spoke up, "Don't stay away so long."

"You'll get tired of seeing me. For now, got to get to my house. Mom is treating me to lunch!"

She grabbed Ashleigh's arm, and they headed toward Ashleigh's sportscar.

It was a perfect Fall Day, so when she dropped JJ off, Ashleigh opened the sunroof and headed toward the Appalachian Mountains, the beginnings of the Blue Ridge Mountains. She blasted the radio as the wind whipped her hair and the sun clarified her thoughts and put her life in perspective. What were her priorities? Her goals? Her place in her work life and love life? What was she willing to give up and what must she have in her life?

When afternoon became evening, she realized she was hungry. She stopped in a picturesque old country store and bought a bottled coke and a pack of peanut butter crackers for her ride home. Her mind was at rest and her soul at peace.

She was going to need Jason. She dialed his number as soon as she settled on her sofa, looking out at Atlanta's skyline.

"Hey, Ash. I didn't think you wanted to talk with me."

"I do. I've decided to carry the baby until birth and give it up for adoption. I need to know that you'll spend time with me when you're home. I will need a friend. I will tell folks that I'm a surrogate for a family, which is not really a lie. I'll be carrying a baby for some mother who can't have children. Therefore, I won't be carrying a stigma and can be open about the pregnancy. I will consider it my community service."

"I don't think it will be that easy. In fact, it won't be easy at all. You'll be carrying a baby. You'll have the discomfort, the limitations and eventually the pain of childbirth and, finally, the pain of giving the baby away."

"I know all that, but I would be helping a couple have a baby and complete their family."

"Altruistic."

"Now, you're insulting me."

"I don't mean to do that. I know you. I can't see you going through with a pregnancy and then discarding the life you've nurtured. I think you will carry guilt."

"No matter what I do I'll carry guilt."

"Even if you keep the baby."

"Especially, if I keep the baby without a father. A child needs a mother and a father."

"I've told you how to solve that problem."

"I will not drag you into my problem and saddle you with the responsibility of a child born out of hate. I called you for support, not advice. Will you help me?"

"You know I'll do anything I can for you. I can't guarantee you when I will be home though. I'm on schedule to work in Atlanta and come to Mississippi every other week, but that is not a guarantee. I'll have to be here when they need me."

"I understand."

"Okay. See you next Monday afternoon or Tuesday morning."

Just hearing Jase's voice gives me comfort. I can do this. I know I can.

Chapter Fifty-Four

Monday afternoon Christine called Ashleigh.

"Sweetheart. How does your week look? I have three friends who are in organizations that might be open to supporting your proposal. I can schedule appointments with them for lunch this week if you're available. I'll introduce you and let you give your sales-pitch to each one. It would be best if we do them all this week, because they will see each other over the weekend and I'm sure they will talk about it. It wouldn't be good if one of them told the others. They all need to have the details from you."

"Mom, that will be great. I can plan my work around lunches. I didn't mean for you to spend your time setting this up for me."

"It's what I do, sweetheart. Okay, I'll call you back when I have the day, time and place set up for each lunch. Have a good rest of the day."

"You're amazing, Mom. Thank you."

Tuesday's lunch was with Annette Charles, President of Women's Service League of Atlanta.

"Mrs. Charles, thank you for having lunch with us."

"Please call me Annette. I am old enough to be your mom, but I'd rather be your friend. When Mr. Charles and I married I worked as an investment advisor. I couldn't give up my career, but as the years and children came and left, I wanted to be a support to his career and do some volunteer work. I made the right choice. The Women's Service League has done so much for the infrastructure support for the city. We raised money to build the children's recreation mall in the central center. We helped raise the money for the children's hospital in Atlanta. We led the fundraising for the new Humane Society building in Grant Park and many other causes.

"But we haven't done anything specifically to support women. Tell me about what your group is doing. I think it's time for us to do something in addition to raising money. I want to hear all the details."

Ashleigh left the lunch meeting with a commitment for her group to make a presentation to the Women's Service League at their next meeting. They would be the first item on the agenda.

As they walked to the car, she looked at her mother in a different light. She felt pride in her mother's ability to be successful in the highly competitive Atlanta's society.

"Mom, I know your influence got me the luncheon and the opportunity to face the whole organization of five hundred women. That's amazing! I'm confident that out of that group several women will want to join our crusade. Maybe the organization will fund some future events to feature us. It would not have happened without you. I guess I can't get beyond your influence."

"Why would you want to?"

"To prove I can make it on my own skills."

"Everyone needs help from other people."

"You don't."

"What did we just do? We got help from a very influential lady. I had the connection, but you impressed her with your knowledge and beliefs in your cause. You sold her.

"It has taken me years to become respected by leaders in the community. I respect them and they reciprocate. I'm trying to do for you what a friend did for me thirty years ago.   "

"Don't you feel like they control your success, because you come to them?"

"Is that what you think? Oh, honey. They aren't controlling me. If they turn me down, I still have my goals. I just go to someone else who might agree with me. That's business. That's the way it's done."

"So, when you try to set me up with a guy or recommend where I should eat or shop or work, you're not trying to control me?"

"Oh, my. No. I'm trying to save you some time, money, and heartache. Maybe I can help you skip some of the mistakes I made. I never want to control you. I want to offer you opportunities. It's up to you to take them, or not.

"Do you want to go forward with the other lunches this week? I can cancel them if you like."

"No. I don't want to do that. The more this topic is talked about, the more likely we are to make enough noise for the legislature to hear us."

The other two lunches went as well as the one with Annette Charles. Ashleigh's group was scheduled to present at both groups' next meeting.

She couldn't wait to tell her group at next Tuesday's meeting at The Brick House.

Chapter Fifty-Five

Jase called on Thursday night.

"I'll be back in town tomorrow night. Can we have dinner?"

"I don't think that's a good idea."

"Okay. If you don't want to go out, I'll pick up some Chinese and we can eat in your apartment."

She thought that might be a good time to end it with him.

"Okay. About seven thirty?"

"Sure. I'll leave a little before lunch. Should make it by seven thirty."

She wanted to see him but continuing to spend time with him did not help her convince him that they couldn't marry and raise Scott's baby. Why couldn't he see that having Scott's baby in their lives would constantly be a reminder of what Scott had done to her.

It was time for her to get in touch with an adoption agency.

Before she met Roger at Dick's house, she called the local social services office and got a referral to a lawyer who was successful with private adoptions. That will be the best way to keep my personal life secret from the press and find a couple who wants a baby to complete their family.

She didn't have time to call the lawyer this morning, but she would have the name to tell Jase about tonight. Maybe then, he would see she was serious about adoption.

Dependable Jase knocked on her door at seven twenty-five with two bags steaming out delicious smells. By the time they opened the containers and filled their plates, she was starving. She asked him about his drive, trying to start a conversation with an innocuous topic.

While they cleaned up the dishes, she casually said, "I contacted social services today and got the name of an adoption attorney. I didn't have time to call him, but I'll get in touch with him Monday morning."

"So, you have completely discounted a possibility that we could marry and keep the baby?"

"Jase, you haven't been hearing me. I cannot keep this baby. What if he/she looks like Scott? Do you think I could look at his face every day of the baby's life? I would never be able to get beyond the rape."

"What if the baby looks like you?"

"We won't know that until it is born."

"Exactly."

"I can't wait until the baby is born to decide to have it adopted. That would feel like I was rejecting the baby. I am not rejecting the baby. I'm rejecting Scott and his rape."

"Either way, you are rejecting the baby. Ashleigh, if that's your decision, I can't be any part of it. I think you will regret it the rest of your life. It could destroy you."

"Think what you will. It is my body and my decision."

"You are absolutely correct."

He stood and put his plate in the dishwasher.

"Goodbye Ashleigh. Don't call me. I can't watch you go through with this."

He closed the door leaving a cold draft that hung in the air the rest of the night.

How dare he try to manipulate me into doing what he wants, not what I want. I wanted our relationship to end, but not this way. Now, I've lost him forever.

Bed was her sanctuary. Tears her companion. Sleep ignored her need.

Chapter Fifty-Six

Tuesday night's good news was eclipsed by her sadness losing Jase. She put on a smile and handed out an agenda to each of the women. The first item on the agenda was to 'Create a Name' for the group.

"It has been hard meeting with strong, powerful women who run large organizations and having to refer to us as 'the ERA group'. You have probably had the same problem. That is not appealing or memorable. Let's think of something people will remember and want to join."

No one had an immediate response that got everyone excited.

Saundra spoke up, "I agree that it's been hard for us to describe who we are and to talk about our goals and have anyone pick-up on it. Since all our brains seem to be empty of suggestions, let's each talk about who we've met with and the outcome of those meetings. Maybe that will inspire a name for the group."

"Excellent idea." Ashleigh was glad to have someone else take charge of the meeting.

Saundra had some luck with the Legal Secretaries Organization. They wanted to set up a date for a presentation. She was working with other groups but had not been able to schedule a meeting with the leaders yet.

Pat was working with the Teachers' Association and felt she could get the group scheduled at their next meeting.

Mary, also, was having a positive response from the Women's CPA group in Fulton County.

They agreed on the date Ashleigh set with the Women's Service League. It would be their first entry into politics, but they must have a name. The four women decided to write down suggestions overnight and get them to Ashleigh. It would be up to her to pick one because she had to let Annette Charles know their name by tomorrow.

Ashleigh called Annette's office Wednesday morning and left the name: Supporters of Sex-Blind Success with Annette's secretary. Smiling as she hung up, "Now that should get some press."

The press was present at the Women's Service League's meeting. The newspaper advertised the meeting and the guest speakers using their new name. A female reporter was intrigued with the name and scheduled herself to attend. Her story was placed on the front page of the business section.

Who are the Supporters of Sex-Blind Success? and what did they say at the local Women's Service League's quarterly meeting?

Lois Lang wrote a thorough and compelling story about the group and their goals for women's rights. When she saw the positive response from readers, she called Ashleigh and asked to join the Supporters.

Ashleigh gave her the dates for the upcoming meetings and asked if she could be at each meeting to report on the responses the organizations had about joining the Supporters group.

Chapter Fifty-Seven

Pregnancy was getting more difficult to deal with. Ashleigh kept putting off the call to the adoption attorney. She wasn't sure why she couldn't seem to make the call. She kept finding excuses that were not reasons.

My dieting is not preventing weight gain. My clothes are beginning to bind my waist. I need to make a commitment to pregnancy and adoption. Without Jase here, it is harder than I thought. I can't run to mom each time I want to rethink this decision. I need to stick to my decision and make plans to move ahead. Maybe I should have an abortion. That would solve everything. I could go back to my life like it was before Scott.

Maybe I'll go see someone at Planned Parenthood.

Roger was trying to be supportive, but he had never dealt with a pregnant woman. He couldn't remember anyone in their firm who had been pregnant. He heard some of the men whose wives were pregnant talk about it some but nothing detailed.

Sometimes Ashleigh would become unbending about a decision they needed to make on a project. She seemed to want to be in charge, even though she was third architect. Other times, she would burst into tears when she couldn't get the numbers to work like she wanted. Roger was losing patience.

One afternoon on their way back to the office from Dick's house, Roger had had enough. "Listen, Ashleigh, I understand your situation. Well, I don't 'understand' your situation but I'm aware of it. I've tried to be patient, but I can't work with you the way you have been lately."

"I'm sorry, Roger. I can't control my emotions some days. I'm torn about what I should do."

His irritation with her showed. "I thought you were going to put the baby up for adoption."

"I did too, but I'm having second thoughts about carrying the baby until term."

"Don't you feel some attachment to the baby yet?"

"Attachment? No. It is a foreign intruder in my body."

Incongruous, he looked at her. "I thought you were a Christian?"

"I am."

"You can't find any empathy for an innocent unborn child?"

"Don't judge me, Roger."

"I'm trying to understand."

"How can you understand. I can't understand."

"Maybe you should talk with someone."

"I've talked until I'm sick of it."

"It is none of my business, except when it involves work. And it does involve work now."

"Do you want me off the project?"

"I don't want you on the project the way you're acting. You make each day very difficult."

"Oh, my. I never thought of you, of the effect on the project, of the effect on Dick. What should I do?"

"Go talk to Edward."

"I will."

Edward was up front with her. "I have noticed the change in you but tried to understand. I remember when my wife was pregnant. She was a different person for a few months, but she mellowed as the baby began to move. That was when she could relate to a little person inside her."

"I'm not there yet. I don't know if I can make it until that time. Besides, I don't want to feel the baby move. I want it gone."

Edward flushed, "Ashleigh, don't say that. So many women would love to have your child. It would be one of the greatest gifts you could give a woman like my daughter, who can't have children."

"I know Edward. This is not me. I'm a loving person. I can't control these thoughts."

"Let's do this. Dick is due to come back to the office for a few hours a week, starting next week. Why don't you take some time off and rethink what you want and how you want to get there. When you feel back in control call me and we'll work out a plan for your return either before or after the baby is born. You are covered by six-months of maternity leave with our company. If you need longer, we can discuss it."

"Are you firing me?"

"No. I said you will be on maternity leave. Your job is secure until you come back."

"Won't Dick and Roger need me for the project?"

"They will be fine until you return. Okay?"

Stunned and dazed, Ashleigh packed up her belongings and left the office. Now, I'm alone. I have no work to concentrate on and no one to take care of me.

The car seemed to pull her away from her office in the same

daze she felt. What do I do now? I can't go home and sit. The Supporters are set for presentations for the next couple of months. JJ is not home for the wedding yet. I don't know where Jase is. Where do I go?

Without thinking the car seemed to have a mind of its own. Then she realized she was in her parking space at her apartment. Filling her arms with her work life, she started up the stairs. By the time she got to the third floor she was tired. Two steps up the fourth flight of stairs, her boxes began to slide.

She let go of the railing and reached for the dismantling tower, leaning back to reposition the bottom box. She felt herself bounce off the railing behind her, which thrust her sideways down the third-floor stairs, boxes landing on top of her, below her and beside her. She tried to move. She had not hit her head. She was conscious but she could not move.

A neighbor heard the commotion and came out to help. When she saw Ashleigh, she called for an ambulance.

Chapter Fifty-Eight

The EMT's gave her a sedative and by the time they arrived at the Emergency Room, she was asleep. Her neighbor took care of the boxes and called Christine.

When she woke, Christine was at her side holding her hand. Carlton was pacing the hallway outside her door.

"Hi, sweetheart."

"Am I in the hospital?"

"Yes."

"I don't need to be in the hospital. I didn't hit my head. I'm probably bruised but I wouldn't have been asleep, if the EMT's hadn't given me a shot. I need to get my stuff I dropped off the stairwell."

"Your neighbor, Sally, took care of your boxes. She said we could come get them when it is convenient. She called the ambulance."

"She is a good neighbor."

Christine squeezed Ashleigh's hand. "Why were you going home in the middle of the day, and why did you have all your personal belongings?"

"Edward put me on maternity leave."

"What? Why?"

"I have been a little disruptive at work. I don't know what's wrong with me?"

Christine smiled. "I do. You're pregnant."

"Did the fall hurt the baby?" Ashleigh was surprised that she cared.

"They ran some tests, and everything looks okay. They say it will be a few hours before they can be sure."

"Can I go home?"

"No. You had a fall. They are going to run some tests on you. You're bruised and scratched. When the pain meds wear off, you will be very sore. It's best if you spend the night."

"I can't believe this. What else can happen to me?"

"You need rest. The hospital is the best place for you. They will give you something to help you sleep tonight. You need that help. I'll stay if you want."

"No. Certainly not. You'd never be able to sleep here. You need your sleep too."

"Here comes your dad. He's so worried about you."

"There's my girl." Carlton approached the bed cautiously and took Ashleigh's hand.

"Hi, Dad. I'm good. Really."

"And you'll be even better tomorrow. Now don't argue about them keeping you. They need to monitor you through the night, but they will let you sleep."

"I hope so. I'm exhausted." Ashleigh looked at Christine with her most pitiful face.

"We'll see you in the morning. Love you."

***

Early the next morning a nurse entered her room. "Miss Justice, we've noticed some troublesome markers in the baby's heartbeat. We will continue monitoring it for a few hours. We need to keep you today, until we understand what's going on."

"Is it serious?"

"We don't know yet. We'll keep you up to date hourly. For now, just rest."

"Rest? How can I rest? This life inside of me is in danger. How could I ever have thought I could harm a life God has created?"

Dear God, help this little one fight. This baby had no part in the hatred and lust that created it. It needs a chance to be the person you created it to be. Forgive me for my hatred of a life I never knew. I will nourish this baby into health if you save it. Your will be done.

A soft knock at the door ended her prayer. Tears streaming down her face, she answered. "Come in."

Jason opened the door far enough to peek at her. "May I come in?"

"Jase. Oh, my Jase, of course you can. How did you know I was here."

"Your mom called last night and said you had fallen down the staircase at your apartment. I had to make sure you were okay. I left early this morning, around five to miss the traffic."

"I am so happy to see you."

She reached out her arms and he leaned in for a hug.

"Are you in pain?"

"Pain? No. I'm a little sore here and there, but it isn't real pain."

"Why are you crying?"

"The nurse just came in and told me there is a problem with the baby's heart. They are monitoring it and will let me know hour by hour if it…"

"Ash, I'm so sorry but this might make your decision for you. You won't have to feel guilty about an abortion. That's what you want. Isn't it?"

"Not anymore. I realize that this baby has a right to live, and I have a responsibility to do everything in my power to make that happen."

"Even if you hate it?"

"I realized a few minutes ago I don't hate the baby. I hate how it was conceived. The baby had nothing to do with that."

"I'm happy you reached that conclusion. I'll pray that it survives. May I stay with you?"

"Yes, of course. I need someone. No. I need you with me."

She reached out her hand. He grabbed it and held on tightly as the baby's lifeline.

The nurse stuck her head in the door and reported that there was no change in the baby's heartbeat.

"That's a good sign, Jase. You brought me and the baby a good sign. Tell me about what's going on with your job."

"You sure you want to hear about that?"

"I want to know everything that's going on with you."

"I'm glad I'm here to share this with you. I wasn't sure you would see me after I told you not to call me.

"Anyway, the city council of Juliet decided they want a complete Urban Development Plan and want me to head the project."

"Jase, that's wonderful."

"I'm excited. I haven't told Harris yet. Just found out yesterday. It means more days in Mississippi, but it is a huge career booster for me and a prize job for the company."

"I'm proud of and for you."

"Yeah. The best part is I get to pick the architect."

"Wow. It won't be Camden, will it?"

"Definitely not. I was hoping it could be you?"

"Me?"

"Yes. You."

"I have a job. I guess I have a job when this is all over. I'm on paid maternity leave now. Edward Northcutt put me on leave early because my behavior became erratic, and I was hard to deal with."

"Wow. You? I can't believe that."

"Quit smiling. I was under a great deal of stress."

"I know. I had to tease you a little."

"Do you think Harris will want the project, since it is so far away?"

"Five hours is nothing. Yes, he wants to expand the reach of the company. This would be a good first start."

"To be honest, Jase, the work at Northcutt doesn't seem as creative. I've worked on one building and the design has not been finalized yet. It is a huge project with major repercussions if everything is not perfect. One building, one success, or one failure. The work at Stockton's took every bit of my creativity. It was challenging every day, but it was rewarding every day.

"I owe Edward so much. He gave me a job when no one else would. He paid me fairly compared to men in the same position. He has bent over backward to work with me during the pregnancy and my changing moods. Now, he is paying me on maternity leave. I can't ignore all that."

"I understand. We won't be ready to put a team together for a couple of months. I'll be working with the city council to get approval for the project and to find funding for it. All I'm asking is that you think about it."

The nurse came into the room. "I have some news. Is this a good time for us to talk?"

Ashleigh looked at Jason, "Will you stay?"

"Of course."

"The baby is still under some distress. It appears from the monitor that it is less than last night. That is a good sign, but it is not a guarantee that the baby will be able to maintain this level of response."

The doctor entered the room, "Miss Justice. We can do a procedure in vitro to support its heart. It would be a major operation for you and the baby with no guarantee it will keep the fetus viable. It is entirely up to you. An operation keeps you in the hospital for about a week. Monitoring could go on that long, but probably not if the fetus is not strong enough."

"I came in here hating the baby. But now that it might not live, I realize it is a person. I need to do whatever I can to help this baby have life. So, I'll have the operation."

"What operation?" Christine walked in at the end of Ashleigh's pronouncement.

"Good morning, Mrs. Justice. I was explaining to your daughter that it is unlikely the baby will live without an in vitro operation. Miss Justice, Ashleigh, would remain in the hospital a week for recovery."

"What procedure?"

"We would go through the umbilical cord and up to the heart with a tiny wire and give the heart a slight charge. It could be enough to keep the heartbeat in rhythm. If it doesn't work, the baby's heart will slow down until it isn't beating at all."

"That sounds dangerous for Ashleigh?"

"Not really, but there is always the chance that the wire could poke a hole in the cord and release the amniotic fluid into her body. It is entirely up to her. I need an answer within the hour."

Carlton walked in as the doctor left. "What's going on?"

As Christine explained to Carlton about the operation, Jase took Ashleigh's hand. "I need to leave so you have privacy to make this decision."

"Jase, I would like for you to be part of the decision."

"I have no legal right to be part of it."

"I'm not talking about legal rights. I'm asking you to be part of it because you have wanted this baby to have a chance at life since the day you found out I'm pregnant."

"That was before there was a danger to you."

"God will look after me. I trust Him. The other issue is that it might be harder to find an adoptive family, if there is a physical condition that would cost a lot of money to fix long term."

"That's a point for you to consider."

The minutes were ticking by quickly. Exactly one hour later, the pediatrician looked in the room. "What's your answer? We need to move quickly."

"Try to save the baby."

Christine looked at her strong daughter, "Are you sure?"

"Yes."

A gurney appeared and she was whisked away minutes later. Christine and Carlton sat in the room without talking about the decision or what it might mean to their lives.

Chapter Fifty-Nine

As soon as Ashleigh was rolled out of the room, Jason said, "I need to think." He left without waiting for their response.

They sat, holding hands, and praying until he returned.

"I need to tell you something. I love Ashleigh. I've loved her for a long time, but she thinks of me as a friend, nothing more. I want to take care of her, and I will love the baby if she decides to keep it. I've had an engagement ring for a couple of months. I'm afraid that a proposal would drive her away from me. If she doesn't want to marry me, I still want to be in her life. I don't know what to do."

Christine grabbed his hands and pulled him into a hug.

"Jason, she loves you too. She just hasn't admitted it to herself yet. When the time is right for you, ask her to marry you. I think her answer will be yes. We would love to have you as a son-in-law."

Carlton stood and man-hugged Jason. "We would be honored to have you as a son-in-law. You have our blessing if you want it."

"Your blessing is a requirement for me to move forward. Thank you both."

A nurse stood in the doorway, "She is out of surgery and in recovery. The doctor will be in to give you the update in a few minutes."

Relief filled the room. The doctor came in a few minutes later.

"Ashleigh is doing fine. However, the stimulation did not improve the baby's heartbeat and it grew slower and slower until it stopped completely. We could not save it. I'm so sorry. We will tell Ashleigh when she wakes up. You might want to be in the room with her."

When he left, all three of them wept for the life that was lost. They gained their composure before they were allowed to see Ashleigh, only to go through the sadness again, but this time with her.

Ashleigh was inconsolable. "I tried. I tried to save that baby. Maybe my hatred at the onset caused a condition inside me that wouldn't allow it to grow and flourish."

"I'm sorry, God. I'm so sorry. Please forgive me."

Christine climbed on the bed and held Ashleigh in her arms. "You didn't cause this tragedy, sweetheart. Scott is to blame for all of it. He should be the one in pain over the loss of this child."

No one could add more to her statement. They all felt it too.

Jason visited Ashleigh every day when she was in the hospital. The week the doctor had predicted was cut to four days, since she wasn't having any pain or infection. The doctor had said it was 'really no different than a regular abortion."

Ashleigh was incensed by that comparison. She couldn't get out of the hospital fast enough.

The next two days, she rested and reviewed all the materials she had gathered on abortion rights. She decided before she left the hospital that she was not going back to work at Northcutt & Associates. After her conversation with Jason, she realized that the job at Northcutt was confining. The projects were large and revolved around one building that took years to bring to fruition.

She had been involved in several projects simultaneously at Stockton & Associates. The job was a good fit, but the unfair pay practices would always be a problem for her. She decided that she would take the next couple of months to work on the legislature to develop laws that held companies accountable for following the guidelines of the ERA.

She felt no guilt about leaving Northcutt because she had been hired as a temporary employee. When she accepted the job, it was for a temporary timeframe. His offer of a fulltime position was made with the idea that Dick Monroe would be out longer than anticipated. Dick's strong will and persistence with exercise and healthy eating made his return happen more quickly than expected. They will not miss her since he was back.

Her mom and dad insisted on taking her home and getting her settled with a refrigerator full of her favorite foods and extra linens and throws, so she could get comfortable regardless of where she wanted to rest. Soon after they left, Jason knocked on the door as he opened it.

"You have everything you need?"

She answered from her snuggled position in the corner of the sofa, covered in a new cashmere throw.

"Mom and dad made sure of that. In fact, they packed the refrigerator so full of cooked dishes, I could never eat all of it. Want to join me for dinner?"

"I am hungry. Let's see what's inside. You weren't kidding. Are you hungry for chicken marsala, beef roast, barbecue pork, garden salad, potato salad, pimento cheese, a variety of fresh fruits, deli meats for sandwiches, fresh sourdough bread, and several deserts."

Jason heated the chicken marsala and put together a green salad. They lingered over strawberry cheesecake and coffee.

"It's getting late. I need to leave and let you sleep. You need to build your strength. Can I come by tomorrow?"

"Please do. Your visits make me happy."

"My visits? Not me?"

"They are the same thing."

"Not really. I'll call before I come tomorrow."

Ashleigh felt an emptiness beyond any other time when he left her.

Chapter Sixty

Jason checked on her every afternoon until he had to return to Juliet Mississippi. She looked forward to his visits.

"Have you told Mr. Northcutt that you are not returning to his company?"

"No. I know I should tell him but something inside me is holding me back. I don't know why."

"Is it because you don't want to make a commitment to work with me?"

"No. Of course not but I've got to finish the work the Supporters group started. I need to know that there is at least one congressman who will continue to actively support us and write a law to force adherence to the statutes of the ERA from all Georgia businesses."

"So, you will not be working at all?"

"That's what I've got to figure out. I've saved a good deal of money, but I don't know if it will be enough."

"I don't know when I'll get back to Atlanta. I'll stay in touch."

"Okay. Thank you, Jase. You've been a true friend."

He held his tongue. Red-faced, he squeezed her hand and slipped out the door.

He didn't kiss me on the cheek like he usually does. He had a strange look on his face when he left. I don't understand him anymore.

She drowned herself in research for a few days. When she rediscovered the article on the National Grange of the Order of Patrons of Husbandry, she became intrigued. Their principles are "equal pay for equal work" and women's suffrage. The social organization encourages families to band together to promote the economic and political well-being of the community and agriculture. They endorsed the Temperance Cause to avoid alcohol and the direct election of Senators. She wanted to know more. She found information on the president of the organization and planned to call her the next day.

Before I start filling my days with appointments, I need to notify Edward Northcutt that I will not return to work. I dread doing that. I'm not sure how to handle it with him and keep his support for me when I no longer work for his company. I respect him and don't want to disappoint him.

I'll talk to Marianne and see what she says. She has known him for years. She'll know how to guide me.

The sportscar skimmed along the road as smooth as skiers on ice. I've needed this emulsion into nature. I've been closeted for too many days. She opened the sunroof and let the wind take her spirits and hair up and away from the interior of the car and her soul. She was eager to see her good friend, Marianne. At least, she thought of Marianne as a good friend. She had been part of the Monroe's family during Dick's difficult cancer days.

Fall's shorter days had stripped many of the leaves off the trees along the ride. Their naked limbs mimicked her vulnerability. Everything about her was out in the open, whether real or imagined. She had been pregnant without a husband; aborted the baby, even though the baby was dead inside her; she was the leader of a group that wanted to fight the status quo with women's jobs; she was perceived as flighty because she left a career she was successful in; but portrayed as a failure because she had walked away from two respected companies in a matter of months.

Marianne opened the door and her arms to welcome Ashleigh. "I've missed you. Come into a quiet house. Dick went into the office today and the kids are in school. How are you? You've had a rough road the past eight months, but you look great."

"You know how to make a girl feel good."

"It's the truth. Let's sit so you can tell me what's going on. Dick said you're on maternity leave, but you haven't had the baby yet. Have you?"

Ashleigh fell apart at the accusation. Wiping tears from her face, she answered simply, "No and yes."

"Explain, please."

"I had decided to carry the baby and give it up for adoption. However, I fell down a flight of stairs at my apartment and went to the hospital with bruises. While there the baby developed an erratic heartbeat. The doctor performed an in vitro stimulation to try to get the heartbeat back to normal. It didn't work. The baby died, so they performed an abortion of the dead fetus. Everything was out of my control."

"Oh, honey. I'm so sorry." Marianne slid over and hugged Ashleigh.

"I'm here to get your advice on what to do about the things within my control."

"Sure. If I can."

"Mr. Northcutt has been great to me. He has treated me respectfully and trusted my work as any other employee. He pays me fairly, which is a blessing. I have no complaints about my employment. I've come to realize while I've been out of the office, that I don't enjoy big projects with multiple architects and a timeframe of years to complete something that is tangible. I like the urban renewal planning of small towns, where there is a grand plan for the city and individual plans for each building and lot within the planning area."

"There's nothing wrong with that, Ashleigh. People change jobs all the time, and you were hired as a temp."

"I know, that's what I mean. Edward has been so good to me. He offered me an extended maternity leave plus a full-time regular job at a nice salary."

"Sounds like him."

"I don't want to hurt him; or disappoint him; or take advantage of him. I just don't want to do the job he has available. To complicate matters, Jason has been given an urban development job as lead project manager in Juliet, Mississippi. He wants to hire me as the architect on his project."

Marianne moved closer to Ashleigh. "You do have some decisions to make."

"And...I don't want to give up my work with the Supporters group. I love working with Jason and that job would be a dream, but I can't do that job here. I'm a wreck. What should I do?"

"I don't want to be insensitive, but you are the only one who can make that decision. Think about it this way. What is the most important thing in your life? Once you decide that, the next decisions will fall into place."

"Several things are important to me."

"Yes, but what is the one thing that would make you very unhappy if you lost it? Once you know that, the other things won't be as important. They will be secondary. In addition to that decision, you need to meet with Edward soon, maybe tomorrow, and tell him how you feel. He will understand, but he needs to know immediately so he can hire someone in your place. They have finalized another massive contract for a building in downtown Atlanta. They will need at least two more architects with your leaving."

"I've been so busy thinking about myself, I haven't taken his position into consideration. You're right. I will make an appointment to see him tomorrow."

"Here's the phone. Call his secretary right now and make that appointment."

Marianne was supportive of Ashleigh, but her allegiance was to Dick's company and his job. Ashleigh's phone call solidified a meeting with Edward.

Ashleigh made the appointment and stood to leave. "Thank you so much for getting me on track. Everything was swirling around in my head. I couldn't stop the merry-go-round of pressures. Meeting with Edward will clear the way for the other decisions. Can I come and see you again sometime?"

"Anytime. You're always welcome here. I didn't say it but I'm sorry about the baby."

"God was in control of that decision. I have accepted it. I didn't even ask you how Dick is managing the hours back in the office. Is he okay?"

"He's getting his strength back each day. Going to the office is the best thing for him. I'll tell him you came by. Take care, Ashleigh and let me know your decisions."

Chapter Sixty-One

Ashleigh was not surprised how gracious Edward Northcutt was about her decision to resign.

"I wish we had met under better conditions for you. You have a lot to offer a company when you settle into the right position. It is a good thing that you recognized early that you aren't a good fit for our mission statement, in other words our architectural goals and purposes for clients.

"I'm sorry about your miscarriage and hope you find peace with that. You will find your place in our profession. Your talent should not be wasted.

"I am happy to know you, Miss Ashleigh Justice. Stay in touch."

The relief from his supportive offer of pardon for her actions and lack of condemnation for her resignation was a boost to her faith in humanity. She knew he was a good man. He deserved to have the best architects working for him. She knew she would miss him.

Restless after she arrived home and exchanged business attire for casual sweatpants and sweatshirt, she decided she would take her first run since her pregnancy. She pulled her hair into a ponytail as she rode the elevator down to the first floor.

Mr. Harrison was at his vegetable cart. "Hey, Ashleigh. You doin' okay? I haven't seen you in a while. I've got some pretty corn and green beans if you're interested."

"I'll think about it while I'm running and check with you when I get back. Good to see you too, Mr. Harrison."

It was so natural to feel the hard surface under her feet and the afternoon sun on her face. With two major decisions taken care of, she was feeling free. God had worked out those choices for her. He was working for her good. She never doubted it.

***

Deciding on the most important thing to her was her starting point. How could she say she wanted just one of the things that were most precious to her. She wanted all three: her career, Jason, her family. One did not outweigh the other two.

God, I'm counting on you again to help me out of this dilemma. Where should I start? Do I have to ignore everything except the one I'm working on? I'm getting less patient, but I will wait for your plan to reveal itself. You are my rock. Amen

After a quarter of a mile, she began to feel weak. She had miscalculated the strength that an abortion could drain from your body. She spotted a bench under the shade of umbrella branches from an old oak tree. The trail was busy, giving her opportunities to people-watch.

Her strength returned slowly. She unsnapped her water bottle from the waist of her sweatpants. Sipping the water slowly, she began to relax and enjoy being free from schedules, appointments, and deadlines. Sitting quietly in nature was refreshing. She couldn't remember the last time she sat and did nothing. After a few minutes, she saw herself working on an Urban Renewal Plan in Juliet with Jason at her side.

Could that happen? Why not? There was no reason she couldn't have a full-time job and vigorously support a social issue at the same time. Women did it all the time. How could she be so rigid. There is no such thing as 'all or nothing' for living the fulfilling life God had planned. There was also room for Jason in those plans. He was always supportive of her project. Why wouldn't he be if they were together?

On her walk back to her apartment, she started making plans for how she could travel back and forth from Juliet to meet with women's groups and congressmen. She needed to talk with Jason for his input on how much time she needed to spend in Juliet.

As soon as she stepped inside her sanctuary, she reached for the phone. Jason answered after several rings.

"Ash, what's up? Are you okay?"

"I know you're working now, so I won't take your time. I wanted to find out how the project is going and if you are in town. Then see if we could have dinner tonight. I'm thinking about taking your offer of a job."

"Whoa, that's a lot of information at one time. I am in Juliet today. I plan to be home late tomorrow or the next day. Can I call you back when I know for sure?"

"Yes. Of course. I miss you, Jason. I can't wait to see you."

"Okay. Later."

He hung up with no further comment. What did that mean? Had he changed his mind about working with her? Had he offered the job to someone else?

Doubts and questions crept into her head, making her unsure of herself.

Stop that! An hour ago, you were sure God put this plan in motion for you. Have a little faith. Remember, wait for his timing. Just because you're ready to move on, doesn't mean He is ready for you to make that move.

In the meantime, I can build a timeline for the Supporters to keep the ball rolling. When we meet on Tuesday, I will get information from them and put together a strategy from where we are and where we want to be in six months. I'll give the other members more responsibility for making that happen.

Chapter Sixty-Two

Jason called Saturday morning to tell her he was on his way home and would have time to meet with her Sunday. He said he would come over after church.

Ashleigh wanted to ask him to go to church with her but something in his tone told her it was not a good idea. When they hung up, she wasn't sure what he would say about her changing her mind to accept his job offer.

The day crept by, but her mind went into overdrive imagining all the potential scenarios that could happen Sunday. She thought about skipping church. Her parents would understand but she knew she would gain comfort from the church service.

Christine and Carlton were glad to see her. "Are you joining us for lunch?"

"Not today, Mom. I'm meeting with Jase this afternoon."

"Meeting with him? Not 'visiting' with him?"

"Mom, why the question on semantics? I am seeing him."

"Kind of touchy today."

"Sorry. I'm under a lot of pressure right now. I have several decisions to make."

"I'm sorry too, dear. I'm sure your body is going through an emotional upheaval over the loss of the baby. Hormones are up and down. I know it will take a while for you to get back to normal."

When she got in her car, emotions took over. She sat crying for a while. She realized she had not mourned the baby's death. She had pushed it to the back of her mind, like it was a problem for months and now was not a problem. Christine's comment made her realize that a life had been taken. Not by her. Not by the doctor. The life inside her died. Did God take the baby's life? Was nature itself at work? Was the fetus not equipped for life outside her body? It didn't matter why but it's life did matter.

Jason was waiting in his car when she drove into the parking space at her apartment. She smiled weakly at him as she opened the door and walked toward him.

"Ash, you've been crying. What's wrong?"

She ushered him into the elevator. "For the first time this morning I realized I have not mourned the baby's death. I've been functioning as if it was not a big deal. Jase, it is a big deal. A little life was inside me and is now gone…forever."

Tears began again. "I'm sorry. I didn't expect this today. It is not why I wanted to see you."

"It's okay. Any reason to see you is sufficient. I know you are not heartless. That's why I wondered if you were going through a denial period because you didn't seem fazed about the baby's death. I guess denial is part of the grieving process."

"I never understood that. I think I did love the baby in some way. It was part of me. I'm sorry it could not live and have a full life."

Jase patted her arm. "Let's go grab some lunch. How about The Brick House?"

"That sounds perfect. I would like to be around people for a little while. I've been isolated."

They waited until they returned to Ashleigh's apartment to have the serious conversation.

***

Ashleigh curled up in her favorite spot on the sofa, expecting Jason to sit beside her as he always did.

Instead, he sat in the side chair so he could look at her, keeping a safe distance away.

"Ashleigh, I heard what you said on the phone. Part of me was excited about the possibility of being with you and us working together again. However, the other part of me was skeptical and afraid that you were jumping at an opportunity to run away from the pain and hurt you've experienced, and that you were not working through the pain. You need to get past your hurt before you make any commitment that affects not just your future, but mine too."

"What are you saying? You don't want to work with me? Have you hired someone else?"

"You're not hearing me. That's what I mean. You're acting like a hurt puppy, running to the first thing that might give you comfort. I don't want to only be that to you. I want to be your safe place and your friend, but I want more than that. You can't accept the job then, when you feel like all this trauma is behind you, leave me and the job and look for another position here in Atlanta.

"I know you don't think that you would do that now, but I don't think you know what you want. You thought you wanted to be part of changing the skyline of Atlanta. Now you think you want to be part of urban renewal projects. They are two different careers."

"Jase, I know that now. Working for Northcutt helped me see the difference and I have not felt fulfilled. I learned a lot from Dick Monroe and Roger, and I can take that knowledge with me to Juliet. It will make me an overall better architect. My lifetime dream of helping change Atlanta's skyline was a child's dream. The reality of how that happens made me know that I'm more suited to smaller projects. I can be creative and work on several designs at one time, helping bring vitality back to small towns that are being devastated by larger cities who draw people to large shopping centers and entertainment venues. There is value in the small-town shopping experience, if it has its own unique design and offers current products."

"Is it the challenge of the job you're looking for or the comfort of a friend, who has your back?"

"Maybe both?"

His disappointment showed on his face. "I see. Well, I have not hired anyone for the job yet. I haven't even started interviewing but I do need to make a decision soon. Think about what I've said. If I offer you the job…"

Ashleigh smiled. "You already have."

Jason ignored her confidence. "If I make an official job offer to you, I need you to be the confident, self-reliant, intelligent, creative woman I worked with at Stocktons. You are not there at this time."

"Wow. That hurts."

"I didn't mean to hurt you. I want you to realize who you are now and get back to who you were. I'll stay in touch."

He stood and smiled at her.

She asked. "When will I see you again?"

"I'm not sure. I'll have to let you know."

Ashleigh could not move. She didn't walk him to the door. She felt that she had lost her best friend. Tears formed as she replayed what he said to her. It felt like there was nothing else in her life for her to lose.

God, what have I done to warrant all the pain I've been through these past months? I've tried to do your will. Has my focus been wrong? Have my motives been selfish? Help me get through this mess. Give me clear guidance. Amen

Chapter Sixty-Three

Ashleigh dreamed that she was walking in the woods, a place she always loved. This walk was different. There was no sun shining through the thick leaves of the summer Oaks, Maples and Poplars. The path was covered with vines, rocks, and last fall's leaves. She stumbled with every step. She could not see where the path led her. The sounds of birds mocking her were not the sweet songs she remembered. The rambling path seemed to go nowhere. She was cold even in the summer's heat, and she was getting tired and weary. The path never ended. She awoke in a sweat.

It was time to shed some light into the darkness of her future. She slid out from the covers and reached for her bedroom slippers and robe. Coffee was the first item on her agenda. While the coffee brewed, she went back to the bedroom and pulled on running pants and a lightweight sweatshirt.

She took her coffee out to the patio. Unlike her dream, the day was beginning to bloom in full sun-filled glory. There was a slight breeze that let her know Fall was turning toward winter. There was no need to rush the morning. She had the luxury of planning her whole day. When the sun reached eye-level with her patio, she decided this was the perfect time to go for her walk/jog.

The air smelled of fresh rain that must have sneaked in during the night. Ashleigh filled her lungs with the intoxicating aroma and let it slide out slowly with each breath she took as she stretched before her trek.

School had started so the trail was a different mixture of users. Elderly couples strolled arm in arm, dodging young professionals running before work. The farther Ashleigh got on the trail, she blended into the assortment of single women pushing strollers and joggers listening to music through earphones. She walked and ran halfway down the trail and then turned around and walked back to her usual entrance. She felt strong. Tomorrow she would attempt to jog the whole way.

She stopped by Mr. Harrison's vegetable bins. There were few vegetables left. He seemed to be packing up for the day. She grabbed some blueberries and watermelon slices before he covered his remaining bins. He told her he would try to be here one more week, but if he couldn't get enough produce to make the trip, he would see her in the Spring. She was going to miss shopping next to her building and hearing his upbeat voice.

The next item on her agenda was to clean the apartment. She put away the fruit and grabbed the vacuum cleaner out of the closet. She was thinking about her day as she finished cleaning the apartment, about buying a variety of vegetables and fruit from Harrison, when Jase knocked on her door and brought her flowers and an afternoon visit.

She took Jase's friendship for granted. She thought of so many ways she could have let Jase know how much he meant to her. She was selfish not to show him. She hoped she had not lost him.

The energy it took to clean helped her clear her head as well as clarify where she wanted to be. To get there, she had to push the state congress and senate into legislating for women's compensation to mirror men's pay. They needed to make a statement again but not like the demonstration on the courthouse steps. The statement should be in accordance with the way other bills were presented. She had an idea.

The Supporters would sponsor a letter-writing campaign to every state representative and senator. The women's groups they had already worked with could get their members to send a personalized copy of the letter she and the Supporters would compose, adding their name and society name to the bottom of the letter and mailing it. If they could get enough buy-in for this approach, they would inundate the legislators' offices with mail. That should get their attention and, hopefully, get the attention of other women's groups the Supporters had not met with.

This approach would be professional, concrete, and factual. It should gain respect for the group and their fight for equal pay. In the meantime, the Supporters would contact every women's group in the state and ask them to participate.

Ashleigh was afraid her plan would overwhelm her friends in the Supporters. She would sell it by stressing how easy it would be to carry out. They would not have to meet personally with each women's group. They would simply blanket the state with their form letter. If a specific group asked one of them to attend a meeting, they could take turns accommodating them.

This could work. I'll start a rough draft of the letter we will send to women's groups and the letter to the legislature. I'll be prepared when we meet on Tuesday night.

God, help the Supports to be open-minded about this idea. If it is your will, help us make this challenge a reality. Amen

Chapter Sixty-Four

The Brick House was overflowing Tuesday night. Thanks to their corner table reservation, they had their spot for the meeting. However, it was so boisterous that they couldn't hear each other.

Aggravated that they couldn't hear her, Ashleigh shrugged.

"Let's just order and eat here and enjoy the fun everyone is having. Afterwards, we can go to my apartment to have our meeting. I live just down the street. Will that be okay with you?"

Everyone agreed. They had never met to eat and talk about their lives and enjoy each other's company. The tension around the table faded into stories about work and families. They left the restaurant after a good meal accompanied by peals of laughter teasing each other for newly learned personal faux pas.

They entered her home with ohs and ahs for her magical view of downtown lit like the sparkling lights on a Christmas tree.

Stretching out on the inviting sofa and loveseat seemed natural for the mood they were in. Ashleigh was proud to have a home that invited her friends to be comfortable and at ease.

"I had an idea that I thought you might agree with, so I took the liberty of working on a rough draft of a couple of letters for you to review and edit."

She gave them a quick summary of her idea and then handed each one a copy of both letters.

"I'll make some decaf coffee while I wait for you to read the letters and digest them."

They were all surprised that Mary was the first one to speak. "As usual you have done a thorough job of assessing and explaining our goals and educating the lawmakers on what we need them to do. I am excited for the first time in a long time about the possibility that we might get some action from the legislative branch of our state government."

Pat, the number-person and not the wordsmith, spoke next. "You always amaze me, Ashleigh. I agree with your assessment and your letters seem perfect to me. What you ask us to do allows us to fit it into our workweek easily. I'm ready to move forward with it."

Saundra paused for a dramatic law-degree-emphasis on her analysis. "I think you came up with a creative idea for getting the word out. I can imagine someone noticing the large mail bags being delivered to the Capitol and a story appearing on the news or in an article in the newspaper. I would like to tweak the letters a little if you don't mind."

"Of course, you are the legal and composition authority in the group. I've written a rough draft. I look to your expertise for making the letters legally sound and understandable in layman's language."

"I'll have them ready by next week."

"While you are doing that, the rest of us can start the list of names and organizations to send the letters to."

Saundra spoke up, "No need for that. Just send me the list of organization names and leaders of each one and their addresses. We have a new piece of equipment at work called a word processor. My secretary can enter the names and addresses on one file and the form letter in another file and the processor will merge the two documents, putting the name and address at the top, the person's name in the salutation and our names and group name at the bottom, using the form letter in the correct place in the middle."

"What a timesaver?" They were all impressed with the new technology."

***

The women's service league was so impressed with the work the Supporters had done, they offered some of their members, who were attorneys, to author legislation for their representatives to use in the legislative session beginning in October.

Other women's groups offered their help in organizing a group to attend the January session. Ashleigh was getting mail daily from groups all over the state. She wanted to get a group of leaders together soon, so they would have time to present a solid force to the legislature.

They didn't have time to use the US mail service to organize the meeting. An electronic e-mail system was becoming popular. The Supporters got on the phone with as many group leaders as they could reach and asked for e-mail addresses. Most of the responders had e-mails. Ashleigh set up an e-mail address for the Supporters and suggested that each of the members set up a personal one themselves. It was a more efficient way to communicate with time-sensitive information.

The hotel with the largest ballroom was rented for a weekend in late October. The Supporters were the hosts and asked for donations to help cover the cost of the room and refreshments. They collected double the amount spent. Ashleigh set up a bank account with the money and paid for everything out of it, saving the rest for future events.

A female business owner from South Georgia was elected Spokesperson for the group. Ashleigh was delighted to have someone else take over.

After the first day, Saundra said, "Ashleigh aren't you upset that you weren't elected Spokesperson? You've done all the prep work for the group."

"No. I'm delighted to get the responsibility off my shoulders. Natalie Birdman is much more qualified to run a large group. She's a businesswoman who has a thriving company and is familiar with all the details that derail a woman's success in business. She's the perfect person for the job."

"But what about all the research you've done?" Pat joined Saundra's concern.

"I'll share it with her to save her some time. We need to work cooperatively if we're going to make any headway with our goals. We can't be protective of what we know or have researched."

Mary summed it up. "You're too giving."

"There's no such thing as being 'too giving'. From what I've observed, some women who have reached the epitome of their profession and pay are prideful about their accomplishments and want to hold other women back, so they can feel superior. This whole effort should be women helping women, so we can all succeed." Ashleigh's passion lit her face.

Natalie turned out to be a star performer. Through her business, she already had a working relationship with several representatives. They would support her presentation to the legislature and would make her feel comfortable.

The Atlanta newspaper heard about the group from several counties in the state. They called Natalie and wrote a story about the group's efforts and promised to follow the progress with regular news stories.

Ashleigh served on a committee but gave her full support to Natalie. It appeared the Supporters' work was in place to move forward as a state group. Ashleigh was on board but not driving.

"I'm free to work on figuring out my life and career. It has been difficult the past year. I'm excited to see where I will be a year from now."

Chapter Sixty-Five

The relationship between Ashleigh and Jason was on a pause. She called and left messages. When she came home, there would be a formal message from Jason. They couldn't seem to be available at the same time.

One afternoon when she arrived home and there was no message from him, an idea popped in her head.

I'll call him and leave him my e-mail address. That way he can e-mail me back with a message longer than an answering machine message and I will get his e-mail address so I can e-mail him instead of calling.

The next morning when she returned from her morning jog, there was a blinking light on her computer.

"Hi, Ash. I'm glad to have a better way to reach you. I am coming home tomorrow. I probably won't be there until late, so

I'll e-mail you and let you know when I can see you the next day. I hope that works for you."

She was excited. He will be here on Friday. She had the whole weekend free. Maybe they could go to church together and have lunch with her parents.

At eleven o'clock Thursday night she got his e-mail. He wanted to go to breakfast Friday morning. He said he would pick her up at nine. She was glad she had stayed awake for his e-mail. She responded quickly that she would be ready at nine and couldn't wait to see him. She was beginning to like technology.

She slept more soundly that night than she had in months.

***

She was ready and waiting when she heard his knock on the door. She opened it with a flourish.

"Good morning Mr. Blunt. You are right on time, as usual."

Her smile lit his face. "Miss Justice, and you're on time, too. Shall I come in, or are you hungry and ready to eat?"

"Both. Can you come back here when we're finished with breakfast?"

"I thought we might take a ride to the lake. It's a perfect late autumn day. We can find a covered table with benches and enjoy the weather and lake, while we talk."

"You have the perfect idea. Let me grab a sweater in case there is a cool breeze at the lake. I've been reluctant to put away summer clothes. This blouse is not thick enough for the lake."

"Always the girl scout."

"Making fun of me already?"

"Not at all. I find you charming and alluring…and always prepared."

She bumped his shoulder, "Let's go eat before this conversation gets ridiculous."

She had never had breakfast at the small café on the water's edge. "I've never known about this place. It's a smart marketing idea. People get hungry when they are around water. Having a place to eat, makes perfect sense."

The October sun was riding the top of the trees across the water, erasing the chill of the night. The tin-roofed rustic café had a walk-up window for take-away orders. Ashleigh and Jason walked past the window and entered a time of yesteryear. The walls were covered with oars, life vests, inflated tire tubes and a rowboat for two, which hung over a small fireplace.

The front counter hosted packs of crackers, chips, and candy bars, while the cooler under a side window was filled with glass bottles of RC Cola, Coke, Orange Crush and Yahoo chocolate drink for customers who only wanted a snack before swimming in the lake.

Jason pulled Ashleigh toward the smell of bacon and ham. They ordered ham biscuits, scrambled eggs, jelly, and coffee. They waited for their order in front of a picturesque window, highlighting a lake view bordered by Maple, Pine, and Oak trees.

"I could get lost in this view. It is so peaceful here. After we eat, can we walk down the ramp to the dock?"

"Sure. We probably need to walk after this huge breakfast." He patted his stomach and smiled at her.

Her gaze lingered on his face, taking in every inch. His day-old beard made him look rugged and at the same time gentle because of his sparkling green eyes. She had never looked into them like she was doing now. What were they showing her? Love? Comfort? Familiarity? Friendship?

"Is that okay?" He had a questioning look on his face.

"What? Is what okay?"

"You weren't listening."

"I guess not. What did you say?"

"I said, we should rent a rowboat one day and float around on the lake for an afternoon."

"That would be heavenly."

"Would you have time for that?"

"Let me tell you where I am with workload."

They moved their conversation out to a picnic table under a covered roof, taking another cup of coffee with them.

Jason listened attentively to her detailed description of everything that happened with the Support group and when she was finished asked.

"You okay giving up leadership of the Supporters? You've worked so hard to get it going?"

"Yes. I reached a point where I needed more help. The movement needed someone to lead it who had more business savvy than I have. Besides, she already has connections in the legislature. It is more likely to get heard with her in the lead. I'll still participate. I'm happy to give up leadership. It leaves me more time to pursue my dream job with you."

Jason smiled at that comment. "I have to tell you; Howard was not happy that I want to hire you. I told him that I had already pitched you to the town leaders and they seemed happy. They offered the job to me, not Stockton & Associates. So, whomever I hire is okay with them, as long as we produce a viable project plan. And afterwards, an updated city center on time and on budget."

"So, he gave in?"

"He didn't have a choice. We will be working in Juliet most of the time. It will be so nice to have you there with me."

"Do you have a job description for me, and a formal job offer?"

"It needs some updating. I need to add a start date. Salary. Additional compensation for housing in Juliet or a suitable housing situation they own. Get them to sign-off on it and then I can present it to you."

"How long will that take?"

"About a week. I'll leave Monday and plan to be back here Friday with everything ready for your review."

"Good. Once again, I've been without an income for a while. I need to get started soon."

"I like an eager beaver."

"Funny. Can we walk to the lake now?"

"Yes mam."

He went to church with her and had lunch with her parents at the Country Club. It seemed natural that he fit in like he was part of her family. As they were leaving to go back to her apartment, she felt someone staring at her. She looked over her shoulder and Scott was sending daggers in her direction. She shivered.

"What's wrong?" Jason sensed her every emotion and body movement.

"It's only Scott. He's creepy. He was staring at me."

"Have you seen him lately?"

"No. The work I've been doing is away from his normal places to 'haunt'."

"Do you feel safe?"

"I don't know. I haven't thought about him in a long time. But he has no reason to approach me. He got his way. The baby is gone." Her voice broke with the last word.

Jason took her arm and squeezed it next to him. She leaned into his comfort and felt safe.

When they got to her apartment, Jason begged off for the afternoon.

"I need to do some laundry and I need to see my mom. I can do both things at her house. I'll call you tonight."

"Okay. I'll be here."

Chapter Sixty-Six

Jason called at 7:30 Sunday night. "You okay?"

"Yes. I'm sitting here watching television, which I haven't done in a long time."

"Good for you."

"How is your mom?"

"She's getting older, but basically okay. I've got to make a couple of phone calls but wanted to make sure you're okay before I get busy with them."

"I'm fine. Thank you, Jase, for checking on me."

"You're welcome. I'll call tomorrow night when I arrive in Juliet."

"Be careful on your drive."

They were not back to their former relationship. They were in an entirely different relationship. She liked it. She sat for a while longer staring at the tv but dreaming of her future with Jason.

Monday morning, she followed her normal routine, even though it was a cold, misty day. While on her jog, which had increased to almost a run, she felt eyes on her again, like she had in church. She looked around but couldn't see anyone who looked suspicious. She kept the eerie feeling during the rest of the run.

She went up the stairs to her door and as she reached into her pocket for her keys, her wet fingers let them fall to the floor. She bent over to retrieve them and felt a blow to her head. Hours later she woke up with hands taped together and legs taped to one of her dining room chairs.

Her mouth was not taped. She started screaming. "What's going on? Who is in here?" Scott rushed from the bathroom with tape in hand.

"Shut up." He screamed back at her, while forcing the tape across her mouth.

She managed to shake her head where he couldn't make it stick.

She yelled, "Help! Help me!"

He slapped her across her face, pulled another strip of tape and pressed it over her lips.

"Now. You can't make any more noise. You're a murderer. You killed my baby."

She shook her head vigorously.

"Oh, yes you did. You should be about six months now. You should be showing. There is no baby inside you. You killed it!"

Once again, she shook her head.

"If I take the tape off, will you promise to be quiet?"

She nodded "yes".

He removed the tape. "How can you deny it? I was in the hospital visiting a friend a few weeks ago and heard a nurse tell another nurse that the abortion on the Justice baby was complete. You can't deny that."

"First of all, I did not kill the baby. I fell down the back stairs and went to the hospital. The baby had heart problems. They tried to stimulate the heart by operating through the umbilical cord. The baby's heart kept beating slower and slower, until it stopped. They couldn't leave a dead baby inside me. They had to remove it."

"You were glad. You didn't want the baby."

"I was going to give the baby up for adoption. No, I didn't want a baby the way it had been conceived, in hate and force."

"If you had loved me back, it wouldn't have been in hatred and force. It would have been love. We could have had it together."

"Scott, I never loved you. I never told you I loved you. Why would you think I would have a baby with you?"

"I loved you. That would have been enough."

"Not for me."

"Shut up."

"Scott, the tape is hurting me. It's time for you to remove it."

"What do you mean? I can't remove the tape. You'll go to the police."

"I should have gone to the police after you raped me, but I didn't. I gave you the benefit of a doubt. I was wrong. What you did to me was a crime. You need to own up to it and pay the price."

"It would ruin my life. I can't have my parents finding out."

"How do you think this will end, Scott?"

"Quit talking and let me think."

The sound of sirens made him look out the window. "Why are they here? How did you call them?"

"I didn't call them. I couldn't. I've been taped up the whole time."

"Miss Justice. Are you okay? Can you let us in?"

"Tell them you're okay."

"No, I'm not okay. I'm taped up and being held hostage,"

"We're going to come in. Okay?"

Scott covered her mouth with the tape.

"Miss Justice? Miss Justice? We're going to break the door down."

Scott opened the door before the policeman's sledgehammer made contact with the door.

"She's okay. I didn't hurt her."

"Put your hands behind your back. You're under arrest. Miss Justice be still. I'll remove the tape as easily as possible."

Ashleigh fell into the policeman's arms. "Thank you so much. How did you know?"

"Your neighbor heard your screams and called us. She knew you were in trouble because you are a quiet neighbor."

"I need to thank her. I'm not sure what he was going to do if you hadn't got here. I don't think Scott is a bad person. He got a little carried away with me. He had false expectations of our relationship."

"He shouldn't be able to bother you. He'll be in jail. Do you need to go to the hospital?"

"No. I want to go to bed. I'll be okay in the morning."

"You need to come down to the police station and sign some paperwork."

"I'll do that tomorrow. I can't do it now."

"Okay, but make sure you come tomorrow. We won't be able to hold him if you don't sign the complaint."

She closed the door and double checked the deadbolt lock. She wasn't afraid but it felt like something she should do. As she walked to her bedroom, she felt a sense of vulnerability. She realized that there were some situations where she was not in control and never would be.

A woman has no defense against a man who wants to do harm to her. What was she thinking to make a public statement about men's assertion that they should make more money than their female counterparts. What if one of them decided to come after her for making waves with employers and legislators? They wanted to keep the status quo and they were strong enough to prevent change.

She pulled her covers close around her and left the bathroom light on the rest of the night.

Chapter Sixty-Seven

Ashleigh left her apartment early the next morning and drove to her parents' house.

"What a surprise, sweetheart. We're so glad to see you. You're early enough to have breakfast with us. I think it's warm enough today for us to eat on the veranda."

"Thanks, Mom. Sure. Whatever you think."

"What is wrong? Where is my daughter?" Christine laughed haltingly with a concerned look at Ashleigh.

Carlton came in from the veranda. "Hey, princess. You're visiting very early today. Did you come for breakfast? Wait a minute, you look fragile. What's the matter?"

"I wanted to call you last night, but I was too upset and didn't want you to think things were worse than they were and come to my apartment at that hour."

"What do you need to tell us? Are you sick? Did something happen to Jason?"

"Nothing like that. Let me start with Jase's visit this weekend and end with last night."

She told them everything. They were pleased that she and Jason were going to work together, even though she would be in Mississippi much of the time. When she started telling them about Scott, she became scared for her father. His face reddened beyond a healthy glow. His breathing was shallow. He got up and paced the floor. He couldn't let her complete a sentence. He questioned every action Scott took. When she finished, she was glad Scott was in jail, afraid her father would do something to him otherwise.

"Dad, please try to calm down. I'm worried about your blood pressure. This is why I didn't call last night. Scott is in jail. He can't hurt me. Now that he knows about the baby, I don't think he will bother me again when he gets out of jail.

"I'm heading to the police station to sign the complaint. I can go after breakfast. Will you go with me?"

"I wouldn't let you go alone. No young woman should be in this position. And my daughter certainly won't be left to handle it by herself."

Christine modified the breakfast menu to consist of toast, fruit, and coffee. She knew their bodies wouldn't be able to digest more than that.

"I'll call Evelyn this morning. I know she'll be upset and need some support.

"Ashleigh, I'm horrified that Scott would do this to you a second time. I guess it's hard for him to accept rejection. Are you sure you don't need to see a doctor?"

"Mom, I'm fine for now. I may have nightmares later. It depends on what happens to Scott."

"It sounds like he needs counseling, and a great deal of it. Maybe I can encourage Evelyn to do that for him."

"Mom, I think he will be in jail for a long time. He should get counseling in jail."

"Jail. Oh my."

"Mom, first he raped me and then he took me as a hostage. Don't you think jail is the least that should happen to him?"

Carlton took her arm and led her toward the car. "We're going to make sure he stays in jail. You're riding with me. We'll let you know what's going on, Christine. Don't get in the middle of this."

"I won't but Evelyn is my friend. She needs comfort and support. Ashleigh is okay. Scott is in jail."

"Ashleigh is not okay. What are you thinking. She has been through hell because of Scott. Christine, think. A few months ago, he raped her. We don't have any idea what her emotions have been over those months. And she has just been through hours of terror being tied up and held hostage by him. She is your daughter. Think about her first."

"I'm sorry, Ashleigh. I didn't mean to diminish your ordeal. You look good though."

"She is a very strong young woman, but she has been through much more than being strong could protect. She is on the verge of a crisis. Can't you see that?"

"Yes. I can. I love you, Ashleigh. You mean the world to me. I don't know what I was thinking."

"I know, Mom. I'll be alright. We'll see you later."

Chapter Sixty-Eight

Her signing a complaint was just a formality, for the record. Scott had committed a felony. The police would hold him regardless of what she said. It would not be a 'he said-she said' situation. The police walked in to see her tied to a chair with tape over her mouth. Her face had a visual handprint on her cheek where he had slapped her.

Carlton told the investigator he did not want to see Scott or his dad. Ashleigh could see his fury boiling just under the surface. She feared he might have a heart attack. They passed the interrogation room where Scott was being questioned. Ashleigh looked straight ahead. Carlton took a side look and almost lost it.

"Mr. Justice, walk this way." The detective took Carlton's arm and guided him away from the window.

"Please tell me that he will not be released on bail."

"There will be a bail hearing Friday morning. I can't tell you what will happen. I'm sure they can afford the best lawyer in town to represent Scott. It depends on which judge is on the bench."

Carlton put a protective hand on Ashleigh's arm. "Let's get this over with, Sweetheart and get out of here."

On the drive home, he said, "I want you to spend the night with us until we know he will not be out of jail Friday morning."

"Okay, Dad. But he is in jail until Friday, at least. I need to go home and pack some clothes if I stay with you. I can spend the night at my apartment tonight. I'll come over sometime tomor-row."

"Please stay with us for a little while this afternoon. We need a more in-depth conversation about what happened."

"Okay. For just a little while."

Ashleigh could see that Christine had been crying when she cautiously approached Ashleigh.

"Sweetheart, I've been thinking about my actions over the past months, since your first incident with Scott. I know I seemed insensitive to you and more concerned about him. I just couldn't bring myself to believe that he could do that…that anyone could do that to you.

"I know you've been in pain, but I didn't know what to say, or how to approach you. I thought you wanted to forget the attack. So, I tried to act as if it didn't happen. I should have encouraged you to talk with me about it. I'm a horrible mother."

"Mother, no one knows how to act or feel after something like that, especially by a friend. I've been confused about it too. Maybe we can talk when I come back tomorrow."

"You're not going home, are you?"

"Yes, just for tonight. Scott is in jail today. I'll be safe. I need to pack some things if I stay here over the weekend.

"Dad wants to talk with me before I go home. I'll come find you before I leave."

Carlton was waiting for her in the library with steaming coffee in floral cups.

"Come here, my precious daughter. Do you feel like telling me about last night? Sit next to me on the sofa."

"Maybe talking about it will make it easier to handle. I don't want nightmares like I've had since the rape."

He took her hand. "You always appear so strong. I can't tell when you're really hurting. You need to let me know when you need to talk."

"The rape was hard to talk about. It was so personal. He took something away from me that I can never get back. I've been learning how to live with that reality."

"I won't ask about that if it makes you uncomfortable. Let's start with last night. Did you know he was coming over?"

"No. If I thought he might come over, I wouldn't have gone home. Jase was in town. We went out to lunch. He took me home and left quickly because he needed to pack for his trip back to Juliet yesterday.

"Yesterday morning I went for a run even though it was misty. I needed to be outside for a while. When I got back to my apartment, I dropped my keys. When I bent over to pick them up, I felt something hit me on the head. When I woke up, I was taped to a chair. I started screaming and Scott came out of the other room and taped my mouth.

"He started ranting about me breaking off our relationship. It wasn't really a relationship as you know. He saw Jason having lunch with us at the Country Club after church on Sunday. I guess he'd been thinking about it since then.

"I'd been having moments when I felt like someone was watching me, but I passed it off as nerves. My neighbor, who called 911 when I fell down the stairs, called 911 after hearing my screams.

"The police came immediately and threatened to break the door down. Scott opened it and let them in. They handcuffed him and took him to jail. That's the extent of it."

"You can stay here tonight and if he is released tomorrow, stay until he is put back in jail."

"Dad, I can't do that. I have a life that I live from my apartment. Scott would be foolish to come near me now. He could add to his problem if he did."

"We're going to get a restraining order against him, then."

"I can agree to that. Let's see if he is kept in jail first."

The bail hearing outcome was a foregone conclusion. Scott was released on a $100,000 bond.

Carlton grabbed Ashleigh's arm and led her down to the first floor of the courthouse and started the process for a Restraining/Protective Order.

"You feel better now, Dad?"

"Somewhat. Have you told Jason yet?"

"No. He's coming home sometime today. I thought it was better to wait until he gets here."

"Let's go get some lunch."

"Okay, but then, I'm going to my apartment. I want to tell Jase when we're alone."

"I understand. We can stop at the house and pick up your mom and head to the Country Club for lunch."

"No, Dad. Not there. Let's go to Rudolph's. I don't want to face your country club friends."

Christine was nervously waiting at the window looking for them to return. Ashleigh got out of the car and ran inside to get her overnight bag. We're going to Rudolph's for lunch, Mom. Dad is waiting in the car."

"Good. You can tell me about the morning once we've ordered."

Chapter Sixty-Nine

Rudolphs encouraged lingering lunches. They all ordered salads with shrimp layered on top. Ashleigh went through the description of her ordeal, while Christine sat staring at her daughter.

"I can't believe Scott turned into a monster. I've always thought of him as a professional, easy-going young man. Where did that side of him reveal itself to you."

"Mom, I'm not sure if he was jealous and felt revenge toward me. Or, if he acts that way under any kind of stress. I had been with him in relaxed situations: dates at a restaurant, trips to the lake, movies, game nights at his friend's house. Our relationship had not developed to more personal times, where we talked about our goals, dreams, plans or needs.

"He was fun to be around, until that weekend at the lake. We never had an intimate moment. He was assuming too much about our relationship."

Carlton glanced over at Christine with flashing eyes, "Well, the Restraining Order should let him know where your relationship stands."

"I understand, Carlton. I haven't spoken to Evelyn, and I won't."

Christine took Ashleigh's hand, "You'll stay with us until this whole mess is over with."

Ashleigh shook her head, "No, Mother. I'm going home to my apartment. I'm going to resume my life. I will not let an incident, horrible as it was, keep me from my life. Jase is coming home today. I want to share everything with him. Hopefully, he has secured a position for me in Mississippi, where I'll be out of reach for Scott, travelling back and forth from here to there. That's my new life. I love you both, but I must live my life."

Christine looked to Carlton for support but got none. She gave Ashleigh a weak smile and let go of her hand.

"Well, I guess we'd better go and let you get ready for Jason."

When Ashleigh walked to her front door, she hesitated for a minute but pushed through and went straight to her glass-sliding doors, opening them with a flourish. She wanted to let fresh air sweep away the stench of Scott's hatred and violence. Her home had been a retreat and a place for peace and renewal. She would not let Scott take that solace away.

As she turned to go into the bedroom with her overnight bag, she saw the red flickering light on the phone. She sighed when she heard JJ's voice.

"Hey, Ash. I got your e-mail with all the plans for my shower and party. It sounds good. I'll be at my mother's that week. Can we get together before the shower? Let me know. Love ya'."

There was some happiness in her life. JJ's wedding and move reminded her that love could be found when you least expect it. She hoped that was going to prove true for her and Jason.

In the middle of straightening the apartment and preparing snacks to share with Jason when he arrived, she got a phone call.

"Ashleigh, I've called several times today. I didn't want to leave a message. I can't come home tonight. In fact, I don't know when I'll get back to Atlanta. The community here in Juliet is having a battle with the whole county. Since a lot of the county is very rural, without much in the way of retail development, they want to argue about spending so much money in one town to revitalize it.

"I'm working day and night with each County Commissioner to make calls, have meetings with churches, PTAs, and several unions, to convince them that making Juliet a hub for retail that isn't available anywhere in the county now would spill over into their communities. We haven't even agreed on how many acres are available to work with, the number of buildings, what types of businesses, where they will get funding or how long before building begins.

"I'm sorry. I wanted to be with you this weekend and on Monday, meet with Mr. Stockton about hiring you as the architect. I don't want to bring you here until I'm sure you have a job."

Ashleigh tried to absorb everything he said but her heart was breaking with each of his words. Nothing was settled: her job's commitment, her relationship with Jason, or her income.

"Ash, are you there?"

"Yes, Jason. I'm here. I heard what you said. I understand. I'm disappointed but I understand."

He couldn't see the waterfall of tears cascading down her face.

"I knew you'd understand. You trust me. I'm going to make this work. I guess it's going to take a little longer than I hoped."

"It is a huge commitment by the county. I can see that. Well, I know you're busy. I won't keep you. I need to check on my dinner cooking on the stove."

"Oh, okay. You sure you're okay? You sound funny. Your voice sounds shaky. "

"I'm fine. I was getting off the sofa to check on dinner. Call when you can. Bye."

"Uh, bye."

There was no dinner cooking. There was no evening to share. There was no joy in her life.

***

She retrieved the snacks she prepared to share with Jason and ate them as her dinner, while she reviewed the plans for JJ's shower. Everything looked in order, so she pulled out the file on the Supporter's plans.

There was a meeting she could attend tomorrow afternoon. She threw her energy into planning to attend.

It was an informal meeting at Natalie Birdman's home. Since it was only a two-hour drive, she could make a day of enjoying the temperate weather on her drive there and back.

Thank you, God for getting me through the week's ordeal and giving me hope where none had existed a few hours ago.

Natalie's stately home rested in the center of twenty acres of gardens, green grass, and pasture for three thoroughbred horses. The white barn nestled under a thicket of pines with white fencing spreading out in front covering ten acres. The floral gardens lined the driveways and fanned out in front of the home on each side of the entrance.

Ashleigh sat mesmerized at the beauty and peacefulness for a few minutes before opening the car door. She ascended four steps to a wide veranda welcoming guest with baskets, buckets and vases filled with cut flowers from the garden, stuck between wicker sofas and chairs on one end and a wood swing and rocking chairs on the other.

The six cars parked in the driveway ahead of hers indicated there would be a small group at this meeting. She looked forward to getting to know these women.

The short walk to the front door gave her an opportunity to breathe in the fresh air of the country. Hearing a horse whinnying in the distance made her want to veer off to the path leading to the barn and horse training rink behind the house. Before she could touch the doorbell, Natalie opened the door and flashed a welcoming smile.

"Ashleigh, I'm so glad you could come. We're just getting started."

She stepped back to let Ashleigh enter a large foyer with an Italian Country entry table in the center, topped with a porcelain urn filled with mums and ferns under a white wood sculptured chandelier. Beyond the table in an open great room, the other guests were lounging on overstuffed leather sofas around a dining-room table-sized coffee table. They all looked up when Ashleigh entered.

Ashleigh could scarcely look away from the glass wall to the left, which highlighted the view of the patio filled with comfortable seating in front of an Olympic-size pool and the vast pasture beyond. When the other women saw Ashleigh, they stood and greeted her with hugs and praise.

"Here's the woman who started this revival. We're glad you are here." They raised their glasses in her honor.

Ashleigh was shocked at the enthusiastic welcome. "We're all doing this. It's not just me."

Natalie motioned for everyone to be seated. "We are all working on it now, but you are the one who reminded us that we had not finished our work with the ERA and that we need to be united to achieve equality for all women. Each woman cannot achieve it alone. Your courage to get the original group together and protest on the courthouse steps woke us up. We thank you for that.

"Now, let's talk about what we should do next."

They discussed the different contacts each person had made with a State Representative and the responses they received.

Natalie summed up the reports, "It appears that we need to identify a new representative who is looking for a cause to get behind to make a name for himself. He could be our voice in the state congress. Too bad we don't have a female congresswoman. It would be easier to convince her to support us.

"Anyway, back to the proposal. Do any of you have someone in mind who might embrace our cause?"

Priscilla Bennett spoke up, "There is a new representative from my region, Bryan Allen, who is eager to get recognition state-wide, but he works harmoniously with other congressmen. I don't know how aggressive he might be with our legislation. I have been in several meetings with him and respect his beliefs and responsibility to his job. I'll be glad to approach him."

Natalie spoke first "That's a great place to start, but we all need to stay in touch with our representatives."

Ashleigh cleared her throat. "The Supporters group has started a letter-writing campaign to our representatives and has sent out letters to every women's group we know about to contact our leader if they are interested in supporting this effort by providing the names of every government elected official to receive a copy of the letter, which talks about our cause and the efforts we're making to assure women that they will receive the pay they've earned alongside males working in the same positions. Have you received your letters yet?

"I hope you support this effort. It is the first concrete move that covers the state. It should get some attention from newspapers and radio. If you don't get your packet by this coming week, let me know and I'll make sure you're added to the list."

The group was interested in Ashleigh's presentation and agreed to let her know if they didn't receive a packet.

As they were preparing to leave, a dignified woman around seventy-five, approached the entrance to the great room, wearing a navy-blue wool, tailored dress, diamond earrings and stockings in navy pumps. She paused, looking at Natalie.

"Hi, Mom. Ladies, this is my mom, Harriet Nelson Woodbridge, a women's activist from the late sixties. She still holds respect from many congressmen. She's the reason I do what I do."

Everyone stood as Harriet entered the room.

"I hope I'm not imposing. I just couldn't help myself." She leaned forward into a conspiratorial shrug with a mischievous smile on her face and an arthritic finger over her lips.

"Please be seated. I'm just an old woman, who led an interesting and frustrating life. Couldn't have gotten through it without my doting husband, Col. Rutherford Woodbridge. He taught me to never give up on a moral fight. I think that's what you ladies are doing now. You're fighting a moral fight.

"Don't know how much you know about the fight for equality in the sixties, but it was both invigorating and challenging and a little more 'in your face' for participants. Have you heard about bra-burning in the sixties?"

They all shook their heads.

"Well, I was in the middle of those stories. Most not accurate…or just downright lies. But we did make a splash. Want to hear about it?"

Everyone slid back in their seats.

Natalie held up her hand. "We need mimosas for this."

Harriet sat in the lone embroidered seat, straight-back mahogany chair with comfortable padded arms across from her audience.

"This is my seat because it makes me sit up straight. Helps my back and legs. Can't sit here long though. Not enough padding on my backside. Here comes Natalie with the mimosas.

"You know how things just happen in your life and you're not in control? You just go with it. Well, some of that is what happened in 1968. We were working long and hard with a plan to force the legislature to recognize women's equal rights.

"Nineteen-sixty-eight had been a troubled time for America. Things were churning all over the country. It was a time for women to be outspoken. The Vietnam War began, Martin Luther King, Jr. was assassinated at the Lorraine Motel in Memphis in April 1968; Robert E. Kennedy was assassinated at the Ambassador Hotel by Sirhan Sirhan in June 1968; the first National Feminist Conference took place in Chicago.

"But the country was still having the Miss America Pageant in New York. So, the Radical Women's Association decided to demonstrate against it. I decided I would go. I wasn't a member of the group, but I didn't want to miss an opportunity to see history being made.

"It was rowdy. It was disruptive and disrespectful.

"It was rumored they set a trash can on fire, containing everything they perceived fostered submissive females. Even though pots, pans, sexual magazines, and bras went into the trash can, they never set it on fire. Many women believed they had.

"And, Ashleigh, I believe they thought your group's demonstration a few months ago would be the perfect reminder of women's power. Those days of unrest did not guarantee enforcement of the laws passed more than twenty years ago. Their mockery of equal rights for women only brought back shocking memories.

"The Civil Rights Movement and other social movements suffered setbacks because of the assassinations. The US economy declined.

"In the early '80s, when I began living a retired life, the Baby Boomers had turned from rebellious activities using drugs, flaunting non-traditional sexual behavior, and ignoring acceptable social standards and laws. With their aging, they fostered a healthy economy.

"However, the residual effects of the troubles of the '60s caused more protests and marches for women's rights.

"The Civil Rights Movement took a back seat to the feminism movement, which shifted in the '70s to more nurturing and focused on ending male dominance at home and in the workplace, working through local, state, and national governments.

"Supporting these events, Gloria Steinman, along with other women, started the National Organization of Women (NOW) and Ms Magazine. The magazine changed the focus for women's magazines from showing women how to improve domestic duties to giving women a voice in business and higher education.

"Women were beginning to be taken seriously and were admitted to colleges in studies such as architecture, science, law, and medicine. They moved into jobs like pilots, doctors, scientists, accountants, lawyers, architects, and business owners. Like jobs many of you have.

"These activities led to the Roe v Wade decision in 1973 and culminated in 1975 with the end to the Vietnam War. That was more than 15 years ago, some of you probably weren't even in high school.

"We made a lot of progress in those years, but not enough. The fight for equal pay must continue until we make it a reality.

"If you need me for help in anything you're working on, just let Natalie know. I still have some clout and can call some congressmen.

The group had sat mesmerized by her. When she stopped talking, it took a minute and then the room erupted into applause.

"It's way past my afternoon nap. I hope to see you ladies again."

Priscilla spoke for the group. "If she can survive through all that, we can too. We can make a difference."

They spent the rest of the afternoon getting to know each other and enjoying Natalie's home and gardens.

Chapter Seventy

On the drive home Ashleigh realized she had a support group of women who, like her, wanted to give women the chance to be appreciated for what they contribute to a job, family, and society in general. It was not just about the 'money'. It was about respect and honor. She felt that they could become good friends as well.

The afterglow from the meeting stayed with her until she stepped inside her empty apartment. Her cleaning and organizing had not taken away the fear and isolation she felt when Scott imprisoned her. She had not been in control of that situation. Was she really in control of any part of her life?

She slipped off her shoes and padded to the bedroom. She slid her skirt off just as the phone rang.

"Hello."

"Hey, Ash. I was hoping you'd be home."

"Jase, I'm so glad to hear your voice. How are you?"

"I'm good. Tired. I called to check on you."

"I'm hanging in there. Had a good meeting with the Supporters this afternoon. There are some impressive women in that group."

"That's good. So, you're staying busy?"

"Well, some. Not enough to keep me busy all day. I can't wait to get a job. Any news about that possibility?"

"The commissioners are pushing me for a preliminary architectural plan. I'm trying to hold them off until I get a commitment from Howard. He's dragging his feet but I'm still working on him."

"I don't know why I expected him to be happy about rehiring me. It may be a lost cause."

"I'm not giving up..."

A background voice interrupted him. "Jase, honey, the movie is about to start."

"Okay, I'll be right there. Well, got to go now. I'll call you tomorrow, Ash."

"Okay, bye." Ashleigh's heart cracked open.

Who is that woman who called Jason, Jase, and told him to come to a movie. Have I waited too long to let him know how I feel? Have I lost him forever?

I need to go for a run. If I leave now, I should be able to get in a couple of miles before dark.

There were few joggers on the trail and the moms with baby carriages had long left for the day. She was glad to hear the flap, flap of her feet on the asphalt. The rhythm comforted her racing mind. The evening had become dusk when she decided to turn back toward her apartment. She couldn't keep the pace of her jog, so she slowed to a fast walk. She passed fewer and fewer people, and it was taking longer to walk than run. By the time she exited the trails, it was dark. She was not afraid, but she was mindful of her surroundings.

She crossed the street wishing Mr. Harrison still had his produce stand with bright lights showering the walk to her staircase. She looked around furtively as she took the first step up the stairwell. She reached her door, shaking uncontrollably. *What is the matter with me? I have never been this afraid. I need to get control of myself. I'm turning into a neurotic.*

She looked in the refrigerator for leftovers. After a few minutes she closed the door and plopped down on the sofa. *What kind of life do I have. I have nothing.* Tears spilled over her cheeks. *I'm all alone and it's my fault.*

She couldn't seem to move from her spot. She gave up and pulled the throw over her and slept.

***

The egg yolk sun covered her face and warmed her awake.

Oh, how glorious the morning is God. Thank you for another chance to do your will. Forgive my weakness yesterday. I know I am not ever alone because you are with me.

She headed for the shower. *I think I'll go out for breakfast. Seeing other people will give me energy and help me plan my day.*

Walking to the corner café, she passed the garden area planted by neighbors in adjoining buildings. The former location of a doctor's office building, which had been raised after a fire and never rebuilt. After a few years, neighbors cleaned off the lot and built planter boxes for flowers. tomatoes, green beans, and a sapling dogwood in a deeper box. There was room for two park benches next to a flowing fountain built around the plumbing left from the doctor's office. Twenty-five residents of the apartments next to and across the street from the garden signed a commitment to continue making payments for the water used at the garden.

The result was a respite from the brick and concrete buildings lining both sides of the street.

As Ashleigh got in front of the garden, she suddenly realized that this strip of land brought life to the whole neighborhood. In renewing towns, it was essential that green space was left to give life to any design. Her mind began working on how she would design a downtown strip in Juliet, Mississippi. She needed to see it to understand the lay of the land and the depth and breadth of the area being considered for renewal.

I can go to Juliet as an excuse to see Jase and let him show me around unofficially? Afterwards, I could draw some basic designs, which he could show Howard. I'm okay using his first name, I will be his employee after he sees my designs.

What if I walk into a relationship between Jase and another woman? Can I handle that? I guess it would be better to know, than to be in the dark.

Her mind was whirling as she completed her walk to the café. Breakfast gave her energy and hope that this was a good move.

She called Christine as soon as she entered her apartment. She wasn't asking permission to go, but her mother took the opportunity to give her an opinion.

"Don't you think you're pushing it with Howard Stockton to just show up and give him designs? And don't you think you're being inconsiderate of Jason by showing up without letting him know?"

"Mother, I've made up my mind. I'm going. I just wanted to let you know where I'll be for a few days. I'm booking the next flight to Mississippi. I'll let you know when I get there, and I'll call you when I leave to come home. Got to go now. Love you."

With a kissing sound on the phone, Ashleigh hung up.

The next flight left in three hours. She flew around the rooms, grabbing suitcases, packing clothes and cosmetics, and filling an artist's canvas bag with her supplies for drawing rough sketches.

She called an airport transportation service to pick her up and was in the ticket line in an hour.

She didn't hear the pilot remind passengers to watch the stewardess for safety instructions. She was giddy for the first time in years. She was sticking her neck out. She was going after what she wanted. She was terrified, forgetting to pray to calm nerves.

The flight was easy and quick. She grabbed a cab at curbside and gave him the hotel's name after he loaded her bags into the trunk. She twiddled her thumbs the entire drive to the hotel. It was dusk when the driver pulled into the circular drive of the two-story Holiday Dream Hotel. It didn't look like the Ritz, but it wasn't a dump. It must be okay; Jason was staying here.

She placed a call to Christine as soon as the bellboy closed the door with her five- dollar tip. The phone call went to the answering machine.

"Mom, I'm here, safe and sound. Talk with you tomorrow."

Now what? Should she call Jase at work or leave a message on his phone here at the hotel? That would be best.

"Jase, surprise. I'm here at the hotel in room two-forty-five. Call me when you get in. Can't wait to see you."

At seven forty-five she was starving and had to find a place to eat. She went to the first floor, looking for a restaurant. Seeing none, she asked at the front desk for the name of a good restaurant within walking distance.

When she entered the restaurant, the hostess sat her at a small table in the corner giving her full view of all the tables. She ordered a light dinner and sipped her sweet tea while she waited for her meal.

Several diners began drifting out as late diners refilled their seats. She enjoyed seeing the couples interactions with each other. One couple was seated at a table near her. The man, dressed in dark slacks, an open collar dress shirt with no tie and a decades old sports coat, thanked the hostess and then held the chair for the woman, patted her shoulder and smiled as he sat opposite her. She smiled back at him, as she adjusted her last season's dress, pulled on her costume jewelry necklace, and reached for his hand resting on the table.

Another couple was led to a table in the same area. The man raised his voice complaining about its location and demanded a different table. He waved his arm adorned with an expensive watch and straightened his tie in a move to show authority. His companion smiled at him and flashed her two-carat ring, when she placed her clutch purse on the new table. Satisfied with the center table, the man began looking around the room and left his wife standing beside her chair. He sat boisterously in his seat and began ignoring his partner, uninterested in any conversation.

The couple that made her want to leave without eating, came into the room, arms around each other. When the hostess showed them to a table, the man started kissing the woman on her cheek. He didn't offer to hold her chair but held her hand as he walked to his side of the table. They threw fake kisses at each other during their entire meal.

She enjoyed people watching, until she saw a tall, handsome man enter with a petite blonde holding her elbow as he often had with her.

Suddenly, she felt sick to her stomach. They looked so comfortable with each other. Thankfully, he didn't see her sitting in her hideaway, partially shielded by a large palm plant. The waitress brought her dinner and she pretended to eat.

Jason and the blonde carried on a continuous conversation, which was obviously sprinkled with amusing comments. The blonde held his full attention. They each had a glass of wine with salad and chicken cordon bleu, followed with crème Brulé.

Ashleigh was having a hard time stretching her meal to last until they left. She wanted to cry, to scream and to curse at him.

He had done nothing wrong. She had been the one to refer to their relationship as a good friendship.

Finally, they rose and headed toward the door with his hand at her back.

Chapter Seventy-One

She spent hours pacing and crying. What should I do? I came here to let Jase know I care for him, but I also came for an opportunity for a job. Jase said he was helping me get a job here. I trust him to be honest about wanting me to work with him.

I need a job. I want this job. I will swallow my pride and wait for his call like any other candidate for a position. He doesn't have to know I was there tonight and saw him.

Sleep didn't come easy or fast. Ashleigh was jarred out of her fitful slumber by the hotel's phone. "Hello."

"Ash, it's me, Jase. I'm so excited you're here. I can't believe it. Sorry I didn't call last night. We had a County Commissioner meeting that lasted until eleven, with only a short break for dinner. I saw your message when I got in my car where my phone resides, but it was too late to call. Can we have breakfast?"

He finally took a breath long enough for her to answer. "I'm still in bed. Can you give me about thirty minutes?"

"Sure. I'll drive over and wait in the lobby. Just come down when you're ready."

She threw back the covers and ran to the shower. Twenty minutes later she had dressed in casual beige slacks and a creamy blue cable knit sweater with comfortable brown shoes. She pulled her hair into a bun at the nape of her neck and added large gold earrings. She swiped her face with loose powder and applied mascara and coral lipstick.

She saw Jason as she exited the elevator. He stood as she approached.

Butterflies in her stomach, she almost ran to him. His smile showed his approval. He met her halfway and picked her up in a hug. He grabbed her hand and pulled her toward the door.

"I know a perfect place for breakfast. You game?"

"Always."

When they were seated, neither one was interested in the country-style breakfast. They nibbled at sausage biscuits and played with the scrambled eggs. The restaurant sat above a small lake outside the business district of Juliet and was filled with local regulars. The buzz of conversations didn't bother Ashleigh or Jason. They spent more time looking at each other than eating.

"I do have to work for a little while this morning. I'm meeting with one of the commissioners who couldn't attend yesterday's meeting. Then I'll be free for the rest of the day. We can meet for lunch and go from there."

"I know I'm intruding into your work, but I couldn't stop myself from coming. I had so much free time, I thought it would be good for me to get a first-hand look at this community, so I'd be better equipped to start with my designs when Howard gives you the okay."

"It just so happens, I talked with him again yesterday morning and he has given me the go-ahead to hire you. I think you'll be happy with the salary. You'll have to wait for the offer package from home office for the amount and other expectations."

She jumped up and hugged him around the neck as he was seated. "I knew you could convince him. He respects you too much to have you upset with the company if they didn't hire me. I guess I'm correct that you would be upset if he didn't hire me. You need an architect. Better me than someone he doesn't know."

"Exactly what I told him."

"What? Better than someone he doesn't know. Are you kidding me?"

"Yes, I'm kidding you. He had to swallow his pride to admit you were the best possible architect for this project and his company. He still had not replaced you."

"You're kidding?"

"You're irreplaceable!"

"I hope you feel that way."

"You do?"

"Yes, I do."

"I have thought that for a long time. I wish we were somewhere else so I could kiss you?"

"Me too."

They rose at the same time. He stopped at the cash register and paid the bill, looking at her the whole time, and then they stopped beside the car. He wrapped her in his arms, and they kissed until catcalls came from passing cars.

"I've got to go work for a little while. Will you be okay by yourself?"

"The hotel is only a few blocks away. I'll walk back and take notes along the way. While I'm waiting for you, I'll start some sketches for you to review."

"You're amazing."

"See you around one?"

"That sounds about right. You'll be in the hotel if I need to extend my work, right?"

"Yes. I'll be waiting."

He drove away and she started note taking on both sides of the street. She wished she had brought her camera so she could have pictures to refresh her mind as she worked.

***

At one thirty the hotel phone rang.

"Ash, sorry I'm late. Would it be okay if I brought one of the commissioners along for lunch. She needs to meet you anyway. She is the main driver of this project and will be your go-to contact for design decisions."

"Sure. We can make this a working lunch if we have tonight to ourselves."

"No problem there. Okay. See you in about fifteen minutes. I'll pull up at the concierge door for you."

Ashleigh went downstairs after she freshened her hair and makeup. She walked out under the canopy to wait for Jason's car.

The first thing she saw as his car pulled up in front of her was a blonde head that barely showed above the doorframe. She stared for a minute before getting into the backseat. Before she settled in, she was struck with the strong aroma of one of the expensive popular perfumes.

"Ashleigh, meet Savannah Rivers, the only female commissioner in the county. Savannah, this is Ashleigh Justice, the talented architect I've told you about."

The women smiled and acknowledged each other.

Savannah spoke first, "What do you think of our little town, Ashleigh? Worth giving it an updated façade?"

"I like what I've seen. I'm interested in the roads leading in and out of town and how far the renewal will stretch."

Jason added, "I'll go over all the blueprints in the morning when we get to work."

"I'm sure you have a lot to show me."

"That I do."

Savannah joined in, "How long have you two worked together?"

"Three or four years." Jason expanded their work time to include their personal time.

During lunch Jason and Savannah brought Ashleigh up to date on the other commissioners and their desires for the project. They were all working hard to get approval for funding for the project they wanted to save the business district.

Ashleigh noticed Savannah's low-cut blouse, tight, short skirt, and spike heels. She realized she had a lot to learn quickly.

"I'll get up-to-speed on everything as quickly as possible."

Lunch was casual and lasted until late afternoon. Ashleigh was eager to get back to the hotel to dress for her dinner with Jason.

"I'll see you in a little while, after I drop Savannah off at her home. She rode into town with her daughter who left to start her second year of college."

He smiled at her as she got out of the car.

"It was a pleasure meeting you. Savannah."

"Likewise. I'm sure we'll be seeing a lot of each other over the next months."

She turned to Jason and put her heavily jeweled hand on his arm.

"We need to scoot. I have a busy evening. Can you join us, Jason?"

"Not tonight, Savannah."

Ashleigh's antenna went up. Is this the reason Jason has stayed in Mississippi? I need to find out more about Savannah Rivers.

Does she have a husband? Is she making a move on Jason? Tonight, I will ask Jase about her.

The afternoon was filled with sketching the current land with buildings and store fronts. Her mind was full of ideas for a new look on current façades if the structural elements were still viable.

She looked at the clock reading six p.m. She jumped up and hurried to the shower. She wanted to look special for tonight.

When she came out from the shower she saw the blinking light on the hotel's phone. She wrapped the towel around her body and pressed the answer button.

"Ash, this is Jase. I hate to do this at the last minute. Some issues have come up with Savannah that I need to take care of. Can we have breakfast in the morning? I promise to make it up to you."

That's my answer. Savannah means more to him than I do. I'm wasting my time here. I'm glad I didn't change my flight for tomorrow morning. I'm going home.

Chapter Seventy-Two

The airport was not busy at seven thirty. She went to a restaurant that served breakfast to wait for the boarding call. She ordered an egg sandwich and coffee, leaving more than half the sandwich but drank two cups of coffee.

God was looking out for me when I chose not to tell Jase I had a flight for this morning. I need to get home to double-check plans for JJ's shower next weekend. If things had worked out, I was going to ask him to come to the wedding with me the following weekend.

The flight was only an hour and a half, but the total travel time was four hours because of the requirements for early arrival, travel, retrieving luggage and taxiing home.

When she entered her apartment, she saw the answering machine light. She knew it was from Jase. She had no desire to hear what he had to say.

Who does he think he is? Who does he think I am? I don't know what's going on with him, but I don't need any more drama in my life.

She spent the day double checking that the guest cottage on the grounds of one of the mansions in the north Atlanta suburbs was being cleaned and prepared for the shower, she also checked with the caterer to be sure the menu was correct and would be delivered a half hour before the shower was to begin and that the florist would have the centerpieces for the tables delivered and in place an hour before the first arrivals. She checked her mailbox for RSVPs to adjust the number of attendees if needed.

The next morning, she called Christine.

"Ashleigh! I'm so happy you called. I was planning a dinner party for next Saturday night. Can you come?"

"I'm busy that Saturday. Remember it's JJ's shower. I thought you were coming."

"Oh, I am. I've got the dinner party catered and having the house cleaned while I'm at the shower. I'll be there. I guess you must stay to clean up from the party and visit with JJ after everyone is gone."

"Yes. I'm devoting that day to JJ and whatever she needs. Can you have lunch today?"

"Not today, honey. I have my ladies Bible study group in a few minutes. Sorry. Will we see you at church Sunday?"

"Yes. I'll be there."

"Lunch after?"

"Yes. I'm free for lunch. See you then."

When she hung up the phone, she realized that life was back to normal for her mom. She had not asked how Ashleigh was doing, when she got home from Mississippi, or if she was going back.

At least I won't have to dodge questions about Jason, or why I'm home. Maybe, it's for the best. I have time for a run before I have lunch and start working on my notes from Juliet. There is so much I can do with what I already know. The truth is, I need Jason to fill in the gaps in my knowledge about conversations the commissioners have had and what they see as a promising approach to the renewal plan.

She found a clean running outfit, put the dirty clothes in the washer and headed out the door. When her feet hit the ground, she realized she needed to run or go back inside for a sweatshirt. The temperature was twenty degrees lower than when she left.

She opted to run. The trail was cleaned by a recent rain. She looked straight ahead and didn't notice squirrels jumping from one tree limb to another or see the cardinals and bluebirds flittering from branches to somewhere deep in the tree. She barely saw the other runners she passed. She moved into her zone. The world was a blur. Just as she wanted.

***

Sunday morning church always boosted her mood. She looked forward to hearing Bible verses read by the minister and his sermon based on the verses. There was usually a sentence or a reference that felt like it was meant for her. It buoyed her spirit and helped her remember that today's trials were temporary. God is in control.

"Do you want to ride to the Country Club with us today, Ashleigh?"

"No, thanks, Mom. I need to run some errands after lunch. I'll meet you there."

Carlton hugged her, "Glad you're home sweetheart. I worry when you're off somewhere alone."

"I'm good, Dad. I take precautions. Thank you for worrying about me."

When she entered the Country Club, she saw Scott across the room with a red head who was hanging on his every word. Caution for the young woman rose in Ashleigh's throat, threatening to choke her. She looked away and headed for her parents' table.

"Hey, honey. You look pale. Are you okay?"

"I will be, Dad. I need a few minutes. I saw Scott when I came in the door."

"Sorry you had to see him, but glad you're with us. He won't approach you when you're not alone. The restraining order is still in effect."

"I'm not afraid. It's just a reaction to seeing him. I'll get past it."

"Sweetheart, do you have everything ready for next Saturday? I can help."

"Everything is ready. I double checked with every vendor when I got home from Juliet."

"I knew you would be prepared. You've learned how to plan a party from me over the years."

"Yes, Mom. I've learned from the best. I'm going to spend the entire day with JJ Wednesday. We haven't been together in a long time. I miss her."

"That's great. You need a social life."

"I always have my Tuesday nights with the Supporters."

"What's that all about anyway. Are you still working to get to the legislature?"

"Yes. We're hoping to get a representative to sponsor a bill to enforce the tenets in the ERA."

"Why?"

"Because it is a law that is not being enforced. Women are not being paid according to their experience, education, and work product the same as men. It is not fair but, most of all, it is not legal. No one else is forcing the issue. We are."

"That just sounds like so much work. You're being paid fairly, aren't you?"

"I wasn't at Stocktons. I was at Northcutt. We'll see when I get the offer from Howard Stockton for a second chance."

"It's just so much work."

"Mom, I thought you supported me."

"I do. I just want you to have fun at this time in your life. You don't seem to be having fun."

"I know. I love you for that, but I must do what I believe in. Fun can come later. Thanks for the lunch, Dad. I'll see you Saturday, Mom."

Relieved, Ashleigh breathed in the cool air. Fall was a time to be outside enjoying the glorious weather in Atlanta.

She was changing into comfortable Sunday clothes when there was a knock at her door. For a moment she thought of Scott. She slowly walked to the door and looked out the peek hole. It wasn't Scott.

"Ash, please let me in. I know you're here. I saw your car in your parking space. I need to see you. Did you get my message the other day?"

"Jason, I can't see any reason to let you in. You showed me how little I mean to you when you didn't show up for dinner the other night."

"I was going to explain at breakfast, but you were gone."

"I didn't need an explanation. I needed you."

"Please let me in. I can't talk to you through the door."

"And I can't talk to you when you never show up."

"You won't open the door?"

"No."

Her heart was pounding, but she didn't relent.

Chapter Seventy-Three

Her light wool black slacks and cable knit beige sweater were perfect for a walk. She waited for twenty minutes and then went down the steps for a stroll down the streets of midtown.

She delighted in the development that was being done to bring this part of town back to its days of family, food, and fun. Several new restaurants had opened in the past year. The park entrances had been cleared and park benches were placed along the route to central city, looping back to midtown.

Her walk led her past Southern Belnew construction where the sun was beginning its descent. She crossed the street and headed back toward her apartment for a different view on this side of the street.

When she reached The Brick House it was nearing dinner time. She opened the door to her favorite smell of grilled steak. She saw a few tables with diners.

"If possible, I'd like to sit near the door so I can see folks coming in."

"Sure. We have a small table in the cubicle near the window. Is that okay?"

"Yes, perfect. I can see the street traffic as well. Thank you."

"You're welcome. Your waitress will be with you in a minute."

As she settled in, she realized that she was a little nervous about being out at night by herself, especially while walking. She had never been afraid before…before Scott. She couldn't blame everything on him, but she felt her nervousness was tied to his actions.

She ordered her favorite steak and a glass of red wine. She might as well get used to dining alone, since JJ and Jase were out of her reach for socializing.

The wine made the walk home a little more comfortable. She slipped into her dark living room, where the glass doors splayed the ethereal skyline of Atlanta. She caught her breath at its beauty. She loved her home, even if there was no one to share it.

Without turning on a light, she settled into the comfort of the sofa and stretched her legs out on its surface. Before long she was asleep.

The phone rang at eleven thirty. She moaned but sat up to answer it, thankful she had left it on the sofa table when she went for her walk. Scott's voice caught her by surprise.

"Ashleigh, this is Scott. Please don't hang up. I would like to meet with you, somewhere public. There are some things I need to say to you. I'm getting control of my anger through counseling. I won't be a problem to you."

"Scott. It is hard for me to even listen to your voice. Do you understand that?"

"Yes. I do now. I will be out of your life after we meet. Will you grant me that favor?"

"I have to think about it. My initial response is no."

"I understand. I know I'm asking more than most people could grant, but I know you to be a forgiving Christian. I think you would be sorry if you don't offer me that gift."

"It would need to be in a public place, somewhere our friends don't frequent."

"You pick the place and time."

"The weather is still nice. Let's meet tomorrow at the second or third bench in the trail across from my apartment at two o'clock."

"I'll be there. Thank you, Ashleigh."

She hung up the phone without answering. She didn't want to do this, but if it would put closure on their relationship, so she would never have to see him again, she could manage through one last meeting.

***

Ashleigh arrived at the bench at one forty-five the next day. She didn't want to be surprised if he had some ulterior motive for the meeting. She did not trust him, but she had granted him some measure of courtesy to meet with him one last time.

Scott arrived at one fifty-five.

She watched him walk toward her with his natural swagger, but with a little less forcefulness. She saw defeat in his eyes.

"Thank you for meeting with me." He reached for her hand.

She withheld any touch. "What did you want to say to me?"

"I'm working with a psychologist to learn how to control my emotions, especially anger. Her approach is somewhat like the twelve-step programs used by addicts in counseling. I've told her all about our relationship and how I treated you before and after the pregnancy. She felt that for your sake as well as mine, I need to tell you how sorry I am about the way I treated you and abused you. While it was abhorrent behavior and a sin, I am asking for your forgiveness.

"I own all the horrible feelings I had and the inexcusable way I abused and threatened you. I've never been that kind of person to the extent I was with you. I put you through hell. I understand that now. You are a good person, and I had no reason to treat you the way I did. I know you were hurting when our baby died. I'm sorry for being so hurtful about that, too."

"You want me to forgive you?"

"Yes. I need you to forgive me. I'm not sure how you can do that. But I need that forgiveness to move forward with my counseling. I want to be a better person. I need to be a better person. I pray God will make me a better person."

Ashleigh saw sincerity in his eyes and heard it in his voice.

"God requires us to forgive those who have harmed us, hurt us, and dishonored us. I believe in forgiveness. God forgave me for my sins, past and future. How can I withhold my forgiveness from you? So, Scott, I forgive you for your actions toward me. I pray you are sincerely sorry and will erase those attitudes and actions from your mind toward anyone else, but those are your decisions…between you and God. My forgiveness is outside of what you do in the future."

"Thank you, Ashleigh. My parents are having a hard time forgiving me for everything I've done to them. I've cost them a lot of money and ruined their reputation in this town. I know they are trying, but it's taking my father a long time to forgive me. Your mercy and forgiveness help me be patient waiting for theirs.

"I won't bother you ever again. I won't speak to you when I see you in public. I won't acknowledge you in restaurants. I will simply nod when I see you in church. In other words, I'll be out of your life."

"Thank you for that assurance, Scott. I wish you well in your recovery. Goodbye."

Ashleigh walked away from Scott and the past that haunted her every waking moment. She felt free for the first time in months. She could resume her life. She could sleep soundly. She could make plans for her evenings without worrying about Scott's whereabouts.

Her forgiveness of Scott freed her through God's promise, "Live justly, love mercy and walk humbly with God."

The day seemed brighter. The air fresher. The joggers friendlier. The wind, softer. The walk, easier.

Maybe it is time to forgive Jason. Although, she wasn't sure what she needed to forgive. She only assumed the worst in his actions. She did not know why he failed to call or why he cancelled dates or why he jumped at every request from Savannah Rivers, even to the point of breaking dates with her at the last minute.

She had not listened to the last messages he left on her answering machine. Maybe she should listen to them. She was being selfish and dismissive of him for not acting as she thought he should act. She didn't have enough information to make that decision.

It was getting dusk when she started up the stairs outside her apartment. She gave no thought to the setting Fall sun. She felt no fear of being attacked outside her door.

She was thinking about the need to pull decorations together for JJ's bachelorette party Saturday night. Happy things were in JJ's future. She was in love and headed for a new life in South Georgia. Ashleigh was happy for her.

She needed to spend more time with her Tuesday night friends and the larger group of women working on legislation requiring adherence to all the ERA, even to the point of garnering support for ratification of the ERA. That could be a full-time job for someone because it would need to include all fifteen Southern states that failed to ratify it.

Even though Natalie Birdman had been elected to serve as lead person, she might need help in achieving that goal.

***

Ashleigh acknowledged the red blinking light on her phone, pressing it with a pen and paper in hand to write down messages from callers over the past week.

The first one was from Jason. "Ash, why did you leave? I know I neglected you while you were here, but you must understand that I'm here working day and night to solidify our contract with the City of Juliet. Savannah happens to control a lot of the decisions made in this county. If I had known you were coming, I could have prepared time to meet with her before you got here. I'm sorry. Please call me back."

There were a couple from her mom, "Just checking in."

There was one from JJ today. "Ashleigh, I'm so excited about this weekend's bachelorette party. Call and let's talk about it. Can't wait for our lunch Wednesday."

The final message was from Howard Stockton. "Ashleigh. Please give me a call. We need to talk about the position Jason promised you. You've got my number."

I'm sure there is no position. Jason didn't give me a formal written offer. What is there to talk about. Savannah Rivers will not want me to be the architect on her project. I will be competition for Jason's time. She wants him all to herself.

Chapter Seventy-Four

The call wouldn't be that hard to make. She knew Howard. After all, she had worked for him for four years. She already knew what he would say. He was going to prove to her that she would not have a position as an architect in his firm.

Might as well get it over with. "May I speak with Mr. Stockton, Angela? This is Ashleigh."

"I know your voice, Ashleigh. So glad to hear from you. Hold on just a minute. He is in his office."

"Ashleigh, where the dickens are you?"

"I'm at home. Why?"

"You were due here a half hour ago."

"What do you mean? Due there."

"Jason said he would tell you about our appointment."

"I haven't talked with Jason."

"Well, nevertheless, get down here. Mr. Phillips will be here in an hour. I need to go over his proposal with you before he gets here."

"What are you talking about? What proposal?"

"Do you want this job, or not?"

"Of course, I want a job."

"Then, you'd better be here in the next half hour." He hung up.

Confused but encouraged, Ashleigh jumped in the shower, put on her favorite business suit, pulled her hair into a bun, swiped on mascara and lipstick, and rode the elevator to ground level to her car.

Maybe I should have listened to Jason's messages.

***

Howard Stockton had a plat, rough drawings, and a lengthy proposal ready for her review.

"Now, Ashleigh, we haven't discussed your employment yet. But since you're here, I'm assuming you agreed to my proposal. We can review it in detail after we meet with Shane Phillips."

He went over everything the new client had requested and showed her the rough drawings.

"Are you ready to listen to his thoughts and timelines?"

"Yes, Howard, I can wing it through this initial meeting."

It felt so good to be back in the place where creative discussions and long-term plans were made. Meeting Shane Phillips and hearing about his dreams started her creative ideas flowing. Her excitement grew. She wasn't sure what her role would be in this project, but she felt in control of whatever it would be.

When Shane left, Howard looked at her and smiled. "I've missed that 'can do' attitude of yours, Ashleigh. I discussed the details of rehiring you with Jason. I hope that was okay. You seemed to be good friends and worked together so well. He went to bat for you. I want you to know that."

"Thank you, Howard. Jason and I have missed communications over the last week or so. Now, tell me about your job offer."

"After you left, I realized the importance you are to this firm. I was short-sighted and a little rough with you. The Deerfield project is in dire need of a manager and talented architect to pull it through to completion. And, as you witnessed, Mr. Phillips is ready to move on his project."

"Yes, it sounds exciting."

"I am offering to make you senior architect over all the other architects in the firm and to pay you what a seventh-year architect should make, plus an additional ten thousand for the added responsibility for the other architects."

Ashleigh was almost speechless. "That sounds more than fair. I assume I'm on the job now."

"Definitely. I let Camden go a couple of weeks ago. I realized you were carrying him over the past four years. I'm sorry I was out of touch with what you were accomplishing. I'm an old man who is stuck in old ways of doing business. I needed your self-confidence and a push from Jason to make me realize how much things have changed."

"I'm glad you came around, Howard. I'm ready to get to work. Is my old office still available?"

"No, I've hired a first-year architect and put her in your office, hoping she would assimilate some of your talent and gumption. She will need mentoring from you. I want you near my office. I had the office next to mine cleaned and set up everything you need to get to work. I'll show you."

Howard's chest puffed a little as he walked Ashleigh to her new office. "I ordered new furniture to suit a woman's style and size. I hired a female designer at Somerset Designs to make sure the office will be comfortable for you to work at your desk and at a drafting table. She assured me you will be comfortable here. However, if anything doesn't suit you, let me know and I'll have it changed."

Ashleigh was taken aback by his desire to please her and make her job comfortable. "This is tremendous, Howard. I'm sure everything will support my work product. Thank you."

"Okay. Well, I'll leave you to get situated and start on the new project. By the way, do you mind checking in on the Deerfield project? I told the staff to expect you today."

"Of course. I'll do that now."

"Thank you. With Jason in Mississippi most of the time and no lead architect, the staff is fledgling. If you can give them a little guidance, they will be able to carry the ball with your oversight. Can you manage that along with the Phillips project and the Juliet project."

"Do you want me on the Juliet project?"

"Yes. Certainly. Jason is the lead, but he needs you as the architect. They are not ready to start yet, because they are still working with the surrounding counties to get support for them using the funds the Juliet project will take from the state budget. That should give you time to get the Phillips project going and finish the Deerfield project."

"You certainly have a master plan."

"That's why I need you. You can handle these projects. I trust you."

Ashleigh blushed at his praise. In the four years she worked for him before, he never gave her a compliment. This moment was surreal.

"I'll do my best Howard. I'll head over to check with the Deerfield team and let you know how it's going."

The day was a whirlwind. She never took a lunch break. She was deep into doing the work she loved. Then she realized it was

Tuesday. She checked her watch and shut down the office. Tonight's dinner with the SOSBS would be an opportunity to share her good news with the group.

Howard saw her leaving the office. "Everything okay today?"

"Yes. I feel comfortable where every project is and have started a plan to coordinate my time among the three projects. The Deerfield team was supportive of my suggestions and made a good deal of progress today. I've started preliminary plans for the Phillips project and scheduled a meeting with Shane for Friday to look at the site. Who will be my engineer on this project?"

"I haven't decided yet. It depends on where Jason is with Juliet."

"Okay. I assume I will be more involved with the progress of this project as time goes along."

"You will. For now, Jason is tiptoeing around the commissioners, encouraging, but not being forceful. You went there, right?"

"Yes, I spent a couple of days there. Started some sketches of the downtown as it is today and got a feel for the people, weather, soil, and their goals for the project."

"Well, done! Have a good evening. See you tomorrow."

"Goodnight, Howard. Thank you for this opportunity. And thank you for recognizing my potential and worth to the company."

Howard's reply showed his inability to acknowledge he had been wrong. "Just don't let me down."

Ashleigh smiled as she walked toward the elevator.

Chapter Seventy-Five

A night out with the girls was exactly what Ashleigh needed. She was the first to arrive at The Brick House. She settled in with a glass of sweet tea, while waiting for the others to arrive. As they arrived and ordered dinner, Ashleigh asked each one to tell her about the progress they had made on getting support for their proposal for the state legislature.

Pat spoke first, "I don't have contacts with any politicians, but many of my clients do. I've been gently asking them questions about their employment opportunities for women and how they are supporting their female employees. At this point, I haven't pushed anything, I'm just trying to build a relationship with them in this area."

Martha was eager to report, "Through the teacher's union I've met senators and legislators over the years. I've had conversations with several of them, who I feel would be supportive of our agenda."

Saundra smiled, "I've gotten the ears of a couple of the partners in my firm, who seem ready to be of help. I need to have something concrete to show them and then I believe they will support us. You remember I told you about Stanley Nelson, a partner in my firm? He is all in. He's ready to make a name for himself in politics. This is the perfect issue to give him a lot of publicity.

Ashleigh brought them back to their project. "Yes, we're making progress. This is great news. I haven't approached Howard Stockton yet. But he just hired me back into the firm with a hefty raise with extra pay for leading the junior architects and coordinating all the architectural staff. I feel he will be supportive of the larger agenda of our group.

"I'm excited to have your reports to take to the state group. We meet in two weeks."

Chapter Seventy-Six

Wednesday night, Ashleigh and JJ met for dinner. Since JJ was staying with her mother until after the wedding, they met at a restaurant near her home.

"I can't believe I will be married in a few days. The time has flown by, even though I haven't accepted many work assignments since we got engaged."

"Planning a wedding and living arrangement afterwards takes time. I think it's a good thing. It gives you time to back out if you want."

"Don't even say that. I can't wait to be Mrs. Ronald Stephens Murray. Ron is the love of my life. Just think, if I had not accepted that job in Warner Robins, I wouldn't have met him."

"It was meant to be, JJ. Are you going to stay in Warner Robins?"

"Yes. He has a good opportunity with a law firm there. I'll miss you, but I won't be working, so I can take some days to come visit often, especially if he is in a lengthy trial."

"How does your mom feel about it?"

"She's happy for me. I guess I'd better head back to her house. We only have a few days to be together. I'll see you at the shower Saturday night."

They stood and hugged. Ashleigh felt a little of her friendship slipping away.

***

Saturday night, as Ashleigh was putting the final centerpieces on the tables, she felt a huge weight lifted off her. The night was the most important thing she had accomplished in a long time. Her social life had been busy and full when she first graduated from college.

She remembered the weekends when she barely got enough sleep to get to work on time. Gradually, weekends didn't mean as much as her job. She let her job become her life. Planning this bachelorette party/shower reminded her how much she enjoyed visiting with friends and partying outside of work socials.

Saturday night, JJ seemed to float into the room filled with college friends, work friends and JJ and Ashleigh's moms. Ashleigh planned the night to focus on JJ without the foolishness younger women would expect.

Soft music played from the speakers in the ceiling; accent lighting highlighted candles flickering around the room from the centerpieces resting on pink tablecloths.

Additional tables with pink tablecloths were set up around the perimeter of the room, each offering a selection of shrimp, crab and other seafood specialties or steak strips, chicken, and finger foods, with the desert table overloaded with delicacies in lady-like sizes.

In the center of the room a table was set up to hold the gifts for the bride.

JJ absorbed the beauty of the night and the friendships honoring her. She greeted each guest and asked about their families.

"JJ, can you believe I have three children?" Shirley Franks pulled out her wallet and, like the other women, showed off pictures of her husband and children.

"A lot has happened in the seven years since I've seen you. Thank you for coming."

"You look beautiful, JJ. Pink is your color with your dark hair and blue eyes. That dress is amazing. You still have your curvaceous figure. Wait until you have children. You won't be able to fit into anything that stunning. I think you've met the man of your dreams."

"I know I have. I'm so blessed."

JJ stood for a moment, looking at the women in the room, friends from her past who took the time to travel back to Atlanta to be with her for her special night. Then she looked at Ashleigh, who was her best friend and had known exactly how to plan this special night for her.

Ashleigh looked across the room at JJ and smiled.

Chapter Seventy-Seven

Being the maid of honor at JJ's wedding made it easier for Ashleigh to attend without a date. This day belonged to JJ.

It was when she kicked off her shoes in her apartment and closed the door, that she felt alone. Her best friend would always be her friend, but she now had a more intimate friend, her husband.

God, how can I be so happy for JJ and yet so lonely for myself? Have I missed some of your plans for my life? I'm trying to stay positive. I know it was you who brought me back to Stockton & Associates and changed Howard's heart about my pay and position.

Maybe I expect too much at one time. I will focus on where you've placed me now and know you already have the rest of my life in your hands. I trust you and love you. Amen

The fullness of the day sapped her energy. She slipped on her robe and made a cup of hot tea. Church with her mom and dad tomorrow would bring her back to reality.

As she sipped the last of her tea, the phone rang.

"Ashleigh, this is Natalie Birdman. I hate to call on a Saturday night, but I couldn't wait to let you know. We've pretty much covered the state and have about a hundred and fifty women leaders who have joined our cause.

"We felt the need to move fast with this group to keep interest growing. I've rented a room in a hotel in Columbus for a weekend meeting next weekend. I know it's short notice, but can you come for the whole weekend? You are the one who stirred up support for us. I'd love you to be there. We have three representatives who have agreed to come and meet with us. There will not be a formal program. We will have discussions with each of them and let them know what we are working toward."

Ashleigh's mind was swirling, "I just started a new job. Let me double check with my boss and make sure he is not assigning me to go out of town next weekend. Otherwise, I'd love to be there. Can I call you sometime tomorrow or Monday? I'm not sure I can get to him this weekend."

"Doesn't he have a cell phone?"

"A what?"

"Don't you have a cell phone?"

"No. Exactly, what is that?"

"It's a digital phone, rather than an analog phone."

"Oh, I've seen a car phone. One of my friends has one."

"No. That's still an analog phone tied to your home phone number. It is cumbersome and only allows calls to your home number. A cell phone works off radio waves sent to towers for radio and television. You have a separate number and anyone who has a cell phone can call you wherever you are. It is small enough to put in your purse. You need one. Look into that this week. Okay?"

"Sure. I'll let you know about next weekend as soon as I can."

"Great. Talk with you then."

Ashleigh was intrigued. She would talk with her dad tomorrow after church.

Sliding under warm covers, she smiled. God was sending her distractions to keep her upbeat and busy.

Chapter Seventy-Eight

"I've been meaning to talk with you about a cell phone, especially since you will be traveling some in your job. You need to have a way to get in touch with us and the police, especially when you're out of town.

"I bought one two weeks ago. Not very many people have one yet, but we're requiring them at work. They are easy to use. The only drawback is that whomever you call must have your new cell number to call you. It won't be long until everyone will carry one."

"This is so exciting. Dad, will you go with me to purchase one tomorrow? I have no idea where to go or what to look for."

"Sure, let's meet for lunch. There is a store near your office. I'll stop by and pick you up."

She rarely had lunch alone with her dad. She was looking forward to time alone with him.

Carlton knew Howard from Rotary Club and the Country Club. They moved in different circles but were acquainted with each other. When Carlton entered the firm Howard happened to be talking with the receptionist.

"Carlton, good to see you. You here to see Ashleigh?"

"Yes. We're going to lunch and then I'm taking her to buy a cell phone."

"You know, I've been thinking about looking into them. It would be good for my staff to have one when they travel. It's difficult to keep up with folks when you only have a hotel number to reach them, and you know they will not be at the hotel during the day. They had better not be at the hotel during the day."

Carlton laughed along with Howard. "I understand. We've required them at the office. I think they will work out nicely. Ah, I see my girl coming this way."

"Hi, Dad. I'm starving and excited. Howard, did dad tell you what we're doing after lunch?"

"Yes. I'm very interested in how you like using it. Have a good lunch. Carlton, good to see you."

"You, too, Howard. Okay, let's head out. I have reservations at Chateau Leon, down the street."

As they settled in, waiting for lunch, Carlton took Ashleigh's hand. "How are you really doing, sweetheart? You look great. Are you managing with Howard?"

"Yes, Dad. It's amazing how receptive he is to my return. He couldn't be a better boss to me. He listens to my ideas and has assigned a couple of important projects to me. I may also get to work with Jason on the Juliet project in Mississippi."

"Well then. I'm glad we're getting this phone for you now."

"I'm excited to use it. It will be better than e-mails because you must be near a computer to get e-mails."

They didn't linger over lunch, eager to get to the phone store.

Ashleigh was amazed that she could get a phone not much

larger than a checkbook. She knew she would feel safe with it in her purse or briefcase. It was easy to use. She couldn't wait to enter phone numbers in the contact list, making her feel even closer to her friends and family.

That night, at home, her first entry was her dad's cell phone, then his office; next her parents' home phone and JJ's phone in Warner Robins.

She added several phone numbers for work and then took a break. She needed to prepare for her weekend in Columbus. Her first call was to Natalie Birdman.

"Hi, Natalie. I'm calling from my cell phone. I feel I'm an explorer in the world of communication. It's great. I'll give it to you now."

"You don't need to give it to me. I can save it from your call to me."

"You're kidding?"

"No. These phones make life easier. What about the weekend?"

"I will be there. I'm excited to see everyone again and hear what the congressmen have to say. Can you give me the hotel's address and phone number?"

"I'm sending out an e-mail tonight. Can I use your work e-mail to send the information?"

"I have a private e-mail. Send it to me here."

After Ashleigh shared her e-mail address, they talked for a few minutes about what was happening in each of their lives.

"I look forward to the weekend, Ashleigh."

"Me, too."

Ashleigh held onto the phone, ready to call JJ. They were back from their honeymoon, and she wanted to share her new phone number and see how JJ liked being married. Then she realized that phone calls to newlyweds at ten o'clock at night might not be a good idea.

Chapter Seventy-Nine

The next few days were filled with challenging projects at work and exciting plans for the state-wide meeting of the SOSBS group.

She packed on Thursday night, loaded the car Friday morning, and left the office at lunchtime. The drive to Columbus should take an hour and a half, but the Atlanta traffic on Friday afternoon was unpredictable. She wanted to be in her hotel room by three o'clock. The first meeting was a dinner with the group at six before the Saturday sessions with the congressmen.

The hotel's meeting room was reserved for the group and dinner was scheduled there. They could take as long as they wanted to meet after eating. Socializing covered the dinner hour and an hour later. Around eight o'clock Natalie took the podium and brought the group to order.

Unexpectedly, she asked Ashleigh to come to the podium to help her describe how the group had been formed and grown. Ashleigh appreciated Natalie's recognition of her efforts and easily told of her determination to find equality for working women, the false starts to forming a group, and finally the formation of the Supporters of Sex-Blind Success.

The room burst into applause when she introduced the other three organizers, Pat, Martha, and Saundra, who blushed at the attention and quickly sat down. The acknowledgement was there. They would be asked to take on responsibility for several committees.

Saturday breakfast in the hotel's dining room gave each participant time to go over the questions they had for the congressmen and discuss how those questions should be asked. After freshening up, the women went to the hotel's meeting room to wait for the congressmen to arrive.

Groups of five women were assigned to each congressman, to guide them to their seat on the podium and get them settled with water, paper, and pens. By eleven o'clock all three congressmen were in their seats, booked in the center of Ashleigh and Natalie.

Natalie came to the lectern, "We welcome each of you to our convention and appreciate your attendance to hear about a cause each of us strongly believes in. I believe, after you hear what we are dedicated to achieving, you will support our efforts and bring our requests to your committees for legislation that is supported and passed.

"First, I ask each of you to give a short summary of your length of service in the legislature and what committees you are assigned to, and to add any personal information you want to share.

"Let's start with Congressman Bryan Allen from here in South Georgia."

Congressman Allen approached the lectern with a big country smile. "I'm just so happy to be here with you ladies today. I appreciate you being interested in the government in our state. I serve on the Budget and Allocations Committee. I've been your congressman for eight years. The economy is struggling in the state as well as across the country. Inflation has run the interest rate up to sixteen percent. It's difficult for families to afford a home loan. Unemployment is at an all-time high. I don't know what you ladies expect to accomplish with your group, but, if it includes money, I wouldn't hold my breath."

The other two congressmen weren't encouraging either. When the presentations were over, Natalie opened the floor for questions to the congressmen.

Saundra was the first to stand. "I am an attorney in a prestigious firm in Atlanta. I have worked as many years in the firm as other attorneys and learned last year that my salary is much lower than younger, less experienced attorneys. I'm not asking the State to give me more money. I'm demanding that my company be required to pay me an equal salary for the equal or higher-level work I do.

"The ERA was passed without Georgia's ratification. I believe Georgia should ratify the tenants of the ERA and make companies abide by them. That is the only way I can assure I am paid equitably."

Other comments made to the congressmen replicated Saundra's story. After each woman spoke, the congressmen gave a lukewarm appreciation speech and alibied that the ERA was in place and contained a statement about equal rights for all residents in the state, which covered equal pay.

Enthusiasm in the meeting began to wane.

Natalie saw that they weren't making progress with these congressmen in a casual setting. However, she let every woman who wanted to speak have her time in front of the congressmen. At least, they would be able to see the passion of the group.

At three o'clock she excused the men with tepid thanks, closed the door after them and approached the lectern with a tirade against the men who had wasted their time.

"It is obvious we need to attack this issue in a different way. Let's break into small groups of twenty or less and come up with solid suggestions on how we move forward. Appoint one person to summarize your thoughts and e-mail them to me tomorrow, I will compile them and share all of them with you next week by e-mail.

"Also, recommend a place we can meet next month to prepare another action plan. Take the evening to relax and have a safe trip home tomorrow."

Ashleigh left the meeting disheartened, as everyone else did.

Chapter Eighty

Shane Phillips' project was named the Rushton Project and focused on a small city southeast of Atlanta. Ashleigh was vaguely familiar with the town. She passed near it each time she drove to Daytona Beach, Florida, for vacations.

Monday morning seemed like a good time to study their plan and drive down Tuesday. She was deep in thought, when a familiar voice came through the open door of her office.

"Hey, beautiful!"

"Jason. You're here."

"For a short visit. You look terrific, Ashleigh." He stepped forward to give her a hug.

She slipped from his embrace, "How are you?"

"Everything's fine. The Juliet project isn't even a project yet after almost a year of trying to pull the commissioners together. They can't see past their own requests."

"How long will Howard let you work on this town?"

"That's what I'm here to discuss. Hey, can we have lunch after my meeting?"

"Sure. I'm planning a trip to Rushton tomorrow to begin work on their Renewal Plan."

"Good. That should be a fun project. Wish I could work on it with you. Anyway, I'll stop by when Howard and I are finished meeting. Okay?"

"I'll be here."

It was long past lunch hour when Jason stuck his head in Ashleigh's door.

"Sorry. Howard went through all the costs and projections for the Juliet project. He is not convinced this is a viable project to keep pursuing. Me either.

"I have worked day and night with those folks. They are all bull-headed, even though they are good people. They can't see beyond their piece of the puzzle. No one, except Savannah, sees the total picture. I think her influence is even waning. I think we should take a break from them until they decide to work as a team with one goal for the whole city."

"So, you're still close with Savannah?"

"Not in the way you're inferring. She has brokered her entire fortune to support a renewal of the city. She stands to lose everything if it fails. I care about that for her. I want her to be successful. She can't be if the city isn't."

"That's a pretty strong hold on you."

"It is, and it isn't in the way you think. She has a husband and family. She includes me in many of their meals and activities because I'm there alone. It upset her that you left without talking to me. She wanted to call you. I said, no. I don't want her in the middle of my relationship with you. She acts like my mom.

"I respect her business acumen, but I don't need another mom."

"Then what do you need?"

"To be happy, I need you. I hope you need me."

Ashleigh was speechless. "You have avoided me for months and now you say that to me."

"I think you were avoiding me. I left you countless messages on your phone. I called you many more times. You never responded. Did you even listen to my messages? I even came to your apartment and knocked on the door. You didn't open it. What else could I do/"

"Do you know how much it hurt me, when I came to Juliet to see you and got rebuffed three times. You left me to be with Savannah."

"I was not rebuffing you. I was trying to save the project. Savannah was in the middle of several confrontations. I went to support her. If I had known you were coming, I could have told Savannah I would be unavailable those days. She already had the meetings set up. It had taken her weeks to get the parties together. I had to be there as her supporter on those days.

"It pained me to miss being with you and it broke my heart when you left without telling me. And then you wouldn't even give me the courtesy of hearing my explanations."

"If you're that upset, maybe you shouldn't be here with me now."

"That's not what I'm saying. I want to be here with you. I just wanted to explain what you wouldn't let me explain weeks ago."

Ashleigh became more frustrated with every sentence from him. She didn't want to believe what he was saying. It would mean she made the mistake.

"I'm headed to Rushton tomorrow. If you're here when I get back Thursday, we can talk again."

She needed to take control of the situation.

"Have a good evening, Jason."

She left him sitting at the table and rushed back to her office. She gathered her project notes, put them in her briefcase and told Angela, Howard's secretary, and Jolene, the receptionist, she would be out of the office until Thursday.

"Here is my cell phone number. I'll always have it with me if you should need me."

She stopped by her apartment to take the mail inside, grab a bottle of water, go to the bathroom, and then locked the apartment. She was leaving earlier than planned, but she needed to be on the move.

Settling into the sports car, she opened the sunroof and blasted the radio. She was in fifth gear by the time she reached the first traffic light.

Why does Jason infuriate me so? I don't know how to handle the situation with him. Can I trust him? Am I a fool? Is he lying about needing me? Wanting me?

The light changed and, since she was still in the city limits, she slowly shifted gears and wove her way onto the expressway, which was bottlenecked for as far as she could see. She turned the radio down in respect for other drivers and poked along for several miles until she exited onto Interstate 20, where the cars were traveling at the speed limit or higher.

Radio back on, she went over the entire conversation with Jason. Was she being stubborn? How did she look to him? Was he frustrated with her? Would he be there Thursday? Thoughts kept running through her mind until she reached the outskirts of Atlanta. There she picked up more speed and enjoyed her car's stereo.

When she reached Rushton, she slowly drove around downtown and then travelled out the main road out of the city. The pastoral setting made her want to pull off the road and breathe in fresh air, while watching horses drinking from sparkling ponds, and cows resting under the canopy of aged trees. She stopped to make pictures of the landscape and then drove back into town and continued taking pictures of the business district.

Her meeting with the county commissioners wasn't until four in the afternoon. She checked into her hotel room and went next door to the sandwich shop to grab a snack or milkshake.

She walked from the sandwich shop to the hardware store in the next block, where the county commissioners held their meetings in the training room in the back. She was a little early, but entered the store and asked if she could go ahead and set up for the meeting. The owner of the store was one of the commissioners and gladly lead her to the room. Two folding tables had been pushed together and chairs for eight people had been placed around the table.

"Miss Justice, you can sit here in the middle seat."

She looked down and saw the seam between the two tables and corresponding table legs as a problem for her with her tight skirt preventing her from placing her legs under the table.

"What if I sit to the side of the center next to the Chairman's seat?"

"Oh, yes. That will be fine. Just make yourself at home. Can I get you a drink from our drink machine?"

"No, thanks. I had a delicious chocolate milkshake from the sandwich shop down the street. I'm good for now. Thank you though."

"Okay. We'll get started in about thirty minutes."

"I'll be ready."

Shane Phillips arrived at four and shook Ashleigh's hand.

"Thank you for coming. As the developer of this project, I presented this idea to the commissioners and wanted to be the one to introduce you. I'll leave after that. I'm not included in all commissioner meetings."

At ten after four, three of the commissioners entered the room and introduced themselves to Ashleigh. They apologized for being late, but according to their normal routine, they were on time. After ten minutes of polite conversation about weather and traffic on the trip down, the other three commissioners entered the room amid raucous laughter. They nodded to Ashleigh and sat across the table from her and Tom Chambers, the Chairman.

Before there was time for introductions, Buster Houston reared back in his chair, smiled at Ashleigh, and said, "Now, who is this little filly? I thought we were meeting with the architect for our project, not a sweet, young thing. Is the architect running late? That doesn't look good for him."

Asleigh's face burned red, while Tom Chambers glared at Buster.

Shane stood. "This is Ashleigh Justice, the architect on our project. She is here for a preliminary discussion with us about our goals for a project of this size. She will be the designer, but will work with a civil engineer, who will study soil composition, water tables, stability of current structures and other aspects of the project. They will work together to present a plan to us.

"Miss Justice was an honor graduate of Southeastern Tech, and the fact that she was even admitted to the program is testament to her capability to guide this project. Since graduating with honors, she has been the lead architect on several projects in and around Atlanta and has proven herself to be a notable professional."

Shane excused himself and Tom Chambers took over.

"Now, let's act like adults and talk about what we want from a renewal project for our town. First, we will hear from Miss Justice about her initial thoughts. She has already driven through town and has some preliminary ideas but needs to know our expectations."

The meeting ran until six o'clock with Buster Houston frequently looking at her and smiling. Ashleigh had a creepy feeling about him and realized she would constantly be on guard against him.

Chapter Eighty-One

Tom asked if she would like to join him and his wife for dinner, knowing she would be dining alone and wouldn't know a good place to eat.

Estelle Chambers entered the hardware store as the meeting was breaking up. She walked toward the back room and greeted the commissioners as they were welcoming Ashleigh and thanking her for her attendance and attention to their list of 'wants'.

Tom took his wife's hand and kissed her on the cheek, "Hi, sweetheart. I want you to meet Miss Ashleigh Justice, the architect on our project. Ashleigh, this is my wife of 20 years, Estelle. I've asked Miss Justice if she will join us for dinner."

"That's terrific. So happy to meet you, Miss Justice."

"Thank you, Mrs. Chambers. Please call me Ashleigh."

"Well, I'm Estelle. Tom's mom is Mrs. Chambers."

Ashleigh liked her immediately. "I would love to join you for dinner."

At dinner, Ashleigh learned that the Chambers had two children, a boy 12, and a girl 15. She was glad they talked about personal things, rather than the project.

"Estelle, you have your hands full with two children. Did you grow up in Rushton?"

"Yes. I'm a local girl. Tom and I met in high school. He's a year older. When he went away to college, I vowed that I would do the same thing. When the time came, my parents were in a financial freefall. I ended up going to the local junior college.

"Tom made it through three years before he had to drop to part-time and get a job to pay for his last year. He was a business major and dreamed of working in Atlanta in a financial investment company. Competition was tough for those jobs. He came home to run his dad's hardware store that was faltering because his dad was sick.

"We believe everything happens for our good. God brought us back to Rushton to help our parents. We were in love and felt we could make a difference for them. Tom has grown the business into a regional success. He knows how and what to stock and keeps relationships with large manufacturers for those special orders our customers need from time to time.

"My parents had a beef farm, with some horse boarding run by my mom. I learned to ride when I was young. I still help with grooming the horses and riding to exercise them. It is something I can do while the kids are in school. Summers, they work with me at the farm. We go to church, help our neighbors, make a living, and have a full life.

"Now it's time to help the town move into the current century. We're glad you're here."

"That sounds like a romance story for the century. Are your parents still living?"

"They are and they are enjoying their families in fairly good health."

"You are blessed." Ashleigh looked at Tom and Estelle and could feel the love between them. She wanted that kind of love.

She left Rushton the next morning with a fresh impression of her goals for this town. She wanted to make the project hurl the town into the vibrant business activity going on in many small towns in the state. She took the recommendations from the commissioners and moved them several steps beyond what they thought could happen.

I need to get with the engineer (I hope it's Jason) to see if I can carry my ideas into fruition.

She used the drive to mentally design renovations of some buildings and demolish and rebuild others. With each mile her belief that Rushton could be revitalized without a major cost to the county became stronger. It all depended on the engineer's evaluation of the buildings' structures and the soil's permeability.

Chapter Eighty-Two

She noticed Jason in the break room Thursday morning, when she arrived at the office.

"Jason, you're still here. Everything okay?"

"Yes. You said you wanted me to be here when you returned. Voila."

A smile crept on her face, even though she tried to hide it.

"Well. I'm glad you stayed. Rushton is a special town. I think we can help those folks. Tom Chambers and his wife are leading the push for renewal of the town. They are a loving family and want the best for their town.

"You and I together could make it happen. What did Howard say about the Deerfield project?"

"He's vacillating. He doesn't want to give up because the company has made a large investment in the work already accomplished. Then again, he doesn't want to keep pouring money into a lost cause. Besides, he and I both, want to see the project completed."

"Would he allow you to work with me on Rushton until the Deerfield folks come around? I think Rushton could be completed quickly."

"Quickly is relative."

"I know but would you ask him?"

"I'll ask him if you will have dinner with me tonight."

"I think I win both ways with that request."

***

She tried on one outfit after another. Nothing seemed right. The air was cooler than just a week ago. She wanted to look amazing for Jase. Since she didn't know where they were going, she decided to dress for mid-season, not too drab but also not too summery.

From the back of her closet, she found her favorite black knit mid-calf dress with three-quarter sleeves and a bit of a plunging neckline. She accessorized it with her diamond drop necklace and matching earrings. For insurance against a cool breeze, she chose a black and white shawl and slipped on black satin strapped sandals.

When she opened the door for Jase, she was happy with her choices. He stood smiling at her in black slacks, a white dress shirt, no tie, but a silk tweed black and white sports coat.

"You look beautiful, Ash."

"Not so bad yourself, Jase."

"Where are we going?"

"I made reservations at Red Rock Restaurant. You seemed to like it when we went before."

"It is my favorite place to go with you. Glad I brought my shawl."

"You're always thinking ahead. It's one of your more endearing qualities."

She swiped at him for his sarcastic remark. He smiled at her and held his arm out for her to hold as they left the apartment. When he turned to check the lock on the door, she caught a whiff of his cologne before they turned toward the elevator.

She squeezed his arm. This was her Jase, the protective, caring, teasing, handsome man she wanted in her life forever.

Chapter Eighty-Three

The trill of a Pine Warbler woke Ashleigh the next morning with its gentle and musical sound. She smiled as she remembered the evening with Jason. Dinner had been perfect, and Georgia's weather cooperated with only an occasional cold breeze.

He didn't try to kiss me goodnight. Does he think I'm too fragile? Doesn't he want to kiss me? Is he afraid I'll reject him?

The night would have been perfect if he had kissed me.

The day's awakening cast deep rose striations across the sky, reflecting in the passing clouds, and canopying above her apartment. She felt she was waking amid one of God's new creations. She prayed the blessings waking her would last throughout the day.

Arriving in the office changed her peacefulness upon opening the door. There was a flurry in every direction.

"What's going on, Jolene?"

"Mr. Stockton is in one of his moods."

"What does that mean?"

"You don't know?"

"No. I've never seen things like this."

"It only happens occasionally. Well, it used to only be occasional. Here lately it has been more frequent. Don't go near him for a little while. Maybe he will calm down."

"What set him off?"

"I'm not sure. Sometimes it's nothing. Today, he got this way after his meeting with Jason."

"Oh, no. Where is Jason?"

"He left the office. He said for you to call him. He has a cell phone. Here is his number."

Ashley went into her office and called Jason's cell.

"Jase, what's going on with Howard?"

"He went into one of his rages when I talked to him about me helping on the Rushton project. He said I was abandoning Deerfield, where I had cost the firm so much money. I tried to tell him I would be able to do both projects. He wouldn't listen."

"Did he fire you?"

"No. He just needs to vent for a while. I thought it best if I got myself out of his line of sight for a few hours. Can you bring the Rushton file and meet me at the coffee shop down the street? There's a nook where we can work."

"Okay. I'll be right there."

He looked over her files and made some notes.

"I think I can put together a reasonable project plan for my time on this project and still have plenty of time to keep up with Deerfield and move Juliet forward. Can I offer you as the architect for Deerfield again?"

"Oh, Jase. That's a big ask."

"I know but I need something to appease Howard for spending some of my time on Rushton, even though my project plan should prove I can do all three. Deerfield is still in a holding mode."

"Okay. I think I'll wait until tomorrow to get an appointment with Howard to discuss Rushton."

"Good idea. See you back in the office in a bit."

Chapter Eighty-Four

Friday night, Natalie Birdman called.

"Ashleigh, can you come to a meeting at my house tomorrow. I'm trying to get the whole team together. We have an opportunity I don't want to miss. The group needs to make the decision about whether to get involved. I'll tell everyone about it tomorrow."

"Of course, what time should I arrive?"

"Try to be here around ten if possible."

"See you then."

Ashleigh was excited but nervous. She wanted something positive to happen with the legislators, but she was beginning to be inundated with projects at work. She wanted to do a masterful job on both.

Her mind churned all night leaving little time for sleep.

The drive to Natalie's home was again relaxing and full of God's beauty. The wind swooped gold and red leaves from Maples and Oaks up and around before depositing their patchwork onto the countryside. The smell of fresh cut grass and the sight of cows and horses grazing were testament to late fall's rejuvenating spirit and wonderment.

Ashleigh was sure she could handle everything…with God's help.

Natalie's home embodied a retreat from everything chaotic in life. Six other cars were already in the driveway when Ashleigh arrived. She lifted her briefcase and left her sunroof sightly open to fresh air. This was not a formal get-together to meet each other. This was a blue jeans and sweatshirt day for digging in and putting together a viable plan.

Ashleigh was taken aback when she entered the great room, and the other women were in wool slacks and cashmere sweaters, drinking mimosas from fine crystal wine glasses. Feeling embarrassed, she smiled and shrugged as she held out the hem of her shirt.

The women smiled.

Natalie said, "Ashleigh you look wonderful in anything you wear. I'm happy you feel comfortable around us. Now, I need to bring you all up to speed on the latest happenings for our cause.

"You may remember these folks from our initial get together. Annette Charles, President of Women's Service League; Lois Lang, reporter; Priscilla Bennett, member from South Georgia and Bryan Allen representative from South Georgia. They have called me wanting to help get the ball rolling in the next legislative session.

"Bryan wants to help with composing the bill. Today, I want us to put together our thoughts and ideas for him to use to craft the legislation.

"If we can put together something quickly, it will give him two months to turn it into a bill before the next legislative session."

The women worked late into Saturday afternoon and left Natalie's home with a product for her to take to Bryan.

Ashleigh was comfortable with their proposal and felt accomplished and satisfied on her drive home.

Chapter Eighty-Five

Monday morning Ashleigh arrived in the office early for her meeting with Howard. He couldn't meet with her on Friday. She wanted to be certain he wouldn't put her off today.

She saw him enter the side door between his office and his secretary's. He stopped at Angela's desk, smiled, and visited for a few minutes.

Ashleigh, relieved to see him in a good mood, grabbed her file and headed to his office.

"Good morning, Howard."

"Good morning, Ashleigh. I hope you had a restful weekend. This week is going to be rather hectic."

"I'm excited to move ahead with the Rushton project and planned to travel there tomorrow for a meeting with the county commission and introduce them to Jason. That is, if you approve him working on this project with me. He told me he met with you last week on it."

"Yes, yes. I've thought about it over the weekend and decided he is the best engineer to work on this type of project. That's where his expertise is. He will be a big help to you when the debate starts over which buildings must go and which ones can be refurbished and redesigned."

"Thank you, Howard. That decision will help move this project along. Jason will make a good impression on the council. I'll let Angela know if we need to spend the night in Rushton. These cell phones make staying connected so easy. You can reach us day or night."

Jason went straight to Ashleigh's office when he got to work. They used the day to prepare a plan to present to the city council.

Tuesday morning, Jason picked Ashleigh up in his Jeep with his engineering paraphernalia poking out like spider's legs from the back seat.

"Is there room for my suitcase and briefcase?" Ashleigh smiled and shook her head, while handing him her necessities.

"Hey, a man has 'necessities' too."

Their trip was slowed by a typical Georgia downpour which made the windshield wipers work overtime and the tires cast buckets of water like butterfly wings on each side of the jeep. Since they had no appointments this morning, Jason was careful to drive slowly because the streets seemed to be freezing into a slushy hazard.

Ashleigh loved driving in the rain and felt safe in the warmth of Jason's jeep under his steady hand. Late fall weather in Georgia was unpredictable and today was no exception.

The meeting was scheduled for six o'clock. They should have no trouble travelling the two-and-a-half hours to Rushton unless the weather got worse.

Ashleigh talked constantly during the first hour of the drive, until she noticed that Jason was concentrating on the road and the weather. She looked out at the road and there was the beginning of ice build-up. She took a sideways glance at Jason and realized he had a concerned look on his face.

The jeep was barely moving, and many cars had pulled off to the side of the road. Jason kept driving.

She didn't question him and sat quietly until they reached a town where there was no build-up on the road. They were far enough South that the warm temperatures turned the ice into rain.

They pulled into Rushton an hour before the start of the meeting.

Jason looked at Ashleigh, "I think it would be best to spend the night rather than try to drive back through icy roads to the north."

"I agree. The hotel is just down the street."

The lone hotel was a two-story white limestone structure with a wide front porch and rocking chairs on each side of the double entry doors. It sat in the middle of the business section of the town with angled parking in front.

"Jase, thank you for being such a careful driver and getting us here safely."

"Thank you for staying quiet so I could concentrate on the road. I've never been a reckless driver and probably would have pulled off the road, but we had a six o'clock commitment and I intended to keep it."

They had no trouble securing two rooms for the night because fall was not the season for travelers in this part of the state. They went to their rooms and freshened up before the meeting. Since the rain had stopped, they carried their equipment the two blocks to the hardware store.

Tom Chambers met them at the door. "Glad you made it. I was a little worried when I saw the weather report for the northern part of the state."

Ashleigh shook his hand, "It was slow going but Jason got us through. Tom, this is Jason Blunt. He will be the engineer on the project. Jason, this is Tom Chambers.:

Jason held out his hand, "Glad to meet you, Tom. How are things going at this point.?"

"Let's talk about that as I show you the meeting room, where you can set up for your presentation. I'm sure you're accustomed to power struggles among commissioners during meetings. We're no different. Some of the guys have a need to flex their muscles a little but they will come around."

Tom left them to set up and, in a few minutes, brought them two cups of steaming coffee and chocolate-chip cookies Estelle had made.

It was a simple gesture, but it made them feel at home before the commissioners arrived.

Buster made it a point to welcome Jason, "Glad we've got some testosterone in the room this time. We enjoyed lookin' at the little filly, but we need a man to get us through a project this complicated."

"There is no architect I know of who is smarter than Miss Justice. We are fortunate to have her in our company and on this project.

"Ashleigh, will you begin the presentation and I'll join you when you need some engineering explanation for the boys here."

Buster didn't speak again during the meeting.

Once again, Tom invited Ashleigh to dinner along with Jason. They met at the hotel's restaurant after Tom picked Estelle up.

Jason seemed to be smiling the whole evening. He looked around the banquet-sized room and studied the Georgian archi-tecture.

"Tom, this building must be a hundred years old, but it is in pristine condition."

"Yeah, Shane Phillips has a love of old buildings and buys every building he can find. He spends a boat load of money in the town. His great-grandparents settled here, and his aunts and uncles stayed, raised their children here and many of them have returned after college. Shane has a lot riding on this renewal plan."

"If your committee approves an initial study and plan, Ashleigh and I will make it a showplace and keep the family-oriented lifestyle. It is too special to change it to something modern. We'll update necessary items, but Ashleigh and I have talked about keeping the 'feel' of the town intact."

"That sounds good to me." Estelle spoke for the first time. "I love this town. I wouldn't want to see skyscrapers or ultra-modern buildings lining the streets."

Jason and Ashleigh kept checking each other's face for reactions, so they would be on the same page. At one point, Jase took Ashleigh's hand under the table and smiled at her.

"Thanks for giving us a reasonable deadline for our next presentation. Since the committee agreed to the initial evaluation phase, I'll be down here next week to start soil testing and walking through each building. Will you make sure every business expects us?"

"Of course. Ashleigh, will you be coming too?"

"Yes. I'll be Jase's...Jason's shadow initially. I need his data to start my design. You'll probably see us together for the first months."

"Good. We enjoy your company. Isn't that right, Estelle."

"Definitely. I've enjoyed their company and look forward to their visits."

"Estelle, thank you for the delicious cookies this afternoon. They saved us. We didn't have time to eat lunch. Hopefully, next time the weather will be better, and we can have a smooth ride and stop for lunch."

Jase added, "Since we are spending the night, we'll spend a little while in the morning to start an evaluation, if that's okay. We won't go into any businesses, but we will look at outside structure."

"Glad to see you're eager to get started."

"I'm ready for a good night's sleep. Ready to call it a night, Ashleigh?"

"Definitely. Estelle and Tom, thank you for your hospitality. I look forward to working with you. Goodnight."

They left the couple at the table and walked up the winding staircase to the second floor.

Estelle looked at Tom, "There's more to their relationship than work. Did you see the way they kept looking at each other. I'm not sure they know it yet, but they are in love."

"Yeah. I saw it too."

Chapter Eighty-Six

Jason and Ashleigh travelled to Rushton at least one day a week.

Ashleigh looked up at Jason from the pile of papers in her lap.

"The weather seems to be getting colder. If it freezes, we'll have to stay overnight."

"I was just thinking that, but we need the meeting today. I'm ready to start digging for the new courthouse and need the commissioner's approval. Maybe you should have stayed in Atlanta. Are your other projects on hold while you are here?"

"Heavens, no. I've got two architects working wonders on Deerfield. We're making great progress, as you already know because you're in the middle of the foundation work, approvals for ordering supplies and adding new staff to facilitate meeting hard deadlines."

"We've got to get back to Joliet next week."

"Do you miss Savannah?" Ashleigh couldn't stop herself from teasing Jason about Savannah.

"Ashleigh, stop. You know there is nothing going on with her. She is our 'insurance' the project will continue."

"I know. I just couldn't resist. When will you need to stay in Juliet for a week as the foundations are being laid?"

"Probably next week, or the next."

"We're only a couple of weeks away from Thanksgiving. Will you be here then?"

"I'll make a point to be here for the holidays. My mom would never forgive me if I didn't see her on Thanksgiving and Christmas."

"Oh, hang on. It looks like it's Phillip calling. Hi, Phillip. I'm so glad to hear from you. What's up?"

"Sis, I have some great news."

"What is it?"

"I've decided to forgo extending my enlistment with the Marines. I've taken a civilian job in cyber security with a start-up company in Mountain View, California."

"Phillip, I'm so glad. When will all this happen?"

"I'm working my last month now. I'll be home for a couple of weeks. Then I'll move to California. I'll not be close, but you can reach me anytime you need me.

"By the way, Dad gave me your cell number. I'm impressed. Never thought you'd be one of the first to use a cell phone."

"Since I'm travelling some, I needed a way to be available at all hours for work and for mom and dad.

"Phillip, I'm so happy you won't be in danger anymore. You can even be with us at Thanksgiving and Christmas."

"Probably not Thanksgiving but definitely Christmas. Well, I won't keep you any longer. My phone number is the same if you want to call me when you are home."

"Jason, that was great news from Phillip. He's out of the military. He has taken a job in Mountain View, California. Now he will be safe."

The day seemed brighter, and some stress seemed to slide away from her heart. She quietly enjoyed the peacefulness of the rest of the ride to Rushton.

Chapter Eighty-Seven

Ashleigh designed the streetscape view of both sides of Main Street in Rushton. Jason had left details about every lot.

"Howard, do you have time to look over my architectural blueprints for Main Street in Rushton?"

"Sure. Give me a minute to tell Jolene something. I'll be right back."

When he returned, Ashleigh jumped into the explanation. "Jason determined that three of the buildings could not be saved. Their structure is already unstable, with cracks in the walls and bouncy floors. They would need to be torn down anyway. The urban renewal plan will help them rebuild cheaper than if they did it on their own.

"So, here's the streetscape of the right side of the road coming into town. Two of the buildings needing demolishing are on this side. I've designed new buildings for both structures with facades to blend in, but not be mirror images of, the other buildings on the street."

Howard took the rendering, "I like the balance you've created, Ashleigh. Do you have the specs for each building's interiors?"

"Yes. You want to see them now?"

"Yes, I have time before my next meeting."

She spent the next two hours going over each building with details inside and out. She showed him colored frontages and blueprint interiors.

"You've done a great job, Ashleigh. I'm impressed with your work but not surprised. Great job."

"When is Jason coming home, Howard?"

"He should be in town tonight and in the office tomorrow. You need something?"

She rolled the rendering and put rubber bands on it. "No. Just wondering. I'm taking the plans to Rushton tomorrow for a preliminary okay. The commissioners are meeting tomorrow night."

"Sounds good. Be careful on the road." Howard patted her on the shoulder and smiled.

"I will Howard. Thanks for your review of the plans."

***

She arrived in Rushton early the next day.

"You're here early, Ashleigh. We don't meet until six thirty tonight."

Tom Chambers greeted her inside his hardware store.

"I know. I wanted to get here in time to let you have a sneak peek before the entire group meets. I need to get back to Atlanta tonight, so if you have questions, we can address them before the meeting and be on the same page when we meet with the rest of the commissioners."

"Estelle is meeting me for lunch today. Will you join us? It seems strange for you to be here without Jason."

"I'm capable of handling my part of the meeting."

"I didn't mean that, Ashleigh. I'm just accustomed to seeing you together."

"Oh. Okay. And yes, I'd love to join you for lunch."

Estelle walked into the store and gave Ashleigh a hug.

"Where is that good-looking Jason today?"

Once again, she felt irritated that Jason's absence was questioned. "He's in Mississippi working on another project this week."

"Tell him hello for me. I bet he misses you."

"What? Why would you say that?"

"Because when you're in love, it's hard to be apart for long." Estelle smiled as she looked at Tom.

"In love?" Ashleigh looked at the couple. "You're wrong."

"Yes. In love. Don't you know he is in love with you? And you love him too. Haven't either one of you admitted it yet?"

"No. We're not...I mean he's not. Do you think he does love me?"

"Without a doubt."

"How do you know?"

"By the way he looks at you and treats you."

"How did you know that I love him?"

"Same way."

"I've been trying to deny it."

"Why?"

"Because I didn't think he loves me."

"No doubt about it. He needs a nudge. Tom, you take it from here with Jason."

"I can do that. When is he coming back?"

Lunch was a blur. The afternoon was eternal. The commission meeting was stilted. The drive home was lonely.

Chapter Eighty-Eight

Ashleigh and Christine were spending more time together, planning Christmas with Phillip.

"I can't believe my son will be home for Christmas this year. There will be no last-minute orders changing his assignment or leave time. Ashleigh it is going to be wonderful."

"I know Mom. It's like a dream."

"We'll have our normal Christmas party but ramped up a few notches."

"I'm not sure how much more elegant you can make it, or how much larger you can make it. It's already the talk of the town."

"Maybe I'll rent the whole Country Club."

"Mom, really?"

"Well, maybe that is a little over the top."

"I'd rather it to be more intimate. I want to enjoy every minute with my brother. Even though he will be out of the Marines, he will still be living a continent away."

"Almost. Do you think Phillip would rather have an intimate Christmas with us?"

"I don't know. He'll be here two weeks. Maybe he would like a party in his honor. It's hard to know."

"You haven't mentioned Jason in a while. Everything okay between you two?"

"We're both busy."

"Would you want to invite him to the Christmas party?"

"Sure. You can finish the guest list without my help. I need to get back to my place and do some chores before church tomorrow. I'll see you there."

"Okay, sweetheart. Anyone else you want to add to the guest list? What about JJ and her husband."

"Of course. Not sure they will be able to come, but I would like them to be invited."

"Get me their address and I'll put them on the list."

***

Ashleigh looked around at her apartment. Her space. Her haven. It wasn't the elegance of her parent's home, but it was cozy. Just what she needed at this point in her life. She had finished scrubbing the bathroom and kitchen and flopped on the sofa to rest before looking for something for lunch.

Where should I put a Christmas tree in this room? I haven't had a desire to have my own tree until this year. Mom and dad have such grandiose decorations, chosen and placed by a local designer. I could never reach that level of perfection. I don't know why I'm interested in a tree this year. Am I thinking of nesting? I'm getting to the age where it would be natural to want to create a home. We're not even at Thanksgiving yet. Why am I thinking about a Christmas tree?

She sat long enough that she relaxed and fell asleep, reading one of the books she bought over the past year, but never had time to read. When she woke, evening was encroaching on her patio and there was a chill in the air. She looked across the room at the gas-burning fireplace and jumped up to turn it on. As she stood warming herself in the heat from the flames, she pictured the perfect place for her tree. The glass sliding doors had a stationary pane and a door that slid in front of it. There was plenty of room to place the tree a few inches away from the sliding door in front of the stationary pane. Her lights would be visible from the buildings across the courtyard and the street below. Perfect.

Sitting in church the next morning, she couldn't wait to start the search for the perfect decorations for her tree. It couldn't be larger than six feet, but it could be her design. She was deep in thought waiting for the sermon to begin, when she felt her mom move away from her and felt Jason slip in between them. He squeezed her arm, and she was home.

They couldn't talk until after the service. Jason grabbed her hand and walked beside her down the aisle, nodding and speaking to several people they passed.

Outside, Christine touched his elbow. "Jason, so good to see you. Will you join us for lunch at the Country Club today?"

"I don't want to intrude."

"You could never intrude. See you there."

It was settled. He would join them for lunch.

"I really wanted to take you to lunch, just the two of us."

"We can decline."

"No. Your parents are so welcoming. I don't want to be impolite. Can we visit after lunch?"

"I'd love that. I've missed you."

"Me too. I'll follow you."

Lunch lasted too long for Jason. When coffee and dessert were cleared away, he asked Ashleigh if she was ready to go.

"Yes. Thanks for lunch Dad. Mom, I'll talk with you tomorrow."

Jason followed, "Thank you for a delicious lunch and the good company."

He took Ashleigh's hand as they walked away from the table. When they got to the entrance hall, he saw Scott and his parents leaving. He tensed up as they got closer.

Scott threw up his hand toward Ashleigh and smiled. His parents nodded her way and left the restaurant.

"What was that all about?"

"Scott went through an anger management program, which required him to ask me for my forgiveness for what he did to me."

"Did you?"

"Yes."

"Ashleigh…"

"God requires us to forgive. I did and feel much better about Scott. He is contrite."

"Just so he leaves you alone."

"He has. Let's not waste our time talking about him. We have a lot of other things to discuss."

"Agreed. Meet you at your place?"

They parked beside each other and walked up the stairs holding hands. When they got inside, Jason pulled her to him. He looked into her eyes and slowly leaned into her lips. She welcomed his kiss and didn't want to let him go.

"I can't tell you how long I've wanted to do that."

"Why did you keep me waiting so long?"

"Because I didn't know you were waiting for it. I thought you wanted to just be friends. I didn't know you wanted more from me."

"I do want us to be friends, but I want much more than that."

He pulled her face to his and kissed her tenderly. "You are my world, Ashleigh."

"Did you miss me that much?"

"Well, yeah. I always miss you when we're apart. But I got a nudge yesterday from Tom Chambers. He called me Friday and asked if I could detour to Rushton on my way home from Juliet. He said he had something important to discuss. Of course, I said yes.

"When I got there, he and Estelle invited me to their home, which is beautiful. We toured his barns and had a snack on their back veranda. Their children were there but involved in their own activities. Tom smiled at Estelle and just laid it on me. 'Do you know you're in love with Ashleigh?'"

"I said, "yes."

'Do you know she loves you?'

"I protested. No, she just wants to be friends."

'No, she doesn't. We asked her. She is in love with you. We think you two are wasting too much time. You need to get on with your lives together, so you can have something like what we have.'

"I was floored. They convinced me. So...here I am. Loving you."

"I've waited a long time for you to say those words, Jason Blunt. I love you too."

Epilogue

Natalie called to let Ashleigh know about the outcome of Bryan Allen's legislation.

"Ashleigh, the agenda was packed, and there were heated and long debates over the piece of legislation regarding voting precincts. Besides being bumped off the agenda for this session, Bryan was unable to get his piece of legislation on the agenda for the next session."

"How disappointing. That means we won't have anything accomplished for another year."

Natalie seemed unaffected. "That's just the way the government works."

Ashleigh tried to take a positive position. "Maybe that will give us enough time to involve more representatives and get their support for getting the legislation on the next agenda. We can't give up on this effort. Women all over the state and country are being subjected to lower pay until we force a law to clearly protect that right."

"I agree. I will stay on this project and will encourage everyone we've worked with to stay engaged too. Ashleigh, thank you for all your enthusiasm and support. We will continue to see each other. Talk soon."

THE END

A Note from the Author

Dear Reader,

Thanks for reading one of my books. **Illusion of Control**

I hope you enjoyed reading it as much as I enjoyed writing it. If you'd like to send feedback to me directly, drop me a line by email at: lorainehaynie211@gmail.com

If you're so inclined, I'd love it if you would post a review for the book – Loved it, Hated it, Whatever — I'd just like to hear your feedback. So please, post a review on Amazon or Goodreads, it helps to introduce the book to new readers who don't know me or my work.

Thank you again for reading one of my stories. It is much appreciated.

Love,
Loraine

Keep on reading. I'm going to keep on writing!

Other Books in the Illusion Series
Illusion of Consent

Also by Loraine Haynie
All the Way
Rescuing Jenny
Confronting the Pitchford Curse

https://www.lorainehaynieauthor.com
lorainehaynie211@gmail.com

About the Author

Award winning author Loraine Haynie writes Southern Contemporary Christian fiction from her home in Hoschton, Georgia. She and husband, Billy, travelled as young retirees. They live in a 55-plus community, where there are activities day and night. Now, they enjoy spending time with their seven grandchildren, six boys and one girl, scattered from San Diego, California, through Austin, Texas, Cumming, Georgia, and Greenville, SC.

Loraine holds a degree in Journalism/Mass Communications and worked in a variety of positions in marketing and public relations. She wrote for two monthly publications and was operations manager for a weekly magazine before buying a weight-loss franchise.

She had a 20-year career as a Director of Human Resources. After retiring, Loraine wrote a monthly column for the local newspaper.

She published her first book, **All the Way,** in 2018, **Rescuing Jenny** in 2019, **Confronting the Pitchford Curse** in 2022, and **Illusion of Consent** in 2023.